1-2012
RS   If you like vampire stories
              not bad

Praise for the novels of

HEATHER GRAHAM

"An incredible storyteller."
—*Los Angeles Daily News*

"Graham does a great job of blending just a bit
of paranormal with real, human evil."
—*Miami Herald*

"Heather Graham has a wonderful talent for taking
bits of history and blending them in with urban
fantasy. With *Night of the Vampires,* set during the
Civil War...vampires [take] advantage of the great
death tolls to feed and replenish their numbers.
Her ability to take interesting little historic tidbits...
could pique even the non-history buff's interest."
—*Fresh Fiction*

"Graham's unique tale cleverly blends Civil War
history, vampire myths and lore and of course,
heart-pounding romance. It's perfect for those
who love intricate historical details, lush scenery
and old-fashioned romance."
—*RT Book Reviews* on *Night of the Vampires*

"Graham's expertise is in weaving a tale
where the unbelievable seems believable."
—*Suspense Magazine*

"Mystery, sex, paranormal events.
What's not to love?"
—*Kirkus Reviews* on *The Death Dealer*

"Heather Graham knows what readers want."
—*Publishers Weekly*

HEATHER GRAHAM

BRIDE OF THE NIGHT

ISBN-13: 978-1-61793-336-3

BRIDE OF THE NIGHT

BRIDE OF THE NIGHT

PROLOGUE

Gettysburg, Pennsylvania
November 19, 1863

"FOUR SCORE AND SEVEN YEARS ago our fathers brought forth on this continent a new nation, conceived in liberty and dedicated to the proposition that all men are created equal."

The breeze picked up, just as President Lincoln began to speak.

Finn Dunne heard a soft crackle from the dead and dying leaves that clung to or fell from the trees in the surrounding forests and hills. It was almost as if the earth itself mourned the tragic loss of life here.

Still mounted atop his large thoroughbred, Finn surveyed the crowd. He had ridden near the president during the procession from the Wills House to Baltimore Street, along the Taneytown Road, and into the Soldiers' National Cemetery. Looking at the president, Finn reassured himself that others equally tasked with the duty of guarding him were likewise vigilant. Vigilant even through the last speaker, Edward Everett—ex-senator, professor and highly acclaimed orator…and certainly a long-winded fellow—had gone on for two hours before giving way to the president.

There were children in the crowd growing very restless, prompting their mothers to take them toward the graves where their antics would be less audible. Other mothers who had lost sons stood near the speakers, dabbing at their tearstained eyes. And since life went on despite the dead, soldiers and civilians stood a little closer to the prettier women, trying to use the occasion, with all of its solemnity, to flirt.

Soldiers, and other Pinkerton men, stood around, the soldiers obvious—some in dress uniforms and some in their well-worn fighting attire—and the Pinkerton men in various combinations of clothing, from dress shirts to frock coats to railway jackets. It was November, and the day had a nip to it: "a cold like the dead," someone had whispered earlier.

The victory at Gettysburg and recent successes along the Mississippi and on the western front had been encouraging. But Abraham Lincoln's reelection remained in doubt. Even now, there were those sick of the war, those who believed they should just let the Confederacy go their own way, and good riddance, too.

But that had not happened, and so Finn was on the lookout for Southern sympathizers, fanatics who might just want the tall, grave man who carried the world on his shoulders *out.*

The president had arrived by train yesterday, and a young local man, Sergeant H. Paxton Bigham, had been assigned to guard the chief executive. Finn had met Bigham, and liked him, and his brother, Rush, as well. Neither had slept during the night. Their loyalty couldn't be questioned. Finn wanted to believe that he could rest easily; Gettysburg was firmly entrenched in the hands of the North. But he never rested, for there was always the possibility that a Confederate spy or sympathizer might just take a shot at Lincoln.

Never before had Finn met a man that he was so completely willing to die for. For Lincoln, he would give his all.

Not that he'd ever die easily.

"Now we are engaged in a great civil war, testing whether that nation, or any nation so conceived and so dedicated, can long endure."

Finn scanned the natural surroundings—acres, hills, trees and beautiful little streams where rivulets sent sparkling water dancing over the rocks by day. There were also rocky tor areas, trails that twisted and turned through narrow paths. Places like Devil's Den...

Where bodies had lain upon bodies... So many men had become trapped in the rugged rock formations, and mown down. More than fifty thousand casualties here alone—Northern and Southern, dead, dying, wounded and captured. Rains brought the masses of hastily buried bodies back to the surface, the decaying corpses a mortal reminder that filled every breath, and which attracted swarms of flies and herds of wild pigs intent upon consuming everything. As the summer heat following the July battle added to the wretchedness of the place, Governor Andrew Curtin of Pennsylvania had to do something, and thus the cemetery had been planned. And the president's consecration of that land today.

Gettysburg would never be the same again. For some, it would be a shrine. For others, it would be remembered as the site of a massacre. Finn was fairly certain that no matter how it was seen by his contemporaries, history would prove that it was the pivotal ground upon which the rest of the war would hang. Here, the South had been forced to retreat. General Lee was said to have all but wept at the loss of life, and that his chance to take the war into the North had surely been lost. And with that, likely the war, as well.

A surge of anguish so strong it was almost physical swept through Finn. He knew General Robert E. Lee. He had been Lincoln's first choice as a commander for his own forces. Lee, so it was said, spent a tortured night pacing the hallway of his Arlington home, trying to decide by light of his conscience and his great belief in God what was the right path to take. The grandson of Lighthorse Harry Lee, a hero of the Revolution, Lee had finally decided that he was a Virginian first, no matter his individual thoughts and feelings on secession.

There.

In the rear, near a gravestone but moving closer to the podium. There was a woman, her shoulders covered by a long cape, her arms and hands concealed by it. Carrying something...

Lincoln—never truly aware of his own personal danger—gave his complete attention and heart to his words. "We are met on a great battlefield of that war. We have come to dedicate a portion of that field as a final resting place for those who here gave their lives that that nation might live. It is altogether fitting and proper that we should do this."

Finn drew his coat more tightly about him as he whispered, "Stay, boy," to Piebald and dismounted. As he slipped through the crowd, most people barely noted him; they were silent, listening. Some, however, smiled as he passed, glad for a break from standing and staring. Many had now wandered off, Everett's speech having left them fatigued.

Finn looked over toward the podium.

He knew that the Bigham brothers and their company were on assignment, and, by the president's request, Finn's own guard kept a perimeter. There shouldn't really have been any trouble. Lincoln's appearance here had actually been a last-minute consideration—after all, tens of thousands of men had died in many locations, and he couldn't be present for every burial. But the battle at Gettysburg had demanded a price of American blood, Northern and Southern, like no other. Finn imagined that Lincoln's host, Attorney Wills, might have believed the president would turn down the invitation to speak. But Finn also imagined that Lincoln had actually been looking for just such an opportunity. A victory like Gettysburg was hard-won, and this was the place to convince the people that the war could be won, and must be won. And that it would end not in retribution against the rebels, but in a true peace for all Americans.

President Lincoln was always hard to guard. He considered himself a man of the people. And he couldn't be a man of the people if he didn't see the people, and if they didn't see him. This, of course, made gave his bodyguards more of a chore.

Finn had almost reached the woman. The president was still speaking, and it seemed that he had thoroughly gripped the attention of the people now. No one noticed as Finn politely slid closer and closer to the woman— who herself moved closer and closer to the president.

"But, in a larger sense, we can not dedicate, we can not consecrate, we can not hallow, this ground. The brave men, living and dead, who struggled here have consecrated it, far above our poor power to add or detract. The world will little note, nor long remember, what we say here, but it can never forget what they did here." Lincoln's voice rang with sincerity, a tremulous quality to it.

And the woman was almost upon him.

"It is for us the living, rather, to be dedicated here to the unfinished work which they who fought here have thus far so nobly advanced," Lincoln intoned somberly. "It is rather for us to be here dedicated to the great task remaining before us—that from these honored dead we take increased devotion to that cause for which they gave the last full measure of devotion—that we here highly resolve that these dead shall not have died in vain, that this nation, under God, shall have a new birth of freedom, and that government of the people, by the people, for the people, shall not perish from the earth."

The president of the United States stepped back from the podium. Some of the crowd applauded enthusiastically. Some stared ahead with such glazed eyes that Finn wondered if they'd really even heard the man.

But Finn's quarry, *she* was a young beauty, and she seemed to be watching the president with rapt, splendorous eyes. Huge, hazel eyes fringed with impossibly dark lashes. Her long wavy hair fell down her back in shades of reddish gold—

A murderous agent didn't have to be ugly on the outside to carry out a heinous deed! Finn reminded himself.

Just as he made it to her side, she reached beneath the encompassing warm cloak.

He'd expected a gun.

Or a knife.

His arms encircled her just as he saw what she carried....

A beautifully knitted scarf in the colors of the American flag.

Her eyes, gold and gleaming, turned on his. They

seemed to burn with a strange fire, and yet, one he knew too well.

"Idiot!" she whispered at him.

She turned away, somehow escaping Finn's grasp and backing out of the crowd.

The scarf fell to the earth.

Blood-soaked earth...

For a moment, Finn lost her, but whether or not she had been carrying nothing more lethal than wool, his instincts told him not to trust her. He moved quickly and saw her again, hurrying away, toward the woods.

The crowd was clearing, enough so that he could whistle for Piebald. His horse came to him, carefully moving through the dispersing crowd. He leaped atop the animal and urged it into a trot to clear the crowd, and then a lope to hurry in pursuit.

The beauty had already disappeared....

Finn rode into the woods and reined in, looking, listening. He heard the rustle of a tree, and quickly turned.

Yes, something moved, just ahead....

He urged his steed on and tore ahead. There...darting from one tree to the next!

When he was almost upon her, he jumped from his horse's back and tackled her back down to the earth. She lay beneath him, staring up at him with hatred and fury.

"What? What?" she demanded. "What do you want from me?"

"What ill intent did you intend President Lincoln?

Who are your coconspirators? *What is the plan?*" he demanded.

"Coconspirators?" she said blankly.

But there was the hint of a soft Southern drawl in her speech....

She took him completely by surprise; that was his downfall. He knew his own power and strength, but he'd been so damned confident in it that he'd not bothered to ascertain hers.

"Ass!" she hissed.

And then she shoved him up off her and backward, much to his surprise.

She was on her feet in seconds. "For your information, I would do anything for that man! Anything at all!"

He leaped up, staring at her. "Then stand here and tell me who and what you are!"

She shook her head, and turned.

He lunged for her, and caught a lock of her hair. She cried out in fury and escaped his hold. And then...

She seemed to disappear into thin air.

He held nothing.... Nothing, save a lock of her hair.

He held on to the red-and-gold lock of that hair, intending to find her, come hell or high water.

He would hold on to it, until he found her again.

And find her he would.

But well over a year of war, bloodshed and death would follow before he did.

CHAPTER ONE

Winter, 1865

"LINCOLN, LINCOLN, LINCOLN," Richard Anderson said, shaking his head sadly. "Frankly, I don't understand your obsession with the man."

Richard pointed out beyond the sand dunes and the scattered pines to the sea—and over the causeway to Fort Zachary Taylor where the North was in control, and had been in control since the beginning of the war, despite Florida being the third state to secede from the Union. He sat down in the pine-laden sand next to Tara, confusion lacing his gray eyes.

"You're at the southernmost tip of the southernmost state. A Confederate state. I don't see you gnawing your lip and chewing down your nails to the nub over Jefferson Davis, who has certainly had his share of trouble, too. Seriously," he said, scooting closer to her, "Tara Fox, if you're not careful, you're going to get yourself killed."

"Getting myself killed is highly unlikely," she murmured. She smiled at Richard, her friend since childhood. They were seated on the small dunes on the edge of the island, away from the homes on the main streets of the town, and far to the east of the fort and any of its troops that might be about. Tara loved to come here. The pines made a soft seat of the sand, and the breeze always seemed to come in gently from the ocean, unless a storm was nearing, and even then she loved it equally. There was something about the sea when the sky turned gray and the wind began to pick up with a soft evil moan that promised of the tempest to come.

"Hardly likely? More than possible!" Richard said hoarsely. "My dearest friend, your passions make you a whirlwind!"

"Honestly, please. This is a war between human beings. The Northern soldiers don't run around killing women—from what I understand, they're only locking up spies when they're women, and not doing a great job keeping any of them in prison at that."

"There's nothing human about war at all."

"But, Richard, I'm not a spy, and I'm not trying to do anything evil. I just keep dreaming about Abraham Lincoln."

"My dear girl, he's not the usual man to fulfill a lass's dreams of fantasy and romance," Richard said, grinning widely.

She cast him a glare in which her effort to control her patience was entirely obvious. "Richard, that's not what I mean at all and you know it."

"It was worth a try," he said wearily. "You are like

a dog with a bone when you start on something, and it terrifies me."

Tara ignored that. "I've already gone north once, Richard." She said the words flatly, as if they proved that she could well manage herself. Yet, even as she spoke with such assurance to him, she was startled to feel a chill of fear.

Yes, she had gone north, and, yes, she had been accosted. By an idiot citizen who seemed to think that she was about to offer harm to President Lincoln. Idiot, yes, but...

Canny and observant, he had watched her—stalked her practically!—and stopped her from getting near Lincoln. If she hadn't been wary...

No, she could take care of herself. If forced into a fighting position, she *could* take care of herself. And, while *highly unlikely,* she *could* be killed, especially if someone really knew or understood just who she was.

What she was.

That was then, long ago now. The man could be dead now, such was the war.

Somehow, she doubted it. She could too easily remember him. Though far shorter than the president, he was well over six feet tall, built of brick, so it appeared, with sharp dark eyes that seemed to rip right through flesh and blood. She remembered his touch all too well. He was a dangerous enemy.

"I've been north before," she repeated to Richard. "I'm not a soldier and I'm not a spy. I'm a traveler. I'm just trying to find a place to live, to find work… I've been there, I've done it before."

"Yes, I know, and I didn't think that it was a good idea then, and I think it's a worse idea now."

She touched his hand gently. She couldn't be afraid, and she couldn't let others be afraid for her. If she could only make her friends understand that it was almost as if she was being *called* to help. "Richard, it's as if he knows me, as if he's communicating with me through his mind. I don't know how to explain, but I dream that we're walking through the White House—and he's talking to me."

Richard stood, paced the soft ground and paused again to look at her. "If you want to go, you know that I'll help you. I just want you to realize what a grave mistake you're making—absolutely no pun intended." He hesitated. "This is home. This is *Key West*. This is where your mother came, and where you are accepted, and where you have friends. It's where *I'm* based."

Tara lifted her chin. "It's where you're based. Half of the time, *you're* off—trying to slip through the blockade. Speak of dangerous."

"It's what I'm supposed to do," he said quietly.

"You never wanted the war," she reminded him. "You said from the beginning that there had to be a way to compromise, that we just needed to realize that slavery was archaic and the great plantation owners could begin a system of payments and schooling and—"

"I was an idiot," he said flatly. "In one thing, the

world will never change. Men will be blind when a system—even an evil one—creates their way of life, their riches and their survival. John Brown might have been a murdering fanatic, but in this, he could have been right." He gazed off into the distance, a bemused look on his face. "The state of Vermont abolished slavery long before your Mr. Lincoln thought of his emancipation proclamation. But do you think that rich farmers anywhere were thinking that they'd have to pick their own cotton if such a law existed? Yes, it can happen, it will happen, but…"

"You're saying the war is over, that we've lost—but you keep going out, running the blockade."

He lifted his hands. "It's what I have to do…. But! You don't have to. You are in a dangerous situation when you leave this place."

"Richard! I don't walk around with a sign on my back with large printed letters that spell out *b-a-s-t-a-r-d!*" she said indignantly.

"Nor do you have a sign that says *Be Wary! Half Vampire!*" Richard warned.

Tara was silence a minute. "And you're my friend," she murmured dryly.

He knelt back down by her in the bracken by the pines near the tiny spit of beach that stretched out along the causeway to the fort. "I am your friend. That's why I'm telling you this. You know I'll take you aboard the *Peace* when you wish…you know that. What I'm trying to tell you is that every journey we make grows more dangerous. The South started the war with no navy, had to scrounge around and build like crazy—beg, borrow and steal other ships—and then count on blockade runners to carry supplies. My ship is good, but the noose is tightening on us, Tara."

He was quiet for a minute, looking downward, and then he looked up at her again. "Tara, I'm saying this to you now, here alone. If I were heard, it might well be construed as that I was speaking as a traitor, and God help me, I'd fight for my state, no matter what. Yet, every word we've spoken here is the truth of it. The war is ending. And we are on our knees, dying. The Confederacy can't hold out much longer, and who knows, maybe God Himself is speaking. General Sherman ripped Atlanta apart, and thankfully Savannah surrendered before being burned to the ground, as well. Since Gettysburg, our victories have been small and sadly sparse."

Tara drew her knees to her chest and hugged them. "Yes," she said softly. "I can read very well," she assured him.

"The death toll is ungodly." He might well have been sadly informing himself.

"I know..." She waved a hand in the air. "I know the tragedy of the whole situation, and all the logic. Grant is grabbing immigrants right off the ships and throwing them into the Union forces. The North has the manufacturing—and what they didn't have, they seized. They're in control of the railroads, and when

the South rips them up, they have the money and supplies to repair them, and we don't. Lee's army is thread-
bare, shoeless, down on ammunition and, half the time,
scrounging desperately for food. I know all that, Richard. Like you, I'd hoped that there wouldn't be a war,
and that most people with any sense would realize that
it wouldn't simply be a massive cost in life for all of us."

She looked at Richard, pain and passion in her eyes.
"I think about you, and my friends fighting for the
South. And I think about Hank Manner, the kind young
Yankee at the fort who helped old Mrs. Bartley when
her carriage fell over. Richard, the concept of any of you
shot and torn and bleeding is horrible. North and South,
we're all human beings." She winced. "Well, you know
what I mean. Hank is a good man, a really good man."
She was quiet for a moment, and then added softly, "I
think I'm just grateful. It really is all over. I just don't
know why we keep fighting."

"Human beings. Yes, as you said—it's the human
beast," Richard said, shaking his head as he looked out
to the sea. "Men can't accept defeat. It hits us at some
primal level, and we just about have to destroy everything, including ourselves...."

"So, it may go on. Please, Richard...?"

"The war *will* go on," he said harshly. "And it will
be chaos while it's still being settled, and, God knows,
far worse after!"

"You can't understand this urgency I feel," she told him.
He gripped her hands. "Tara, it makes no sense! Why

in hell are you worried about Abraham Lincoln? He's been elected, again. He'll be inaugurated soon, again. He'll be the conquering hero of the United States. What, are you crazy? There are *professional* military guards who worry about his safety, friends who watch over him. And Pinkerton guards..."

"He surely can't imagine the amount of enemies he must have."

"But, Tara—" Richard began, and then he just shook his head and went silent with frustration.

She smiled, touching his face tenderly. They'd known each other so long. She almost smiled, thinking about how most of the people they knew couldn't understand why they hadn't married. But, of course, they could never marry. They were closer than a sister and a brother. They had grown up as outcasts who'd had to prove themselves, even to survive in the bawdy, salvaging, raw world of Key West, where nationalities mingled with the nationless pirates, and, yes, where the War of Northern Aggression went on, though most often as idle threats and fists raised to the sky. At Fort Zachary Taylor, the Union troops died far more frequently from disease than from battle, though Union ships ever tightened their grip on the blockade. Beer, wine, rum, Scottish whiskey and all manner of alcohol ran rich at the taverns. Fishermen mingled with the architects of the fine new houses, and only at night, behind the wooden walls of their houses—poor or splendid—did the system of class mean much in Key West.

Tara thought that she and Richard were far closer than they might have been had they been born blood sister and brother. Tara's mother had returned from an excursion to the mainland with a new name and child, but no husband. Richard's mother had deserted his pirating father, who had eventually been seized and hanged for his criminal ways. Lorna Douglas Fox had taken Richard in when he'd been just eight years old, ignoring all speculations that the boy would surely grow to be as bad as his father. Lorna had already weathered rumor and whispers; she didn't care what people said, no matter how tiny the island community. She had been born in Key West, and her father had been there before Florida had even become a U.S. territory, much less a state. And, of course, at the beginning, statehood had meant little in Key West. Its population had remained Spanish, Bahamian, English and American...and that really only at shifting intervals, since so many came just to fish, drink and rest, and move on back to nearby island homes.

Tara stood. Richard eyed her warily but stood, too.

"Where is your ship?" she asked flatly.

"I haven't dissuaded you at all, have I?"

She wagged a finger at him. "You have given me a lecture. Now, I shall give you one! I think—however he might have been hated in the South—that Abraham Lincoln is an incredibly good man. I believe that of many of our leaders and generals, as well. And, I think that we need him. I think that we'll need many men of his ilk if we're ever to repair the great rift that's been cre-ated. As you said, John Brown might have been an out-and-out murderer, and certainly, by the law, his sentence was just, but he did have the right idea. Here's where we are, though, about to surrender to a furious power that will have to have any remnant inklings of vengeance held in check, or else the South will be truly doomed. I have to try to get close to the man. I believe that he needs me—and that's not turning traitor, because *my state* will need a strong, enlightened man in control when the giant foot of victory stomps down on us as if we were a pile of ants. Maybe God did decree that we lose the war, but I don't believe that even God wants more horror than what we've already seen to follow it."

Richard looked downward for a moment, and then met her eyes again. "I'm so afraid anytime you leave, Tara. Here…here, you're safe. You have me—and even if I'm not here, you have the threat of me! You have people who know you and love you, and if the general population somewhere knew everything about you—or if they suspected the truth about you—we have stock! We have plenty of beef, we have…blood."

THE UNION SHIP *USS Montgomery* found anchor in the deep harbor at Key West.

Soon the ship's tender drew to the dockside entry of Fort Zachary Taylor on a crystal-clear winter's morn-ing, and Finn took a moment to enjoy the sun stream-ing down on him through a cloudless blue sky. Palms and pines lined deep-water accesses on the island and joined with the bracken that collided on small spits of sandy beach.

The fort itself was a handsome structure, joined to the island by a causeway that was equipped with a draw-bridge. When the Union had first maintained the fort, there had been fears that the citizens of Key West would rise up and try to take it, hence the drawbridge, and the ten cannons set toward the shore. The walls were thick, and dominating the northwest tip of the island, the for-tress was an imposing structure to those at sea.

However, despite these fears, it had yet to see real action in the war, and at this point, it was not likely to. Still, the fort had been a major player by enforcing the Union's dominance of the shipping lanes. The Union blockade was strangling the South, and many of the men stationed at the barracks at Fort Zachary Taylor had been the sailors who prevented Bahamian goods and British guns from reinforcing the rebels.

Finn mused that, from the outset, the North had been at a disadvantage when it had come to true mili-tary genius, since many of the mainstays of the Union army—men who had fought and prevailed valiantly in the Mexican conflict—had chosen to lead the troops in their own states. An agrarian society, the South had naturally bred many fine horsemen, and their cavalry had been exceptional. But the North had the manufac-turing, a greater supply of men upon which to draw and what Finn considered the key in finally winning the war: tenacity. That tenacity, of course, came in the form of the one man who stayed his course no matter how bitter and brutal and disillusioned many had become: Lincoln.

"Agent Dunne!" a smartly saluting soldier proclaimed, offering assistance with his travel bags. Finn greeted him in return, leaping upon the dock.

"I'm Lieutenant Bowers. We've been expecting you, sir! And, please, whatever you've heard about the island and the fort, don't condemn us before you've had your stay. Winter is the time to be here. Though it can grow cold, the days are dawning beautifully! It's not wet and humid like the summer, and mosquitoes are at a minimum. There's hardly a man in the hospital ward, and we're praying we'll not see another summer of war, sir, so we are."

"We can all pray," Finn assured him.

"Come along, sir."

The fort was impressive, Finn thought as they entered. The causeway and drawbridge gave it a bastion against the island, and its high thick walls and multiple guns aimed at the sea provided for a threat against invaders from the water. On the grounds, the barracks seemed clean and even bright in the winter's sun, while within the walls, Finn was certain, there was ample space for supplies, ammunition and further arms. As they walked, Lieutenant Bowers pointed out the dorm-style rooms where many of the fort's occupants slept, the guard stations and the desalination plant, supplying the fort with its own mechanism for providing clean, potable water.

"Started out with cisterns here, but the rain didn't come as thought. Then the seawater came in and the salt started eating away at the foundations," Bowers said cheerfully. "We expected much more difficulty from the population, but...well, the citizens may call themselves Southern as we're in a state in secession, but the place was filled with speculators, fishermen, a few rich and a few down and trodden. None has risen at arms, and while the few moneyed families are careful to keep their daughters under close guard, most of our men have managed to carry on decent relations with the Rebels. Oh, there's a bit of jeering and even some spitting here and there, but nothing too bad!"

"And yet, you know that some of the populace must be plotting," Finn said.

"Sir?" Bowers asked.

Finn smiled at him. "Please. Those running the blockade surely sift right through here. In small boats, there are many ways to move undetected or unnoticed. Fishermen still make a living, rum is reaching the bars and taverns. It would be impossible to police every transaction taking place."

"True, of course," Bowers said. "But you'll note the east and west martello towers across the causeway on the mainland, sir. We are not a huge garrison, but we do manage something of control. Our power, however, is on the sea. We've learned well through the years."

"We've learned a great deal through the years," Finn agreed. "Where there is a will, dedicated men will always find a way."

Finn was led to an office in one of the wooden barracks constructed on the grounds. Bowers opened the door and introduced Finn to his commanding officer, Captain Calloway, and then left.

"Agent Dunne," Calloway said, standing. The captain had the weathered look of a man long familiar with the sea, and the very fact that his skin had begun to resemble one of the state's famed alligators made him a man well worth his salt to Finn. Here was no pretty boy, no educated rich man sitting in power through academic hobnobbing. He'd been on a hard ride in service to his country.

Finn wondered what the captain saw in *him,* since he seemed to be measuring his worth in return. Finally, Calloway indicated a chair. "Sit, Agent Dunne, please. I must admit, I was surprised to hear that you were coming, and I hope we'll be able to help you. I find it incredibly curious that you're here, when President Lincoln is at the capital, and that still, in the midst of mayhem, you're willing to track down every threat, obscure though some may be."

"There is no threat against the president we deem obscure," Finn told him.

Calloway nodded gravely. "Yes, but…well, I'm sure that President Lincoln has enemies everywhere—North and South. There are those in his own camp who believe he should have let the secessionist go. Those who were furious over the draft— Hell, there were draft *riots*. He surely has political enemies. Quite frankly, I'm surprised you have enough men to cover all threats. But to come here…"

"Here, to this is faraway, other world, you mean?" Finn suggested. "I certainly see your point, but we've learned through the years to separate what is probably an idle threat—angry talk—from what may well be a concerted plot being put into motion. My superiors consider this plot by the blockade runners and their co-conspirators serious. We have a man incarcerated in the capital now, and the correspondence he carried was damning. Better to stop the situation at the seed than allow it to become a giant tree with branches sweeping across the continent."

"I see," Calloway said, though Finn was pretty sure he didn't really. "And yet, in truth, how easily the president could be stopped by a single bullet, while riding in his carriage around the mall…"

Finn didn't want to admit that it wasn't an easy task protecting the man. While Lincoln was plagued with strange dreams and a sense that his lifespan would be cut short, he seemed unwilling to take the necessary steps to prevent such an outcome. "In the capital, and when the president travels, he is still under protection. He has the military, and he has Pinkerton agents. Pinkerton himself stopped an assassination attempt in Maryland. We have men in the capital, and we have men covertly stationed throughout the Southern armies. Captain, the point is not just to be at the president's side and stop individual bullets. It's also to stop what could become an event in which many people are involved, if you will—a situation in which the entire government is brought down."

"Like, say, a civil war," Calloway said gravely, still looking puzzled, though introspective. "Do you usually succeed in these intelligence missions?"

"We do, sir." Inwardly, Finn flinched. *Usually.* Usually, he discovered the truth of every situation. But he still chafed over one particular failure: the day he had lost the woman at Gettysburg. Ostensibly, she'd carried nothing but a harmless scarf. But there had been something strange about the beauty, something he felt he recognized and that portended danger. The memories of that day had haunted him since.

"Well," Calloway said, "I'm not privy to your means of intelligence, sir, but we're pleased to offer all the assistance that we may. I believe that you want to set out tomorrow night?"

"Indeed. The moon will be all but black, and I understand that this time of year lends itself to good cloud cover. If I were setting out with contraband and communications, it's the night I would choose to take flight."

"You'll be sailing with Captain John Tremblay, an excellent sailor, and a rare man—a native of St. Augustine. And," Calloway admitted, "he pointed out to me himself that the date you have chosen does seem optimal for such a runner to take flight. I hope, sir, that you are not on a wild-goose chase, and that you catch your man. May God help us all in this."

THE WAR, EVEN IN DISTANT Key West where little happened, had changed life.

Tara could remember being a child when it was easy to run down to the wharf at any time, when a friend might head out fishing or just take sail because it was a beautiful day. She remembered shopping the fish market without tension in the air, and when the cats and seabirds shrieked and cried out, trying to steal the best fish heads and the refuse tossed aside by the men and women working the stalls.

She remembered when the great ships had brought in new supplies from the Northeast, the Bahamas or even Europe. Women on the island would receive their copies of *Godey's Lady's Book,* and they had oohed and aahed over the newest fashions and determined what they should buy, what they could sew and what they could practicably wear on an island where heat was king.

Some merchant ships still came, though they were heavily patrolled by the Union. Women still looked at fashions, but they could seldom afford to buy. The fish markets were quiet, with only the birds and the cats unaware of the unspoken tensions.

And it was no longer easy to set sail from the tiny island, not without proper credentials. Unless, of course, it was by darkness, in a small craft, and with someone who knew the lay of the land.

That being, Tara left the island of Key West on a single-mast fishing boat with Seminole Pete, who had long kept a bar in town. Pete had outlasted the Seminole Wars, and he had never surrendered or succumbed—he had just kept moving, and now his bar was a fixture. In his spare time, Pete "fished," and in doing so he helped his friends, who numbered many. There were only friends and those who were not his friends. In his day, he'd seen half his people decimated in the Seminole Wars, and there was no white man in a uniform he trusted, North or South. Tara was Pete's friend, and she loved that he was one of the few people who seemed to know everything about her without ever being told.

When Tara's mother had died, just as the war had commenced, Tara had rented out the beautiful home on Caroline Street her grandfather had built, and took residence in a few rooms in the huge and rambling home Pete owned. Pete and Richard had both insisted she do so; it was dangerous for her to be alone.

That was fine with her. She'd always thought her mother would eventually marry Pete, but while the two were close and constantly together, they'd never taken vows. It was nice to be around him after her passing.

As they neared the small island just north of Key West, Tara became aware of the scents on the air: cows, pigs, chickens and other animals. The Union-held fort and the Confederate citizens of the lower Keys all found their sustenance through the remarkable resources of the island.

"We are near. You are in plenty of time," Pete said, his voice expressionless.

Pete didn't question the power of dreams; when she had explained to him that she felt that she had to get close to the American president, he merely nodded. He'd taken many a person through the years to Richard's ship, hidden behind the mangroves. An Indian out in a small fishing boat was not someone with whom the Yankee troops would bother.

Besides, not even the Union troops questioned *where* Seminole Pete secured his beverages. Off-duty, they were far too pleased to enjoy his bar. In fact, at times, the situation there would have been comical if there weren't a country pathetically at war all around them. Customers sometimes shouted taunts, or made them beneath their breath, but all kept it peaceful, as if they were but placing bets on different horses in a race.

She looked over at Pete. The sail was down, so he rowed steadily, his sculpted face impassive. He watched her as he steadfastly drew the oars, one easy, even stroke after another.

"You think I'm crazy," she said quietly, breaking through the rhythmic sound of the oars on the water.

"You said you must do this. Then you must," he said. "Will I worry about you? Indeed, child, I will."

"Have you ever had anything like this happen to you?" Tara asked. "I mean, where your dreams were of someone else and came upon you like a sickness of worry?"

"I know many people who have had such dreams," Pete said gravely. "But were they dreams? Or did we know that the guns were coming to our shores, and that we would be driven farther and farther into the swamps? Perhaps we rush to bring these things into our minds, and dreams are the culminations of our fear—fear for what we can't stop."

"But if we see omens, doesn't that mean there's at least a prayer we can stop a catastrophe?"

"Perhaps," Pete said, gazing out across the darkness. "Sometimes we see a path, and think that we must take it, and then there's a fork in the road. We may not go to the same destination."

She smiled. "You're confusing me, Pete."

"Life is confusion. Now, more than ever. Or it is not. We just live. Time will come and go, and this war will end, and there will be new wars. I understand that any man or woman must do what they believe is asked of them by a great power. So, do what you must. And then come home. This is where you belong. Where you are known and where you are loved. There will be bitter days ahead, and harsh punishment, and our tiny island world will be far enough from the heaviest part of the boot when it falls."

"The war isn't over yet," she half protested, though she didn't know why.

"All but the tail end of the dying. Trust me—I've seen war. At the end, there is nothing but blood."

"There is already blood," Tara said softly.

Pete didn't disagree; he had spoken his mind.

She was aware of the sound of the oars striking the water again and listened to them for a while. Then Pete nodded his head toward the horizon.

Squinting, Tara could see Richard's *Peace,* sails down, at deep anchor off the stock island. It was barely a silhouette against the dark sky. She was surprised that Pete had seen it, but he had spent much of his life fighting and running through the darkness and the marsh.

Peace was a beautiful ship. Richard had commissioned her for his salvage and merchandising business before secession, and before he had ever dreamed of operating her as a war vessel. She had three masts and a square rig, which meant that at full sail she was quite a sight to behold. She could move swiftly over the open water, but since the decline of the clipper had begun with the advent of steam, Richard had modernized her by equipping her with a steamer, as well. She had a shallow draft, and could easily navigate the coral reefs and shoals, especially with a captain like Richard manning her; he knew the waters around the Florida Keys as well as he knew his own image in a mirror, if not better.

Richard had sailed out on a dark night many a time, evading the enemy ships. He hid the *Peace* and walked about Key West as an average citizen, avoiding the Yankee troops in the town these past four years.

Pete ceased to row, letting his small boat drift toward the larger ship. A man on guard on the deck quickly called down to them. "State your business, and speak quickly!"

"It's Tara Fox!" she called quickly.

"Come aboard!"

A rope ladder was thrown down, and Tara leaned over to plant a kiss on Pete's face. She imagined he might have blushed. "Don't worry. I will make it home," she promised him.

Grabbing her satchel and securing it around her shoulders, she reached for the rope and carefully climbed her way up to the deck. Richard was there to help her on board.

"You know, you are insane," he told her huskily.

"Just following the lead of my captain!" she returned. He turned quickly, introducing her to the man on guard.

"Tara, I think you know Grant Quimbly here. Lawrence Seville is at the helm, and Gary French is working the steam engine. Make yourself at home in the cabin. We'll be on our way."

"Thank you, Richard," she told him.

He nodded. "Lawrence, let's get her under way!"

Tara looked down to the dark sea; she could barely make out Pete's small boat.

The darkness seemed overwhelming.

But just as she thought so, the cloud cover shifted, and a pale glow of starlight filled the sky. She could see the barest sliver of a moon. It was the night of the new moon, and yet, it almost looked as if, for a moment, it was waxing crescent.

It almost appeared to be grinning.

She shivered. It seemed as if even the moon was mocking her.

CHAPTER TWO

"THEY'RE GOOD—THE BLOCKADE runners around these waters," Captain John Tremblay told Finn, looking out at the darkness. "They're very, very good—the men who sail in the night and the darkness. They know when to make their runs. They know how to make use of moonless nights, when cloud cover erases even the stars." He turned and looked at Finn. "But, of course, you chose the date."

The sea and the sky seemed to combine that night, as if they might have been sailing off the earth's surface into a stygian void of nothingness. Setting out on the captain's steamer, *USS Punisher,* they had navigated easily enough; the Key West lighthouse helped ships on both sides avoid calamity on the reefs. But Tremblay and crew were now beyond its glow, heading north, and the moonless, starless night created an eerie realm where even the truth and the horror of the war seemed of another world. The stars, of course, were out there. But cloud cover was blocking even their gentle light. The world was one, water and air merged. Watching the vastness of the ocean at night, Finn could well un-

derstand how the medieval population had believed that
the world was flat.

He'd been at sea enough to comprehend winds and
tides; he'd kept a small sailboat on the river for years.
But here, tonight, the sky was deep velvet and blue-
black, and the sea seemed to be a glass sheet as vast as
the endless dark heavens above them. Though Calloway had been apprised of his mission, Captain Tremblay had not been told any of the particulars, other than
a Pinkerton was seeking a certain man, and he believed
that he'd find him in these waters.

Finn found himself admiring both the Union navy
seamen who plied these waters and the blockade runners themselves. Of course, there was money in running the blockade, but at this stage of the war, many
of the men willing to risk the noose of the Union navy
did so out of a sense of patriotism; money only meant
something if you were alive. Of course, there were those
reckless would-be pirates who were willing to take a
chance at anything, but at this stage of the game, many
were also die-hard heroes, continuing to fight a losing
battle in the hope of keeping the Confederacy alive long
enough for the North to tire of the war before the South
was completely decimated.

"What makes you think your man is a blockade
runner?" Captain Tremblay asked him, handing him
the spyglass.

"We intercepted communications," Finn said. He

looked through the glass, and still there was nothing to see but blackness.

"About a blockade runner?" Tremblay asked. He seemed puzzled, and then said, "Blockade runners are not often spies, except, of course, they will carry whatever information they acquire. They're seldom assassins."

"This one is an unusual circumstance. The man is apparently obsessed with his hatred, though I don't suppose that's so unusual at this time…. But he has a vendetta against Lincoln, and he just happens to be a blockade runner, and since he's able to move around quickly and communicate with others, he's especially dangerous."

Finn hesitated a minute, looking at Tremblay, but he was afraid that if they didn't catch the man tonight, whether his name was known or not wasn't going to matter much. "He's a man who goes by the code name of Gator. His brother was killed at Gettysburg, and one of his conspirators was apprehended in the capital— with an incriminating correspondence."

"Many good men were killed at Gettysburg. Tens of thousands," Tremblay said, a hoarse note in his voice. "But putting together a conspiracy… What fool puts that information in a letter?"

"Most of it was code, but we have code-breakers. This Gator is moving supplies to the Jacksonville area— there are scores of inlets that connect with the St. Johns River. A Florida militia is planning a movement somewhere in the north of the state. Gator is bringing up arms procured in the Bahamas, and beef from the Keys. His delivery made, he will continue north, without stock or arms, and gain entry close to the capital, possibly around northern Virginia or Maryland. He'll carry nothing but legal sales goods at that point, in case he's stopped. Once he makes land, he'll find his way to the capital, working then as some kind of a sutler. He has fellow conspirators in the North, who will supply him with arms when the time comes. I don't think he cares if he's shot on the spot himself—not if he manages to kill President Lincoln. That's why it's imperative that we stop him now, while he's bearing goods to break the blockade. Once he divests himself of arms, it will be difficult—even in war—to recognize him, detain him and stop him."

"Then we'll do our best to bring him down," Tremblay said.

Finn lowered the spyglass. "Thank you, Captain."

Tremblay nodded. He was an old-timer, a man who had spent his life in naval service. His beard and hair were white, his eyes were blue and his stance was square and steady. As he looked at Finn, he added, "We've lost many a good ship to the Confederates, you know. We had to scuttle three in the river up at Jacksonville just last November. Many of the blockade runners have guns aboard as well, but they're not fighters. They keep themselves light and shallow for speed and the ability to slip through narrow channels and rivers. But if we come across your man, there may be a fight."

"Captain," Finn said, a note of bitter amusement in his voice. "Do I look like a man who's never seen a fight?"

Tremblay studied him a moment, and then grinned sheepishly. "No, sir, you do not. But fighting as a Pinkerton is different, of course, from a fight at sea."

"Don't worry, Captain. I've seen my share of action—on land *and* on sea."

Finn looked through the glass again. Nothing. His vision tended to be excellent, no matter the velvety blue-black of the night. But there was nothing to see, as yet.

And, of course, this mission could be a futile one.

Still, better futile through overexertion than through laziness and bad surveillance.

No matter how much energy it took, Finn couldn't let this *Gator* make his connections, definitely could not let him reach the capital and their leader. No matter how many times guards, generals, friends and fellow politicians warned him, President Lincoln was a man of the people. He rode his carriage along the mall. He invited his constituents to speak with him. Quite simply, Lincoln believed to the core that if he was not available, then he was not serving anyone. To try to change him might well be an effort to change the very soul of the man they all strove so diligently and with such love and admiration to protect.

Finn didn't know that he and others *could* prevail,

not forever. He did know, however, that there had been many times when his abilities helped him single out the right person to stop in a crowd. That he had protected his charge on that particular day. He didn't necessarily face an assassin every time, but often someone bent on harassment, or ready to throw rotten food at the president, or to create a riot out of a rally. He had done well so far, but it only took one mistake....

Like the woman at Gettysburg. Moving toward him, reaching beneath her cloak...

She had carried a scarf, he reminded himself. She might have meant nothing but a show of worship.

Yet, she had been so strange. So beautiful, and so different, dangerous...dangerous even if what she had produced had been a hand-knitted scarf. She had wanted to get close to the president, and there had just been that strange difference about her....

He still had that narrow lock of her hair in his wallet. And he still believed that she was out there somewhere, and that, one day, he would find her.

Of course, now he was here.

And still thinking about his failure that day!

Finn chafed at this assignment. He felt better serving the president nearer to him; he was ready to stop a bullet for the man at any time. He felt himself well qualified to do so.

But he also knew something about the sea, and it was true—he had seen many a naval battle and survived.

He'd seen battles the good captain couldn't begin to imagine.

Staring into the darkness, assigned to stop a blooming threat before it could fully materialize.

"You needn't worry about me," Finn said. "Whatever course is called, I will be ready."

"Bosun!" the captain called, looking to the man up on the fantail behind them, a sailor who was studying the night with his own spyglass. "Any signs of life?"

"No, Captain, sir!" the sailor called back. "Not a whisper as of yet!"

Captain Tremblay looked through the glass again. "I see nothing."

Finn narrowed his eyes suddenly, looking toward the shore. He knew that they were in an area where mangrove swamp gave way to rivers and waterways. They were now north in the Florida Keys, nearing the mainland. It was an area where the Atlantic frequently gave way to channels between the islands, where little mangrove spits were in the tectonic process of gathering silt and debris to become islands, and where trim, shallow-draft ships could easily disappear in the blink of an eye.

"There!" Finn announced suddenly.

"Where?"

"There...hugging the shore. He must know of an inlet."

"Bosun!" the captain called.

"Nothing. I see nothing, sir!" called the lookout.

"It's there, believe me," Finn said. "We didn't see her,

but she's seen us, and she's ducking through a channel now, heading for the gulf."

As Finn spoke, a break formed in the cloud cover overhead. The moon might be new on this January night, so crisp and cool even, but with cloud cover gone, the sky seemed to be filled with a sudden burst of starlight. Perhaps God himself was on the side of the North, Finn mused.

And there, just disappearing before them, was what almost appeared to be a ghost ship, a steam clipper, gliding away, her sails down but her masts just caught in a pale sparkle of starlight.

"Full speed ahead, sir!" Finn said.

"Man your guns!" the captain bellowed.

And the chase was on.

TARA HAD BEGUN TO FEEL that her fears had been entirely unjustified. They had set out with a light wind, cutting through the islands midway between Key West and the mainland and then out to the Atlantic, where they had run parallel with the coast. A breeze had picked up, perfect for the sails, and for a while, she had gone to the cabin, far too restless for sleep, but determined to at least lie down awhile.

And it had been while she had been there, planning a route once she reached land, that she heard Richard's anxious shout.

"Union steamer starboard. Down the sails! Steam power, with all due speed!"

Tara jerked up and raced out to the deck. The men

were grimly pulling down the sails. Richard was at the helm, and they were under steam power once again. The *Peace* moved quickly. Richard knew how to avoid the reefs, and she was certain that he would head back into the inlets and perhaps the gulf, doing his best to ground the enemy ship as it came in pursuit.

He cast her a glance as she hurried to him at the helm. "She's heavily gunned," he said tersely, indicating the enemy ship. "If the firing starts...do whatever you need to do to get out of here. Even if you haven't the strength to go far, you'll know where you can find shelter along the islands and the coast."

"I'm fine, Richard."

"You're not listening to me. That ship is *heavily gunned.* I have a few small cannons. If I can't outrun her..."

"If you can't outrun her, you surrender," Tara said, feeling a choking sensation in her throat. "Richard, do you hear me? You *surrender.* They don't shoot down blockade runners in cold blood. They're trying to stop the flow of supplies, not murder people."

The look he gave her was one that clearly told her his thoughts.

No. In principle, the enemy was not out to commit murder.

But this was war.

And tempers flared and shots fired easily....

"Men die in the camps," Richard said flatly.

"And men live in the camps!" Tara insisted.

"You should get out of here, now," he told her.

"No."

"You're stubborn!"

"I know my own resources." It was difficult to see the Union ship, but she could make out its ominous silhouette.

"Take the helm!" Richard told her.

She did, and he reached for his spyglass, looking over at the enemy ship.

"He should be over the reef any minute…grounding, I pray…." And then he swore, quickly looking at her apologetically. "He rounded it. He knows the game I'm playing."

"You'll outrun him," Tara said with confidence—far more confidence than she was feeling. Few people knew these waters like a native son.

Save another native son.

"I'm heading for the channel. Maybe there…" Richard said.

"You will outrun him," she repeated staunchly.

But the echo of her words had barely died when the sound of a cannon boom burst through the night.

The ball fell short of its target, causing the water in their wake to burst from the sea like a geyser.

"That was too close," Richard murmured.

"Damned close!" Lawrence said.

"Aye, Grant. You and Lawrence, man the rear cannon!" Richard commanded. "Quickly. We must pray for a strike and hobble here on the reef!"

His men scurried to do as bidden. Before they could reach their posts belowdeck, a second volley came their way, closer this time. The *Peace* shook in the water, the waves rose and Tara quickly grabbed hold of the mast to keep her feet.

"Tara, do something to save yourself!" Richard said firmly.

"No! I'm not leaving you!"

Richard stared at her in frustration and yelled out to his men below. "Fire!"

A second later, their cannon fire boomed.

Tara stared out at the enemy ship, relieved to see a small burst of fire explode near her aft section.

"Direct hit, first volley!" she said.

Richard had his spyglass on the ship.

"She's lamed, she isn't dead," he said flatly.

As he spoke, another volley exploded from the enemy ship.

"Hold on!" Richard roared to her, bracing himself.

The water exploded to their front aft side. A miss, though the *Peace* rocked precariously.

Tara held tight to the mast, weighing the possible consequences of the battle. It might be time for them to abandon ship, and use Richard's knowledge of the islands and the water to survive. "Where are we?" she asked him quickly.

"Near the mainland," he told her. "Just a few islands southwest of the mainland. And it's time for you to go. Head northeast—"

"I will not leave you. You're—well, you've a safety net in me, if we're together. We'll head northeast. By ship, or by foot. They will flounder in the channel—they're floundering now! I'm not leaving you, so please don't waste your time trying to get me to do so."

He stared at her with exasperation. But even as he did so, he bellowed to his men below.

"Fire!"

THE UNION SHIP WAS ROCKING like a cradle in the water, ablaze in the aft section, and Tremblay was shouting orders to his men.

Finn balanced easily enough, watching as men hurried about, stumbling here and there, and turning a slight shade of green at the pitch and heave of the ship.

Tremblay was a seasoned captain. He held his sea legs steady, moving with the motion of the ship, a pitch and roll he probably knew far too well.

"Gunners!" he shouted out, his voice calm and powerful. "Stay your posts! Seamen, douse that fire! See if we're taking on water!"

Tremblay swore beneath his breath. "She hit us! The lucky Reb actually hit us.... *Keep us steady men!* We'll come apart on the reef! Gunners, fire! Take to the cannons, boy, and give her a long volley, one after the other, all ablaze!"

Finn turned to him. "Captain, we don't want all aboard killed."

"We'll man the boats, and bring them in. We must

stop her—before she stops us." He stared at Finn. "We may be floundering already. If she scrapes coral now…"

"Demand her surrender," Finn urged.

"Her surrender? We've been hit!" Tremblay said.

"Aye, but she is listing worse. Demand her surrender," Finn insisted. "She can't know that we're taking on water just as badly."

"Hold fire!" Tremblay called.

His order came just as someone fired a gun prematurely.

THE NIGHT WAS SPLIT again with a great boom of sound, and the earth itself seemed to tremble.

That time, the thunder in the air was followed by a shuddering explosion; they'd been hit again, and hard. The repercussion swept Tara off her feet. She fell and discovered that she was lying under Richard. She quickly eased from beneath and rose above him, touching his face. "Richard, Richard…"

He opened his eyes slowly, and then blinked rapidly. "We've been hit…we've been hit a death blow…. Take the helm and try to steady her until we can abandon ship. I've got to get below…to the others…."

"Richard, it's burning. It's—it's too late!"

"Have to…have to get down there… My men…"

He staggered to his feet; she feared he wouldn't make it to the deck below, but there would be no stopping him. The night that had been so pleasantly dark and quiet was now ominous in its silence between small bursts of fire that ignited about the ship. Black smoke was heavy on the air.

"Richard, please," she said softly.

He grabbed her by the shoulders; his eyes seemed almost blank. He was shell-shocked, she knew, but she couldn't stop him.

"I have to see," he said thickly. "You know I have to see…. Someone could be…injured."

No. She wished that it was true, but no one could have survived that explosion.

He thrust himself from her, heading for the steps below.

Tara staggered back and grabbed the wildly jerking wheel, using all her strength to steady the ship, trying to keep her limping forward. But another volley followed, and another. It was all she could do, just to hold tight.

Richard burst out from the deck below, his face covered in soot, his features twisted in a grim mask.

He grabbed her by the shoulders, jerking her around to face him. "They're dead…the men are dead, and we're taking on water. Get out of here, now!"

Past Richard, she could see that the enemy steamer was moving in on them.

They stared at each other—Richard angry and impotent to get her away, Tara determined that she'd never leave him, not at any cost.

Then thunder burst through the sky again, so loud that it was painful, and when the ship shuddered, it was as if they'd been hit by the hand of God.

Perhaps they had been....

Tara landed hard, stunned and breathless. For a moment, even she was completely disoriented, seeing only darkness. Then color and light returned to her world. She grasped a trunk and pulled herself to her feet. Looking around desperately for Richard, she saw that he was hanging over the portside of the ship.

A wave crested over the ship. Water washed around her friend.

And when the water was gone, Richard was gone.

With a scream, Tara rushed to the rail, and saw his body being swallowed by the darkness of the ocean.

She pitched herself over the rail to follow him.

"JESUS, MARY AND JOSEPH!" Tremblay raged. "Who's responsible? The last volley wasn't on order!"

Finn could have echoed his furious sentiments, but it would do no good. A gunner ran up to them, soot-faced and frantic.

"Captain! There was a spark that flew from the match…it caught the wick. We didn't fire to destroy her!"

"Destroyed or not, I *need* the men aboard that ship," Finn said.

Another filthy man ran up to the captain. "Sir, we're taking on water—heavily. We're working the pumps, bailing…. She's on a reef, sir. Cut by the coral as well as their return fire!"

"Lower the longboats!" Tremblay ordered in a booming voice.

As the men hurried to do as told, Finn stared out at
the Rebel runner.

"We're sinking, Agent Dunne!" Tremblay told him.

"I am aware, sir."

He stood his ground, staring at the enemy ship. The
masts were shattered; she was listing badly to the land-
ward side. Fire had broken out in her aft; he'd seen the
explosion that had hit her there. The way that flames
were leaping and burning, he assumed they'd hit her
powder supply.

Whatever cargo she carried would soon be lost.

Anyone caught in the aft was dead; they had, at the
least, died swiftly. The portside of the ship and her fore
still stood in the night, though the fire would soon con-
sume them, as well.

He quickly reckoned the distance from the dying ship
to the shore; a strong swimmer could make it. Theoreti-
cally, others—if not killed by the blast—might well still
be aboard, dead or dying, or unconscious.

Finn didn't want to wait for the tenders; he stripped
off his jacket and headed for the rail.

"Agent Dunne!" Tremblay called. "Sir! The boats
will be speedy—"

"Not speedy enough."

Finn dove from the ship's deck, hitting the water
hard and pitching downward. The water was cold, a
hard slap of ice against his flesh as he landed and thrust
through its density. In the night, not even his eyesight
was much against the depths, but he had little interest

in what was around him. When his legs scraped coral, it only confirmed that their ship would have floundered had it come out this far. The Rebel captain they chased knew his landscape, and knew it well.

Finn swam hard, picking up greater speed with every length he cleared from the Union boat. He could see the Rebel ship burning and listing, and he swam harder; it was war, of course. A Union ship destroying a blockade runner and all aboard was a regrettable fact of war.

To Finn, it meant a dead end. If all aboard had perished, he might never know if he had found Gator, if this threat to Lincoln still remained; if failed, he might not be able to return to the president's side.

There were shouts audible in the air. The Union men had lowered the longboats, and crews were coming in his wake.

He reached the burning ship. It listed so badly to the side, he could climb straight aboard. The remnants of her shell would remain where it was in the days to come, her skeleton caught on the reef.

Despite the heavy smoke on the air, he could smell the sickly sweet scent of burning flesh, and he prayed that those caught in the inferno had been baked before the fire even reached them. Crawling aboard, dripping with seawater, he lifted his arm against the rise of the flame to protect his face. He quickly ascertained that there was no getting belowdeck; anyone caught there was gone.

But a hurried search topside against the rip of the

flames in the night revealed no bodies consumed by fire or otherwise. And if anyone had survived, they had not gone for their longboats—they had done as he had, diving into the night.

Someone was out there. Even if the ship's crew had been small, there had been someone topside. Someone running the operation.

Gator?

In just another second, Finn realized that the heat of the fire had already nearly dried his sea-soaked clothing.

He could feel his flesh beginning to sear.

He dove back into the water, and began to swim again, aware that the water felt even more frigid against the heat of his body. The difference between the fire heat aboard the ship and the winter water was extreme; he knew that he had to keep moving, and move fast. The fire illuminated the night, and he looked toward the shore. He could just see a tangle of mangroves, and beyond that, the small spit of a beach.

The island was some distance. And though it might be far warmer than any sea farther north, the icy hand of winter had stretched even down here. Could an injured man have possibly survived?

Yes.

Possibly.

Whatever it took, he had to know.

Finn couldn't help his thoughts from spinning, even as he kept his arms and legs moving in swift, even strokes through the water. He was sick at the thought of the men caught by the cannons as the ship exploded. He was angry that he had come so far, and that he might never know if they had or hadn't killed Gator.

No.

Someone had to have been topside. And that person had survived.

Someone was out there, alive and well, or dying, in the midst of the mangrove isle, and he was going to find them.

CHAPTER THREE

TARA'S DESPERATE DIVES beneath the surface had paid off—she'd found Richard and quickly brought him to the surface.

But he wasn't conscious, and with the frigid water washing around her, salt waves rocking hard against them minute after minute, it was difficult to even ascertain at first if he was alive. Mindless of the water, she squeezed his torso to force water from him...and he coughed, and he breathed.

And he lived.

"Tara...." he gasped.

"I've got you, Richard, I've got you," she assured him.

"Too far from shore. I can't make it. Go...for the love of God, go."

"Ease back. I've got you."

"Tara, you can get—" Richard's words were cut off as a wave washed over them. He coughed violently again. "Get away!"

"Shut up! Quit talking. Keep your mouth closed and lie back. Damn you, Richard, I can swim with you. Stop fighting me or I'll knock you out and drag you, so don't make it harder for me," she warned him with a note of steel in her voice.

Water washed over him again. He sputtered it out, and she took advantage of his weakness to force him flat and slip her left arm around his chest in a hold that would allow him to keep his head above the surface while she fought the waves with her right arm and legs. She had a reserve of strength that was deep, fortunately, as the sea itself seemed to be against them that night.

As she kicked harder, she was dimly aware of some form of shadow that seemed to linger over Richard's boat.

Death?

She gave herself a mental shake; she couldn't think that way. She had to use her entire concentration to get her friend to the shore. She didn't even dare look back at the Yankee ship. Richard had been thrown severely about his wounded ship, and if she didn't get him to land, nothing else about the night would really matter.

An explosion suddenly burst through the night and Tara realized that a powder keg had exploded.

The resulting mass of waves wrenched Richard from her arms. Skyrocketing flames illuminated the water, and she couldn't see Richard anymore.

Even with her exceptional sight and strength, it seemed like an eternity in agony, diving and searching, diving and searching.

While the blazing fire on the ship illuminated the surface of the water, creating an almost beautiful array of golden splendor on the now-gentling waves, beneath the glowing sheen the water remained stygian in the night. She could barely see, and while she knew about where Richard had gone in, she couldn't pinpoint the precise location, and she might not have found him at all had he not bobbed to the surface.

Facedown.

"Richard!" she shouted, swimming to him, turning him over in the water. His eyes were closed; his form was limp.

"Richard!" she cried again, and then squeezed his torso with gentle pressure, fighting the waves around them. To her relief, he coughed and choked, and water spewed from his mouth. A wave lapped around them, covering his face, and he coughed again, trying to fight the water that seemed so ready to claim him.

"Easy, easy, just float, I've got you!" Tara assured him.

"The ship...the men," Richard said, and choked as icy salt water moved over his mouth again.

"Shhh... Stop talking." She wondered if he'd been struck in the head.... But he was breathing; he was alive and breathing and she was going to make sure nothing changed that.

"The men..." he repeated.

"Stop. We've been through this." She was terribly afraid that her friend didn't want to live, that guilt over his men would infect his thoughts and keep him from assisting her rescue attempt. "Richard! Shut up! The war has taken many lives—I won't let it take yours."

Richard wasn't a small man, and the water felt bitterly cold, and it wasn't easy managing the weight and length of his lean and muscled body—especially when he wasn't cooperating.

"Fire," he said, as if he hadn't heard her, glazed eyes reflecting the burst of fire in the sky.

She was tempted to knock him out again. He was the dearest friend she'd ever had, or would have, and she would not lose him.

"Quiet!" she whispered softly. She hooked her arm around his body, trying to get him to relax and let her use the power of her right arm and legs against the water. "Lay back, Richard, and let me take you. Please. Please…" Just when she thought she couldn't wrestle with him for one minute more, he mercifully passed out once again. She felt the fight leave his muscles.

Finally, she was able to begin a hard crawl toward the shore.

The water was deep; the ship had floundered in the channel between isles, where a coral shelf rested just to the Atlantic side. They couldn't be in more than thirty feet of water, and yet, now the length of her body burned with the exertion of her muscles and her lips continued to quiver from the cold.

She had never felt so strained, nor so exhausted, in her life.

Just when she thought that the agony in her arms and

legs would cripple her, she felt ground at the tips of her feet. She realized that she could stand, having reached the gnarled toes of the island. She slipped off the submerged root, dragging Richard with her. Doggedly, she found a foothold again, paused, breathed and waited. She looked back to the Yankee ship, on fire now.

At last, she managed to drag him up on a spit of sand between the gnarled and twisted "legs" of a spiderlike clump of mangroves. She lay there next to him, panting, and feeling as if her muscles burned with the same fire that still illuminated the night sky. She breathed in the acrid and smoky air.

Turning then to Richard, she felt for his pulse—faint, but steady—and warmth jumped in her heart. She allowed herself to fall back for another moment, just breathing and gathering her strength. She was drenched, and her skirts were heavy with water. She felt the winter's nip that lay around her, even here.

She thanked God that they hadn't gone in farther north, where temperatures would have been far more wicked.

She rested, and then, even as she breathed more easily, she bolted up. Looking out over the dying remnants of the *Peace,* she could see that the Union ship floundered, too.

She had grounded herself; she wasn't injured and limping, but she was caught on the reef, and there was no escape for her. The Union boat would have a number of longboats, easy to send into the inlets, saving the lives of the men aboard.

Richard was alive, she knew that, and she believed in her heart that he would survive. But he wasn't coming around, and they had to leave their present position; they were like sitting ducks at a county fair.

She dragged herself to her feet. Half of the heaviness of the weight she had borne, she realized, had been that of her skirts. She wrenched off the cumbersome petticoat that had nicely provided warmth—before becoming saturated with seawater. Rolling the cotton and lace into a ball, she stuffed it into a gap in the tree roots, shoving up a pile of seaweed and sand to hide the telltale sign that this was where survivors had come ashore.

Something in the water caught her eye, some form of movement. It might have just been a shadow created on the water by the rise and fall of flames that still tore from the desiccating ship. Soon, the *Peace* would be down to charred, skeletal remains, and she would sink to the seabed. At the moment, enough of the hull remained above the surface to allow the flames to continue to lap at the sky, shooting upward with dying sparks now and then.

A shadow on the water... The Unionists would be coming...coming after a blockade runner.

She reached down, dragging Richard's body up. He was far bigger than she was, but she managed to get him over her shoulder. Taking a last glance back at the flame-riddled night, she started to move through the mangroves that rimmed the edge of the isle.

THE FIRE ON THE BLOCKADE runner was just beginning to subside, but Finn could still hear the lick of the flames as they consumed tinder, and the split of wood as it disintegrated in the conflagration. Soon, however, the sea would claim the fire, and the night would be lit by only the stars.

He couldn't wait for the longboats; he surveyed his surroundings from the mangrove roots he stood upon.

This side of the islet—new to time and history, created by the tenacious roots and the silt and debris caught with those roots—was really nothing more than a tangle of gnarled tree, slick ponds and beds of seaweed. But looking toward the east, he could see that there was a spit of sand. He began crawling over the roots, heedless when he stepped knee-deep in a cache of water. Tiny crabs scurried around his intrusion, and he could hear the squish of his boots. When he cleared the heaviest thicket, he paused, leaning on a tree, to empty the water from his boots.

Shortly after he resumed moving through the thinning foliage, he heard a grunting sound. He paused. Alligators roamed the freshwater areas of the upper Keys, and even crocodiles made a home in the brackish waters off the southern coast. But Finn wasn't hearing the odd, piglike grunt of a gator. He was hearing the snuffling grunt made by wild pigs. There was hope that water was to be found on the island, and if pigs were surviving here, then man could, too. Good to know, in case this was a long excursion.

Something along the terrain caught his eye and he paused. The remaining fire that had lit the sky was all but gone, little more than a flicker. He paused, seeing nothing, and retraced his footsteps, wincing as he stepped knee-deep into a pool again. But even with this, his efforts were rewarded. There, deep in a crevice, was something. He reached for it, and was surprised when something big and white and heavily laden with seawater fell into his hands. He frowned, puzzled for a moment, and then smiled grimly.

A petticoat. A woman's petticoat. Soaked and salty, ripped and torn and encrusted with sand and muck.

It hadn't been there long. It hadn't been there long at all.

He looked ahead to the beach, where a survivor might conceivably find a dry spot in the chill night. Where a survivor just might have to risk building a fire, or freeze. There was certainly no snow this far south, but it was a bitter night. They were probably hitting down close to freezing.

He set the petticoat down, studying it, and felt a sweep of tension wash over him. He did his work well, and he knew that he did, and he felt passionately that the future of the country—the decency, the healing—were in the hands of a good man. He had followed through on every threat, perceived or real, and he had lost his suspect only once.

At Gettysburg.

The woman had slipped cleanly through his fingers, and he had never forgotten, and now...

He couldn't help but look at the petticoat, and wonder, as impossible as the odds might be, if he hadn't come upon her again.

Was *she* Gator?

TARA FOUND A SPOT SHIELDED by a strip of land where pines had taken root. She looked around carefully before lowering Richard's body to the soft, chill ground, and then paused for a minute to stretch her agonized muscles. She fell into a seated position next to Richard and leaned her head against one of the protecting trees. She was exhausted and, despite her exertion, very cold.

She checked Richard's pulse and breathing again, and assured herself that he was going to make it. But his limbs felt like ice. She forced herself back to her feet. She would gather fallen palm branches to make a blanket for her friend. Now that she had gotten him out of the water, she wished that he would come to—there were others out there in the night, and it was imperative that they stay hidden until she could find a way off the island. Another blockade runner would eventually come by. They would survive; they both knew how to hold out in such an environment. If there were palms on the island, there were coconuts. And she had heard the scurry of wildlife. But they had to get through the night.

And avoid the men from the Union ship that had gone down. They would be seeking shelter, as well.

"Richard?" she whispered, caressing his cheek. He didn't open his eyes; he didn't acknowledge her in any way. She groaned inwardly, checking for his pulse once again.

Still steady.

She wanted to build a fire; she didn't dare. "Richard, I so wish that you would wake up and speak!"

His chest rose and fell as he breathed. But his eyes didn't open. She consoled herself that it was better that he got some rest; the death of his men was a crushing blow to him. It had almost been a fatal blow.

She eased against him, trying to use her body to warm his. The winter breeze seemed to rise with a low moan, as if it wailed for the bloodshed that night.

She listened to the sound of the wind, and the waves, and she watched as the fire left the sky, and cloud cover came over. The night became dark again, as if it had consumed all the events that had taken place, and nature had been the victor.

She knew she needed rest also, but she didn't want to doze. She had to stay awake.

And listen.

So Gator just might be a woman. No matter, he told himself, she had to be dealt with as harshly as a man. He wasn't sure at all why women were considered to be the weaker sex; he'd met many who could make strong men cower. But still…

In the darkness, he did his best to follow a trail. It was difficult with the watery sand washing over every footprint. Finally, however, he cleared the mangroves, and found the part of the isle that had surely found birth at the beginning, and had gained substance from the passing sea. There was one beautiful, clear area of beach, residing almost like a haven, visible only in the pale starlight that fell upon it, and, in that starlight, almost magical. As he stood there for a moment, he thought of the great majesty of the sea and the sky. He might have been at the ends of the earth, he was so far removed from Washington, D.C. No troops marched through the streets, no civilians at work and play, and no great buildings rising around him. There were no buildings at all. Just the crisp darkness of the night, the wash of the waves and the soft whimpering of the wind.

Actually, he wasn't sure he was glad for the wind; he was slowly drying, but the air was cold, and his flesh felt like ice. He'd had matches in his pocket, but they were quite worthless now.

He hunkered down to see the sand.

Footprints. The foot was fairly small, but the indentations were deep, and they almost dragged, as if the imprinter had carried a heavy load. There seemed to be drag marks in the sand, as well.

A seabird let out a raucous cry in the night, a sound so sudden and eerie in the darkness that even he tensed, spinning around. He stood quickly.

The last of the fires had burned out. There seemed to be nothing in the darkness.

He looked toward the center of the island where pines and palms had taken root, and where someone, evading capture, might well seek sanctuary.

TARA COULD SEE HIM coming.

The man was tall. The darkness wouldn't allow much more information than that, but she had a sense about him. It was almost like she was being stalked by a jungle cat, one of the panthers that prowled the hammocks of the Everglades up on the mainland. He didn't slouch. He didn't creep along the beach. He just stood there, perhaps doing the same as she—trying to *sense* the very air around him.

He couldn't possibly see her in the dark, and yet, she felt as if he was looking right through her.

He saw her!

Or he saw something. He started walking right toward her little palm-and-pine sanctuary, and in a minute, he'd discover where she'd hidden Richard.

Tara eased to her feet; as silently as she could, she made her way behind the stand of pines and crept back into the brush and palms. Once there, she fled back toward the west, allowing the foliage to slap around her, giving a clear path to anyone who wanted to follow her.

She did well. Turning back, she saw the man was no longer on the beach. He had disappeared as if he'd been no more than a shadow in the night.

She weighed her situation. Looking up, she saw the

outstretched branch of a sea grape tree. She measured the distance, lowered herself and bounded onto the high branch. Then she sat silent, waiting.

EVEN FOR FINN, PURSUIT in the dark was not easy, though it was usually more of a friend to him, and an enemy to those he sought.

He had followed the trail, and yet, it seemed amazing that, now, the same person who had made those foot-prints was bounding as light as a bird through the trees. He followed with all speed, running through brush, a copse of pines and through a thicket containing a dozen different trees. He followed the thrashing he had heard, the bracken breaking underfoot, and he burst through the trees onto a higher spit of ragged brush and poor sand.

Which was empty.

He held still, listening again.

He let go of the natural sounds of the island.

The now-slightly distant roll of the waves, the rustle of branches. He heard again a sound that was guttural, like a rooting sound, as if animals—wild pigs? boars?—sought deep in the ground for some kind of food. He heard the wings of a bird as it took flight from one of the tall trees.

He knew that the Spaniards had found native tribes living on most of the islands; fishermen and others had come and gone forever. Pirates had made use of the channels and the reefs to escape capture. They'd brought new species to the little islands, and there might well be anything—plant or animal—hunting in a semitropic climate here.

Pigs, birds, insects, crabs.

He kept listening, concentrating his extrasensory abilities.

Then he could hear it.

The beating of a heart.

The sound was fast, a strong rhythm.

And then Finn knew; he was being watched, just as he was watching.

He stood where he was for a long time, and then he started back to the beach. As he did so, he heard a wild flurry of activity behind him; he turned, and he saw the figure running back into the trees.

He raced after the fleeting form, but in the midst of trees again, the subject of his chase disappeared once again. He didn't hesitate that time.

He stopped cold, and he *listened*.

And found that heartbeat again.

He waited a very long time, until he was certain, until the *thump-thump-thump* grew stronger and so familiar to him that it almost seemed a cacophony.

He took aim, and jumped, certainly taking his culprit by complete surprise.

Even though the thought had crossed his mind upon uncovering the petticoat, he had not fully accepted that he might actually find the woman he had lost in Gettysburg. The experience had been such a sword in his side; he had chafed at losing her, been haunted even by what had happened, and now...

She screamed, not so much with fear, but with complete surprise, as he made his way to the branch, capturing her in his arms and bringing them both slamming down to the ground below. He looked into her eyes, amazed that he remembered them so well, and as she stared up at him, he realized that she found instant recognition, as well.

She stared at him as if fighting for the right words of loathing to hurl his way. She was winded, he realized, even if he'd twisted himself to take the brunt of the fall. And so he spoke first.

"Why, miss. Fancy meeting you here, on such a dark and lonely night."

She looked back at him, gasping for breath, and he eased his hold.

"Let me go—move. You're an oaf. You're a disgrace to your uniform," she spat out.

"I don't wear a uniform. But I *am* taking you in—"

"You have no power to take me anywhere."

"You're a blockade runner. And I believe your name is Gator, and that you're plotting against the president of the United States of America. You will face a military tribunal, and you will hang, my dear," he said most pleasantly.

Of course, it was doubtful that she would hang. Southern spies—women—had been incarcerated in D.C., but the judges and leaders seemed loath to take action against such a woman. Hanging one damsel—however clawed and vicious she might be—would just be another knife in the side of the Southern ethic.

And, of course, Finn thought, what a waste if she

were to hang. Even now, in half-dry, tattered clothing, hair tangled in clumps around her features, she was stunning. The same uncanny beauty he'd reflected upon since Gettysburg. She had a perfect face, with large eyes that dominated the fine, slender structure of her cheeks and jawline. Her brows were clean and even and fly-away, and if she were to smile…

She didn't smile. "You're in a Southern state, you fool," she told him.

"There's a massive Union fort down at the tip, in case you hadn't noticed. And let's see, the Union has held St. Augustine since '62. Plus, there's a host of Union sailors about to land on this little islet, while I'm not seeing any boys in butternut and gray marching along the sand to save you. Oh—and since we're at war, I think I'm doing okay," he told her pleasantly.

To his amazement, she smiled, giving no resistance.

And then she did.

He had eased his hold to something far too gentle; she was small, but apparently built of steel. She suddenly shoved him aside with exceptional strength, kicked out hard, catching him entirely by surprise and with a sound assault, and leaped to her feet.

"Ass!" she hissed.

And he was, of course, because she was gone.

IT WAS EASY ENOUGH to escape him; she could move quietly and with the speed of light when she chose. Of course, she was exhausted, and laden with the heaviness of the salt water still soaked into her clothing. And still, she had managed to take him by surprise.

As he had done with her.

But now she knew; now, she would not take her eyes off him.

Even with this resolve, her heart sank; she was certain that he was telling the truth. The Yankee ship was going to go down, but not as Richard's *Peace* had.

The men aboard the Union ship had survived, and they would be coming to the island.

Trying to keep a step ahead of him, and draw him away from Richard, she headed toward the western side of the island. Moving through the trees and brush, she burst out somewhere near the southwest, at a copse leading straight out to the water, to an inlet where old coral formed some kind of a seawall.

She bent over, breathing hard, pondering her next move—*her way to save Richard*—when she heard his voice again, and jackknifed instantly to a straightened position.

"You are stubborn, my dear. But you'll not get away. Not this time."

She stared at him, incredulous. How was he standing before her? How had he reached the copse before she had managed to?

"You're supposedly some kind of officer of the law, is that what it is? Well, you're insane. I wasn't in Gettysburg to hurt anyone. And I'm not hurting anyone on this island. What, did they put you in charge of the blockade? Are you trying to starve women and children?" she demanded.

"I'm not in charge of the blockade. And the blockade isn't to starve anyone, but instead to stop a war, and any reasonable student of military history is surely aware of that fact. But, no, I'm not in charge of the blockade. I'm in charge of rounding up would-be assassins."

Up close, within an arm's breadth, he did tower well over her and, while he appeared lean in what remained of his white cotton shirt, muscle rippled at his chest where the buttons had given way from throat to midabdomen. She looked into his eyes, however; his physical prowess was not something that really worried her.

"There are no assassins on this island," she said. "In fact, this is my home. You're rude. You're trespassing."

"You came off the blockade runner. This is not your home."

"It's certainly far more my home than it is yours, or the North's."

"It's not a qualifying point at all—this island is deserted, and you came off the blockade runner. For that, you will answer to the government of the United States of America."

His eyes glowed so darkly that they almost appeared to be red fire in the night. His features might have been chiseled for a great warrior statue, and he seemed to have the ego and arrogance of a god to go with the hard-wrought classicism of his face. She felt the urge to take a step back, but, of course, she would never do so. She wouldn't lose.

"I am not a citizen of the United States of America, sir, and therefore, I will not answer to any government other than my own."

He stared at her without speaking, and then shook his head sadly. "You people would prolong this war forever. You would watch thousands and thousands more die."

"I am not fond of war!" she snapped back sharply. "But, sadly, I am not in charge of the state of affairs, and to my knowledge, the war still exists."

She felt a strange chill; it was what she believed, and she so wanted it to be over. Every day was futile now; every day was just more loss of life.

"I have no intention of discussing my feelings regarding this war—or anything, for that matter—with you, sir." She set her hands on her hips, trying for some form of dignity, which was actually quite ridiculous under the circumstances. Had someone called her *bedraggled* at that moment, it would have surely been a compliment.

He didn't take a step toward her, but, hands folded behind his back, he took a step around her, making her far more uneasy than she wanted to admit.

"What is your name, and where are your accomplices?"

"I don't have accomplices," she replied.

"You were sailing that ship on your own?"

"I didn't come off that ship. I live here."

"You didn't come off the ship, yet you're caked with sand and seawater."

"If I choose to take a dip at night, it's no one's concern."

"The water just about has frost in it," he said dryly.

"I am from here. I am accustomed to bathing through the year. One can become quite adept at the water in the islands," she assured him.

"Interesting. I last saw you in Gettysburg. Stalking the president."

"I was not stalking the president," she said.

"I suggest that you tell me about your companions— or hang alone," he said agreeably.

"You are an arrogant and extremely rude person, and I know your countrymen far too well to believe that many share your total lack of courtesy. I am guilty of nothing, and I suggest you leave me be, or the fate that awaits you will be far worse than hanging."

He laughed, and for a moment she was, despite the circumstances, struck by just how appealing his dark good looks were.

Except, of course, he was an ass.

"I weary of this. Leave me be, and no harm will come to you."

He shook his head, still smiling, and amused that she would dare to threaten him.

"You'll excuse me?" she said, her tone equally modulated, as if they were in a fine drawing room.

He didn't move. She stepped toward him, took one hand and set it on his chest, and pushed.

She had expected that he would go flying. He did not; she took him by surprise again, but he barely budged. His movement, however, did give her the escape she needed. With the foot and half that lay between them, she turned, and burst back through the brush and trees.

Where to go? Oh, God, where to go? She couldn't lead him back to Richard....

Had Richard awakened to consciousness yet?

She tried leading the tall stranger deep into the trees, and far from the eastern spit of beach where Richard lay covered in the sheet of branches. To the northwest... that was the way she had to go. Again, she ran, swift as sound and the darkness.

But she could sense her pursuer at every turn.

She burst into another copse, aware that her strength was waning.

She turned back; she could hear noise on the island. The men from the Union ship had reached the shore at last.

How many men had survived from the Union ship? Oh, God, if the men thought that one of them was an assassin, indeed, they might not make the night.

She wanted to sink to the sand in exhaustion; she must not.

She turned again, forming a plan in her mind. She had to keep them away from Richard through the night, and in the morning steal one of their longboats. No one

knew the coast and channels and the islands like Richard did. If she could steal one of the longboats, they
could escape. That was it, a simple plan.

She stiffened, her muscles suddenly burning again
as if the fire on the ship raged near once more; she *felt*
him behind her, *knew* that he was there.

How?

She turned, and he was.

Just behind her, so close she could feel the heat of his
body, sense him there.

He stared at her, waiting; she didn't speak. "Agent
Finn Dunne, miss. Pinkerton. By the power invested in
me by the United States of America, I'm placing you
under arrest for seditions and attempted murder."

She gasped. "I'm not attempting to murder anyone!
And you're still an ass. I will not go anywhere with
you."

"I honestly suggest that you do. I can chase you
around the island all night, or you can come with me
now. You can bring me to your companion, and when
the others arrive, we can administer medical aid to
him."

"I don't have a companion."

"Really, miss. I've seen whereabouts you've hidden
your friend. Not very endurable alone and injured, and
he probably does need medical attention." He shrugged.
"Such as we can offer."

She shook her head, feeling lost, impotent and helpless.

She could escape. Eventually, she could escape.

But Richard...

"Whatever you're thinking someone is guilty of doing, it's not us."

"You were on a blockade runner."

"We are still at war," she reminded him.

"Choice is yours," he said softly. "Show me to your friend, and we can see to him. Keep trying to escape, and I will keep coming after you. I never give up, miss. And if my companions come upon *your* companion without my protection, well, I'm not sure how things will go."

"You will not hurt Richard?"

"That I swear."

"And I should believe you? Why?"

"My word is sacred to me. And besides, you really have no choice. I don't know if you've heard it yet or not, but the Yankee longboats have reached the shore."

"Then we will return to Richard," she said.

He nodded. She was surprised when he looked at her curiously, head at a slant, dark eyes seeming to have that ripple of fire again. "Richard. Richard...?"

"Richard Anderson," she said. "Captain Richard Anderson."

He nodded and came closer to her. She bit her lip. She wasn't going to move.

"And you?" he said politely. "Who are you? I don't know your name, or who you are—even though I'm quite sure that I know exactly *what* you are."

CHAPTER FOUR

TARA STOOD STILL, for a moment not sure that he'd said what she thought he'd said. Maybe her fear of discovery was becoming irrational. Maybe she was imagining things.

She stared back at him, desperately praying that she would show no emotion.

There were others of her kind; she knew that. And that "her kind" came in full-blood and half-blood—those who had an ancestor generations before, and had inherited certain traits. Her mother had done her best to teach Tara everything that she had known, that she had learned from Tara's father. Tara had never actually met another of "her kind," but she knew that someone was out there; she also had half siblings, and she often felt an emptiness inside, wishing desperately that she might know them. She had sisters and brothers and....

And a father.

Finn was staring at her. She tried to stare back at him, her head cast at an angle, a slight smile curving her lips.

"Yes," Finn told her. "I said exactly that—I know *what* you are."

She waved a hand in the air. "A Southerner?"

He laughed. "Well, that would be true, too, I imagine. No, I know what you *really* are. Half-breed. Bloodsucker. Vampire. Some might call you a succubus, demon or lamia. What they call you doesn't matter."

She shook her head, incredibly wary of the man who seemed to have her at his mercy. He'd been ahead of her all night long—even though she had managed a smooth escape from him at Gettysburg. She could have escaped him tonight, too, but for Richard.

"No tricks," he told her.

"I don't know what you're talking about," she assured him.

He indicated the path where they had ripped through the foliage in their chase. "I'm going to suggest that we head back—before the angry men who just lost their ship come upon your friend."

She hesitated. "I'm telling you, neither of us is a spy. And neither of us is an assassin."

"You're both blockade runners."

"Richard is a merchant, nothing more."

He sighed. "Of course. But merchants running arms at times of war are by definition blockade runners. I am a tremendous believer in due process of law. If you come with me now, I can guarantee that nothing will happen to either of you on my watch. So, if you value your friend's life…" He let his voice trail and indicated she begin walking.

Tara did so. She turned and began moving quickly

through the brush, doing her best to make sure that every branch she passed slapped back into his face.

He didn't say a word, he simply caught the branches.

She let her words trail over her shoulder at him, along with her anger. "Due process of law. That means you get us into a puppet military court, and see that we're hanged."

"If you're innocent, you have nothing to fear."

"You're looking for someone called Gator. I'm not Gator. Richard isn't Gator. There's no reason that you should suspect either of us as your man."

"We'll see, won't we?" was all he replied.

"You should be worried, you know," she said smoothly.

"Oh?"

"Lamia! You see me now, but I'll turn to smoke, and you'll find me behind your back, slipping around your side, seeking your jugular vein."

"That's always possible."

"You should tremble. You shouldn't push my temper," she warned.

"I'm a mass of trembling flesh. Please keep moving."

As she walked, she became aware of the shouts and instructions of the other Union men in the distance— one booming voice, and then others that rang back and forth as they scurried to obey the commander.

Tara quickened her pace. Finn Dunne hurried behind her.

When she at last neared the little copse where she had left Richard, she ran the last few steps.

She raced by the last tree. From there she could see that men had pulled longboats up on the beach, and that they were being sent out to gather firewood.

There seemed to be a lot of them.

Tara slid down to her knees at Richard's side. His eyes were still closed; he had barely moved. But a quick check assured her that he was still breathing. His pulse even ticked a little stronger than before.

Finn Dunne was down beside her. He could move with an astonishing ease, especially for a man so tall. She tried to ignore him, but could not.

"Richard Anderson," he said.

"Yes, his name is Richard Anderson."

"And your name is…?"

"Tara. Tara Fox."

"What?" His tone was so sharp that it stunned her.

She looked at him. His features were hard and tense; his eyes seemed to be burning as he stared at her. They were such unusual eyes.

"Tara Fox," she repeated.

To her surprise, his eyes said he knew her name.

"Look, I don't know what information you've been given, but you're mistaken in me. I would never hurt Lincoln. Never. I would do anything to stop any evil being done to the man. Even a fool knows that we'll need his strong leadership when it's time to make peace and reconstruct the South. Stop looking at me like that. I am not a monster."

"That's debatable," he murmured, getting to his feet.

As he did so, a loud shout rose in the air.

"Dunne! Agent Dunne! Are you here?"

Tara touched Richard's face gently and rose, as well. On the beach, she counted ten men. Several were still securing their boats.

The others had their guns at the ready.

"Here!" Finn Dunne called out. "I have the survivors from the Rebel ship. They're unarmed. Hold your fire!"

Tara looked at him, feeling a sudden surge of anxiety. The Union men could have come upon them after the sea battle with guns blazing. This man had prevented that. She could only pray that the Pinkerton meant his words, that they wouldn't be harmed.

In her heart, she honestly believed that most men were honorable. Union men would not murder a man in cold blood. And yet, despite the decency and courtesy displayed by commanders on both sides, horrible murders had occurred. While she understood that John Brown had wanted to make all men free with his campaign against slavery, he had in fact committed murder—and in the Kansas and Nebraska territories, men had committed murder in retaliation.

Wasn't war just sanctified murder?

She just stood there, tense, terrified and praying. The philosophy of man wasn't something she could solve, and certainly not at this moment.

Please, God, don't let them hurt Richard.

A young soldier came through the trees. She thought that she recognized him—that bit of scruffy beard on his chin—but he was so covered in soot that she couldn't be sure. He looked at Tara with surprise, his brows shooting up. Then he looked at the man on the ground and spoke to the Pinkerton agent.

"Sir!" the young man said, addressing Finn Dunne. "The men are busy setting up on the beach, sir. Captain Tremblay set off a flare, and he says we can expect a Union ship by tomorrow. There are always ships ready to move with all speed from the fort." His eyes kept darting with surprise toward Tara. He gasped suddenly. "Tara!"

"Billy Seabold?" she asked.

Billy nodded.

"You two know each other?" Finn asked sharply.

Billy nodded. "Well, a bit, anyway." He scrambled to take off his military jacket, and offered it to Tara.

"I'm fine, thank you, really."

"Please, Miss Fox, allow me the courtesy," Billy said.

She thought to refuse would be rude, and so she accepted the jacket. Dunne was looking from one of them to the other, as if mentally shaking his head over the naivety of youth—in his mind, apparently, Billy was offering comfort to a venomous snake.

Finn cleared his throat.

"Oh…oh! If you'll follow me to the beachfront, please?" Billy said.

Tara hunkered back down by Richard. Finn lowered himself as well, moving her aside with the breadth of his shoulders. "I will take him," Finn said.

"He's—he's my friend. My brother, really," she added softly. "I will tend to him."

Finn's voice lowered. "You want everyone wondering how you have the strength of ten men?" he queried.

She fell silent, lowering her eyes. He could, if he chose, kill her—he knew how. Why didn't he? Was he actually decent in his way, loathe to murder without the facts established?

Finn took care as he lifted Richard's form, keeping the man's head rested in the crook of his arm. Tara rose with him and followed them to the beachhead.

Men were already busy setting up makeshift tarps for a shelter. Two others were collecting wood for a fire.

An elderly man, dead straight and dignified, was the one calling out the orders.

"Captain Tremblay, Agent Dunne is here, sir! With the, um, the Rebs," Billy said.

Tremblay seemed equally surprised to see a woman. "Well, Agent Dunne. Are these the culprits you meant to apprehend?" Tremblay asked.

"It's hard to know for certain, sir, until I'm able to question them thoroughly, and as you can see, this one is scarcely in shape for questioning."

Tremblay looked at Richard, still in Dunne's arms.

"He lives?" Tremblay asked.

"Yes, sir."

"We'll have the good doctor see to him, then," Tremblay said. "MacKay! Doc MacKay! We've a man in need of your tender touch, sir!"

One of the men building the fire came over and nodded to Finn. "Bring him under the tarp, will you, please, Agent Dunne? Billy, I'll need some light—will you see to it, lad?"

"Aye, sir," the young soldier said.

Finn Dunne walked with the doctor and beneath the canvas tarp that had been lifted about fifty yards in from the shoreline. There were already blankets spread out beneath it, along with a captain's portable desk; the men of the Union ship had known they were in trouble, and they had salvaged all that they could.

"Fresh water might be in order," Doc MacKay said, preceding the others.

Tara found herself longing to follow, and yet, under the scrutiny of Captain Tremblay.

She looked up at him. He appeared to be a fine and gentle man, and she wondered how he went to war, and watched everything that happened around him, and still maintained that sensibility.

"So," he said, "you're our culprit. You're from Key West, child?"

"My name is Tara Fox," she told him. "And I'm not a spy. I have no intention of bringing harm to anyone."

Except, she thought, *maybe Agent Finn Dunne. I'd love to give him a good slap right across that smug face!*

"Tara Fox..." the captain murmured, looking at her speculatively.

"Seminole Pete is a dear friend," she told him.

Tremblay smiled. "I don't frequent the taverns of the island, my dear. Mine is to set an example."

Tara stood there awkwardly, wondering what she was supposed to do. No one seemed ready to tie her up or confine her. Maybe they realized that she would be making no escape attempts when Richard Anderson was in their care.

Or, perhaps, they didn't think that she was capable.

Tara smiled, looking at the captain. He was reassuring; she didn't believe that she had fallen into the hands of cold-blooded murderers. "Sir, I promise you, I don't sit around the tavern gulping down rum or beer. Pete is like a father to me, just as the young man now in your care, Richard Anderson, is like a brother."

"Your young 'brother' is one hell of a seaman, Miss Fox. And, I admit, I wish that he were on my side. But as he is not, he is not a man in my good graces, as my ship will soon be at the bottom of the sea, providing a home for the fish."

"He is not a man who seeks to harm others."

"He's a blockade runner," Tremblay said flatly. "Let me rephrase—*was* a blockade runner."

"You will never be able to prove that Richard is anything other than a merchant, carrying food—"

"Young woman, do I look like a fool?" Tremblay demanded.

She shook her head. "No, sir, you don't. I merely mention that in any legal court of law—"

"War changes everything, doesn't it?" he said plainly.

"What will you do with us?" Tara asked politely, switching tactics.

"Well, had I just brought down the ship, I'd have seen that you were held at the fort, confined until this weary bloodbath limps to its halt. But you are prisoners of Agent Dunne, and I believe it's his pleasure that you be brought to the capital."

"Sir, we are not the cold-blooded killers he thinks us to be," she said.

"The problem with war is that it makes cold-blooded killers out of all of us, now, doesn't it?" Tremblay asked. "Never mind, child, the weary philosophy of an old tar. I believe you are standing there anxiously awaiting a chance to see to the welfare of your young seaman. You are free to do so."

Thus encouraged, Tara gave him a grateful nod and headed for the tarp. A pallet had been set up for Richard. Doc MacKay was down on his knees. And seeing that Richard had come to, she let out a little cry of joy and slid down next to them both.

"Easy, now," MacKay said. "The boy has taken a good rap to the head."

"Richard!" Tara said happily. He looked at her, his face still ashen. He tried to smile. He caught her hand. "Thanks, my friend," he murmured.

"You got him here—you swam?" MacKay asked, studying her. She flushed slightly, just imagining what she must have looked like in her tattered, salt-, sand-

and debris-covered clothing, and sodden hair plastered to her face.

"I'm from Key West. I'm a strong swimmer," Tara said.

"So you must be," MacKay said. "I don't believe there's more than bruising to the skull—I can find no crack or rift—and I believe that Mr. Anderson will make a full recovery. Rest is in order now, but as we are awaiting rescue, rest can be easily procured." He looked at Tara again. "What about you? You must be thirsty, my dear."

She suddenly realized how thirsty she was. For water, at the moment.

MacKay offered her a canteen. She accepted it gratefully. After drinking a long swallow of cool freshwater, she looked at the doctor, who was studying her in return. She felt a flush come to her cheeks. "Thank you. We are receiving far greater kindness than I expected."

"This is a war wherein fathers fight sons, and sons fight brothers. The intent is not to torture others, just to bring the conflict to an end." He grinned, and she liked his grin. "Besides, I have taken an oath to save lives," he reminded her.

"The truth, however, will be known."

Tara hadn't seen Finn Dunne return to stand near Richard's head beneath the tarp, but she knew the sound of his voice instantly.

She looked up at him. "Well, Agent Dunne, I am certainly eager that the truth shall be known. Two survived the explosion of Richard's ship, the *Peace*—Richard and myself—and neither of us has ever been called Gator, gone by the name Gator or had any particular affinity for gators in the wild, or in any so-called human form. So bring on your truth, sir. We are innocent of what you seem so desperate to find as fact."

"We'll see, won't we?" he asked.

He turned and walked away. The manner in which he did so—dismissing her words as if she were obviously the most heinous liar—disturbed her. She leaped to her feet, following him. He had been heading back toward the bracken and she caught up with him away from the tarp and the fires that burned on the beach.

She slammed a hand against his back, hard. He turned to stare at her, a scowl tensing his features.

"What?"

"I'm not a spy! I'm not an assassin! Neither is Richard."

"Spy, assassin—those facts need corroboration and truth. Your friend is a blockade runner, at the very least."

"Not *Gator!*"

"And you?" he asked, an edge to his voice.

She let out an exasperated sigh. "I am not Gator! You have it all wrong. I am Lincoln's greatest supporter. I know that he is wise, war-weary, decent and kind. He saw saving the country—a united country—as his calling, his duty under God. I believe he is our salvation. I would never want to hurt the man!" she told him.

"Pretty speech, now that you are captured," he told her.

She set her hands on her hips. "Well, you're just a fool, because you're holding us, and the man who you know as Gator is still out there somewhere!"

"And, assuming you're not Gator, how do you know that your friend isn't?"

She stared at him, speechless for a minute. "Because he's not! Because I know Richard. He's no murderer. Yes, fine, he's a blockade runner. Until the war is over, this is the Confederate States of America. He's doing what he can to see that Southern children eat!"

"So noble," Finn said mockingly.

"He is noble. You have no right to run around judging people you don't know."

"No, I am not a judge. We'll see to it that you are brought before a tribunal."

"I would think that you need evidence to convict us of anything."

"We have a witness sitting in prison right now, ready to do just that. His life will be spared when he identifies Gator," Finn said. "You'll be decently treated in transit and while awaiting trial. As will the suspect."

He started to walk away. Incensed, she followed him, pushed past and stopped in front of him, blocking his way.

"You're an idiot!" she told him.

"And you're a prisoner. Leave me alone—before I see that you're shackled."

She drew herself up with dignity. "You can't shackle me, not really," she informed him.

"Believe it or not, I can."

"You said that you know what I am," she said softly. "But do you? Do you really know exactly what I am?"

"I do."

"And how can that be?"

"Because, Miss Fox," he began, pushing past her, "I am what you are."

HE SHOULD PUT HIS PRISONER into shackles, Finn thought. *His* shackles, specially designed of wood and silver, with a unique configuration of crosses intricately laid into the woodwork. They had been blessed and could contain almost any creature.

High in a treetop, looking out as the night slowly began to ease into the golden rays of dawn, he mused on his captive.

At the moment, it wasn't really necessary. He couldn't shake her off if he wanted to. She wouldn't attempt escape without her friend.

No, she wouldn't need restraints.

He found himself wondering about the relationship between the two, and he was surprised to discover that he was annoyed with his own turn of thought. He'd wanted to capture the wretched woman since she'd eluded him at Gettysburg. He hadn't realized then exactly why she had escaped so easily, because her—*their*—hereditary disposition was rare.

He should have known then. He should have at least suspected.

But he hadn't.

And now, he knew. This, of course, made her all the more dangerous, and made him more intrigued.

"Agent Dunne!"

He heard his name called through the scruffy brush and trees that dotted the central area of the island. It was Billy.

He leaped down easily, soundlessly, and walked along the path created by his own forage through the growth until he reached the young man's back.

"Agent Dunne!" Billy shouted again.

"Yes, seaman," he said, standing just behind the boy's back.

Billy spun around, startled.

"There's water, sir. The army must have come through here before. There's a cistern, filled with water. The captain wanted me to let you know. We've also salvaged a trunk of fresh clothing. He thought you might be feeling the discomfort of the dried salt water and be wishing for something a bit fresher."

"That's very courteous."

Billy produced a neatly folded stack of clothing—plain blue breeches and a cotton shirt. They'd probably do well enough; he was taller than Tremblay, but not by much. And the clothing would be far more comfortable than the now-stiff and clammy shirt he was wearing.

"The captain respects your mission, sir," Billy told him.

Finn nodded in return to the statement. "Where would this cistern be, Billy? I saw a fair amount of the island, but not a cistern."

"Extreme northeastern side, Agent Dunne. I can escort you there."

Finn started to tell him that it wouldn't be necessary, but he remembered that Billy was familiar with the island of Key West—and its inhabitants.

"So, Billy, how long have you been at Fort Zachary Taylor?" Finn asked him.

"Oh, a long time now, Agent Dunne. I was there at the outbreak of the war. I was there when the Union forces dug in—after Florida joined secession."

Finn looked over at the man. "You don't look old enough to be in uniform—much less have spent years at the fort."

"I'm twenty-three, Agent Dunne. Older than many a man dead on the field."

"True," Finn agreed.

"So, where did you hail from?"

"Chicago. And will you head back when the war is over?"

Billy smiled and shook his head. "No, sir, I will not. I love the island. There's a breeze in the air, even on the hottest day. And the ocean is there, and the folks…

well, some are a little lost. Some are starting over. Many are different, and in a world where they are accepted. Men grew rich on salvage, and then no one questioned where they came from before or what they do. It's my home now. I'll go where they command me while this war goes on, then I will be home in Key West."

"So, you know the local population fairly well," Finn said.

"Indeed."

"And they are Southern sympathizers, living by a Union fort," Finn said.

Billy shrugged. "The state was split on the vote from the beginning. There's been talk of an 'East' and a 'West' Florida. Sure, like men everywhere, the men spew their opinions on the war, on the generals." He paused. "Talk has changed, though, since the actual fighting started. No one is running around saying, 'We're going to whip their tails in two weeks,' or any other such nonsense, neither side. No one has really had their tail whipped, and we've all watched two weeks turn into four bitter years.... God alone knows how long it can go on. Some folks, of course, talk about the draft riots in New York, but, hell, Lincoln is president again, and that man is as tenacious as a rat terrier! So, the old coots at the bars talk, and sometimes they're rude when the Union soldiers are about, and sometimes, some lets out a squeak for the Union. Mostly, folks just want to make a living and get by, and it is an island, so we're pretty isolated."

"Except for the blockade runners."

Billy shrugged.

"And you know the two we captured tonight—Miss Fox and Mr. Anderson."

Billy nodded.

"What kind of talk have you heard from them?"

Billy looked at him and exhaled. "I've seen Miss Fox a fair amount—Mr. Anderson, not so much. Miss Fox is always courteous to everyone. Kind of grave and somber, but courteous. She serves sometimes at Seminole Pete's. Her mom and Pete were awful close. From what I heard, her father wasn't around much. Came down to the Keys, lived with Tara's mom, and I guess most folks thought they were married, exceptin' legally, I guess they weren't. There's some girls on the island who think they're all social princesses or the like, 'cause their fathers or grandfathers or uncles or what have you were the first Americans down in the area and they live in those big fancy houses. But you ask me? Miss Fox, she's the real deal. She knows her manners. Oh, her momma died a few years back, and I guess that hurt her bad. But she's good. She helps out at the church, helps with the sick and injured—and she's never seemed to care if it was a Yank from the fort or a Rebel off the island."

"Sounds like you've something of a fancy for the lass, seaman," Finn said.

Billy flushed. "Oh, she's not for me, Agent Dunne. No, no, she's not for me."

"And why do you say that?"

Billy looked at him, studying his face for a moment. "Because you can just tell, Agent Dunne. You can tell by the way a woman looks at you, as if you could be the man she wanted. She looks upon me kindly enough, but there's nothing of magic or mischief in her eyes when she does so, and I know—I'd not be what she was wanting."

Finn thought about that. He was silent as they walked, thrashing through the trees as morning's first light began to cut through.

"Some women have an agenda, Billy. They can be more like a man. They see a purpose in life, and they have to follow that purpose."

"Maybe that's what it is, sir. But what purpose would that be? I think she loves her home. Loves Key West."

"And does she love Richard Anderson?" Finn asked.

Billy grinned. "I don't see the locals all that much, but, yes, from what I've seen and heard, yes. Why, you see, his father was hanged. His father was a pirate. And the two of them, well…not a nice thing to say regarding a lady, but legal truth is truth, so…a bastard and a pirate? Even in Key West, such a state of birth calls for the whispers. And the rich girls—half of them ugly as sin—keep up a barrier. Tara—she's just not one of them, you see."

He was surprised to feel that he was thinking defensively of her position.

No, she would not be one of them. She would speak her mind, she would fight for what was right....

Like her love for the South?

And, yes, when she had spoken about Lincoln, there had been such a depth of sincerity in her words.

Almost as if they shared their opinion of the man who was still holding the country together—while being lampooned in papers and magazines across the country, belittled by his political opponents and appearing years older on a daily basis.

"The cistern is ahead, sir, just ahead," Billy said.

"Thank you. Extend my gratitude to the captain, as well. It seems that the sun is rising, and there's hope we will see a rescue ship on the horizon soon," Finn said.

Billy nodded and stepped back.

Finn continued forward and then paused.

Ahead of him lay a bricked-in cistern. He was not an engineer, but he could see that the planning had been well executed. The ground here was higher. It must have been the oldest section of the island. The coral rock beneath the scrub in the area made an excellent filter, while the water flowed from the catch basin of the cistern to form a little freshwater pool. Had it been only the cistern there, what fresh water that was collected would have grown stagnant.

As he came closer, he realized that he was not alone.

The sun was just rising in the east and the sky was slowly becoming pink and yellow, but those colors were still vibrant between layers of mauve, the remnants of the night.

And there, silhouetted on the horizon, was the woman who seemed to be consuming his thoughts.

Angel—or demon? he wondered.

At the moment, she was pure angel, though she seemed to offer pleasures of the deepest, darkest delight. She had shed her salt-logged clothing, and done her best in the cold water to bathe.

She was there, body slightly arched, head thrown back as she rinsed and tossed her hair, body at a graceful arch that allowed an almost mystical, mermaid-view of her torso, waist and breasts. The moment was so sudden, the vision so striking....

He stood there, dead still and silent, and aching.

The war... It took so much from one.

He'd forgotten what it was like to see something so beautiful. To want...want a woman with such an aching, all-consuming desire.

He stepped back.

He closed his eyes, and willed the vision to leave his mind. He realized that it never would.

He opened his eyes. She still didn't know that he was there. She emerged, looking around. She found her clothing on the shore, and quickly slipped back into it, shivering. The morning air was cold.

Finn waited, not breathing.

She paused for a moment, tense as she looked at the

sky. For a moment, he could almost feel her intense desire to escape. Her shoulders fell.

Richard. The son of the hanged pirate.

She was going to return to the camp.

Of course, he thought. Richard was there.

For a moment, he envied the man with an intensity that was frightening. And then he remembered that he had a cause himself, that he'd never been a fool for a woman, and this was not the time he could neglect duty.

He waited until he watched her walk toward the foliage closer to the beach, intent on returning to the camp.

As she turned down the trail, the sun rose higher, and it caught the dark vibrant red within the tresses of her freshly washed hair.

Longing wedged in his throat, and he felt that he missed something, something precious in life.

When she was gone, he gritted his teeth and mentally willed himself to remember his quest. He hurried to the little pool created by the cistern, stripped his clothing and nearly dove into the shallows, he was so eager to feel the icy blast of the water.

And it was cold....

He stayed, and he washed away the seawater, but for the life of him, he could not wash away the vision that had so entranced him.

CHAPTER FIVE

THE STRANGEST THING about the visions or dreams that plagued Tara was that they were so real.

This time, she was walking down a long corridor. The walls were painted, and hung with scenes from American history. She could see men talking at the end of the corridor, and she could catch snatches of their conversation. Something was said that referred to Sherman's next move, and someone else was bemoaning the relentless tactics of General Grant, while another was arguing that he was getting the job done. "I know Robert Lee," another man was saying, "and he's a brilliant, brilliant man, and general. He sees that there is little hope. I don't believe that the fighting can go on much longer."

"But we might well be looking at draft riots again," another man said.

She was walking toward them, where they stood, all awaiting an audience with the president. She thought that they had to be his advisers, or perhaps even members of Congress. She was sure that arguments regarding the war had gone on at the end of that corridor since the fighting had first begun.

She wasn't going to reach the men. The president's door was ahead, on the left.

She entered.

Lincoln was not seated behind his great desk. He was in a chair near the door, and she was certain that he could hear every word being said. His head was bowed; he rubbed his temples as he listened.

She didn't want to interrupt him; he looked as sad and weary as if he had carried the weight of the world on his shoulders, and of course, he had been carrying the weight of his own world. He'd seen a child die while in office, and for years he'd born the ridicule of the people when his generals had lost battle after battle, and the count of the dead had steadily risen to unthinkable numbers.

He looked up, aware that she was there. And he offered her a weak smile, standing as a gentleman would do.

"You've come. I've been expecting you, waiting for you."

"Thank you, Mr. President. I've come to beg you take care. You know that you have enemies all around you."

"I entered the great fray of politics—no man in politics is at a lack for enemies," Lincoln assured her.

She shook her head. "You know that your situation is different. Sir, you can't be so open. You expose yourself to the trust of the people far too often. You must understand how fragile you are as a human being."

He walked to the window, and stared out at the length of the mall. His hands were folded behind his back.

"I am not worthy. How can I serve people, if I cannot be among them? I can't give them the answers they want far too often. But I can see that they know that my heart breaks when a man or a boy is killed. They can know that I spend my every waking hour thinking of ways to end this horror as soon as possible. I pray that we win the battles, so that the bloodshed can stop. We have come this far—we cannot be swayed from our position." He turned back to her. "I feel that we are close. Having stayed our course, we will be triumphant.

"I sometimes fear for myself, but more often I think of Mary. She weeps so often. Her family is Southern, and they suffer so. She is delicate. 'Spiritualism' became so popular in the Midwest when we were home, and at first, it seemed that she enjoyed exploring the possibilities—and, of course, the social interaction. But then our Willie died. She's had séances here, in the Red Room. I have been, and I have seen, and we've had Dr. Henry—the head of the Smithsonian—in to investigate. And while he finds shenanigans among the mediums, Mary is unconvinced. She has seen the ghosts of my predecessors here, in the White House. She has seen Thomas Jefferson and Andrew Jackson and John Tyler. I know how troubled her mind is, but I…well, I have felt that I have known who will win a battle, and often my instincts have proven true. And I—"

"Sir," Tara interrupted, hurrying over to him. "What's

important is that you realize your physical danger. You are mortal. Any man might be an enemy."

He turned to her, and she could feel his hand as he touched her hair, smiling as gently as a father. "I will see you soon, I believe. I will see you soon."

Suddenly, she felt as if she was being pulled away from him. Great shadows that insinuated diabolical faces rushed between them. She was being hurled away, farther and farther, and she cried out, fighting the swarm of shadows.

"Hey!"

She awoke with a start, and became aware of the hands firmly holding her shoulders. When she tried to bolt up, she was pushed back down.

There were no shadows around her. She was lying on a blanket on the sand, her bed beneath the shelter of the tarp, the world around bursting with sunlight. She was even aware of the smell of something roasting, and the aroma was provocative.

And she was facing the Pinkerton agent, Finn Dunne.

"You're dreaming. Calling out and fighting in your sleep," he told her.

She stared at him a moment, trying to shake off the shadows and fog of the dream. She had no intention of giving him any explanations.

The sun had really risen high, but then she hadn't gone to sleep until it had started to rise. She smoothed back her hair, grateful that she'd been given a bit of soap by Captain Tremblay, and that she didn't feel like a complete salt block.

"Richard?" she asked. Her voice was thick.

Finn offered her a canteen of water. She accepted it. The water was cool, crisp like the day, and it tasted delicious.

"Richard fares quite well. He has been up and about, and is working with some of the men on salvage. Some of the goods aboard both ships survived. A few trunks floated to the surface, and Richard has suggested that we arrange a diving party to bring others up from the seabed."

"He knows how to dive," Tara said, setting a hand on Finn's chest to force him far enough away so that she could push up to a sitting position. "I'm excellent. I can help."

"And you can disappear in the water, too," he said crisply, rising.

"You know that I won't leave. You know quite well that I could have left already," she said, finding her feet, as well.

"Richard in the water, you in the water…not a good scenario for me, I dare to think. The men hunted down a boar, and there's coffee and dried meat that came from one of the rescued barrels. I left a special canteen, just for you, near the palm where you watched over Richard yesterday…"

He turned away from her.

"And where are you going?" she called after him.

He paused, as if surprised by the question, or surprised that she would dare to question him.

"To help with the salvage, of course," he told her. "I'm not from an island, I fear, but time has taught me well. Billy is tending the camp, should you need assistance."

He had been by her side…and he had refused to let her dive while Richard was doing so, and yet, he seemed to think that it was safe to leave her to roam the island. Well, it was, of course; he knew that she would certainly try to escape—but only if she had Richard at her side.

She splashed some of the canteen's water on her face and rinsed her mouth, then headed for the tantalizing scent of the boar that continued to sizzle on the stake.

She found Billy tending coffee and the meat by the fire.

"Good morning, Tara," he said pleasantly.

"Good morning, Billy."

He had a soldier's mess kit out, and quickly poured her some of the hot coffee. "There's still a chill here. Seems that winter's cold can seep into the bones, even if it doesn't begin to compare with the brutal snow and sleet of the north."

"It's a wet cold, Billy, and that's why we feel it," she murmured.

"The meat's a bit stringy, but decent," he told her, cutting her a slice from the carcass.

She accepted the plate and sat on one of the logs that had been dragged close to the fire. Tasting the meat, she realized that she was ravenous. She didn't eat daintily, but devoured the portion.

Billy poured himself more coffee, looking over their camp area. Blankets and a few pallets lay in order beneath the tarp. With their longboats, the Union men had managed to come away with a fair amount of supplies. She had the feeling that Tremblay was a man who had sailed the sea so long that any situation was a matter of following regulation. His ship was floundering and going down, and therefore you set to the task of securing the most necessary supplies. When survivors became beached on an island, there was still order, and men were set to work.

Billy cleared his throat, looking at her.

"There are books in Dr. MacKay's trunk, if you would like something to occupy your time," he suggested.

"Thank you, Billy. I will most certainly see what reading material the doctor carries. But I thought I would amble about a bit—if your job isn't to stop me from doing so?"

"You are free to wander the island."

She smiled, rose and started for the spit of ground where she had buried Richard beneath the branches the day before.

Just as Finn had said, there was a canteen leaning against one of the palms, half-hidden by branches. She unscrewed the top, and discovered that it was indeed filled with blood. She sniffed it.

Boar's blood.

Tara drank her fill, and discovered that she yearned for more, and then more. The previous day had taken a great deal of her strength, and the blood washed through her body like an elixir.

She drank it all down, and returned the canteen to its place, wondering if she should have been so selfish. How odd—the man seemed out to prove she was guilty of the most horrible offenses, and yet, he meant to see to it that she was supplied with this secret necessity.

The better to keep her alive and torment her, she thought.

However, with her new sense of energy filling her limbs, she couldn't help but be grateful. He knew what she was; he could present her to the others as a monster.

But then, wouldn't he have to admit himself a monster, as well?

She couldn't begin to fathom the working of his mind.

Tara left the little copse and started walking along the beach. She waved to Billy, and kept walking back around to the tangle of mangroves she'd stumbled upon the night before. From there, she could see that a number of the Union longboats were out in the vicinity of where *Peace* had gone down. One trunk bobbed in the water, and three sailors in a boat were trying to capture it with a hook. Tremblay himself was aboard another of the boats, and, as she watched, Richard surfaced, dragging a rope. Tremblay and another man reached for the salvage he had secured from the ocean floor, dragging the barrel aboard their ship. A moment later, Finn surfaced, another of the barrels in his arms. He managed to lift his arms high above the water himself, and Tremblay needed only to lower the barrel to the boat.

Out by the remains of the Union ship—its masts all that rode above the waterline—she could see that the men were busy. They had apparently fashioned a diving bell out of scrap metal, and they had a man down to find what he could.

She chafed, being on shore. She knew that she would be excellent at finding whatever treasures might have been blown clear of Richard's ship.

She noted, however, that hanging on the longboat catching their breath, Finn and Richard seemed to have easy enough conversations.

Did Finn seriously believe that she or Richard could be Gator, the spy supposedly known to be heading north to attempt an assassination attempt? She had expected grueling interrogation, not collective efforts to secure supplies.

She watched the work, a sense of bitterness overriding the moment's goodwill she had felt toward Finn Dunne. He couldn't begin to imagine how tormented she was, longing to help the man he seemed convinced she wanted to kill.

And, of course, he should be careful with her; perhaps he had a matching strength, but he should really know better than to underestimate her.

Tara hesitated another minute, and then could stand it no longer. She was already down to little more clothing than a cotton blouse, pantelettes and skirt. She doffed her shoes, made her way over the mangrove roots and dove in.

It didn't take her long to near the area where the Union longboat awaited the divers. She surfaced there and faced Tremblay.

"Captain, I can help," she told him.

He looked at her, and smiled slowly. "There was chloroform on the *Peace,* so Richard has told us. I believe we have thus far raised coffee and rum, clothing and a score of boots."

She nodded. "The chloroform is heavily wrapped, sealed in a barrel, sir. It might have exploded, you know, along with the gunpowder."

"We will search a while longer," Tremblay said.

As she clung to the hull of the boat, speaking with Tremblay, Finn surfaced again, bearing a carpetbag that was the worse for wear, but still closed. She knew the travel bag; it was her own.

Finn gave no thought to the bag, tossing it into the boat. He stared at her, his eyes burning with that red tinge that seemed to warn of danger, his brows knit in a scowl. "You were told not to assist, I believe, Miss Fox!"

He was shirtless, down to his breeches. Water sluiced over his shoulders and she saw the sun-bronzed ripple of his shoulder and back muscles. Sleek dark hair slashed in wet disarray over his forehead, and she was disturbed to realize that, even wet and dripping, he was an imposing man. And an attractive one.

"I can help," she said, wishing there wasn't quite so much of a plea in her voice. She didn't look at Finn; she gave her attention to Captain Tremblay. "I'm an excellent diver, sir. Very, very good."

"Find the chloroform," Tremblay said. "God knows, enough soldiers, both sides, will be needing that."

She didn't look back at Finn, but gave herself a push from the boat and pitched downward, passing Richard on his way up as she dove. Today, despite the cold of the water that remained like an icy bath, the sea was beautiful. They were by the side of the reef that had been the final death grip for Tremblay's ship, and fish were about in a burst of color. Tangs, yellow and blue, swam by as she propelled herself along the outskirts of the reef, searching the sandy bottom and the jagged coral for signs of the sealed barrel that carried the chloroform. She saw another barrel on the sand bottom and dove for it; this barrel had split. It had carried salt or sugar, she thought, but the contents were now lost. She pushed herself harder and farther, was forced to surface, and then pitched down in a dive again. The water, even where there was an absence of coral, was no more than forty or forty-five feet deep.

This time, she found a barrel that had been thrown clean and clear. She went for it, and realized that she needed rope and buoy to get it up.

Or Finn.

Twenty feet from Tremblay's longboat, she surfaced again. Finn was hanging on the bow, about to take another dive. Richard was now aboard, a blanket around his shoulders; he was shivering. She didn't think that he'd been ordered out for his health, but rather because she was in the water now. That was well; she hadn't received a massive conk on the head.

"Agent Dunne!" she called, treading water. It didn't do well to stay in one position long; the water became colder and colder as she did so.

He turned to her.

"I need help!" she called to him.

She couldn't really see his face clearly from her distance; she didn't know why she was certain that he wore a quick look of suspicion before joining her.

He swam to her as easily as any of the fish in the sea. "Straight down," she said.

"I'll follow you."

She met his eyes, nodded and dove down, kicking hard. They came to the large barrel. She might have managed the weight, but the bulk of it was more than she could get her arms around. He grabbed it by the lip, pulling it to stand straight, then gripped it around on the other side as well, and thrust off from the ocean bed to reach the surface with the weight. She kicked off, too, streaking after him, but when she reached the boat, Tremblay and Richard had already leaned over to help Finn take the precious barrel from the water.

"That's it," Richard said. "There's the marking." He pointed to an etched-out scrawl in the wood at the top of the barrel. "That's the chloroform."

She thought that, most likely, unless there was some kind of rescue from heaven for the two of them, Richard would wind up being sent to a prisoner-of-war camp. She wasn't sure what would happen to her.

But Richard still seemed as pleased as the others that such a precious piece of cargo might be saved.

"Let's bring it in. We've done well," Tremblay said.

Finn hiked himself out of the water and reached for Tara. She accepted his assistance into the boat, and she was grateful when Tremblay set a blanket around her shoulders. Finn took up the oars, while Tremblay called out to the other divers; it was time to come in.

They brought the longboats back around to the beachhead, and pulled the boats out of the water. The men began emptying the day's treasure, laying the items out on the beach.

Tara wandered to the side, clutching the blanket around her, as they assessed the day's haul. Richard pounced upon her carpetbag, and brought it, still dripping, to set before her. "Some things may be salvageable," he said.

"Yes, of course, thank you. I guess I'll bring them to the cistern and freshwater pool and rinse them out and…they won't be salty, at least," she said.

He looked at her, and touched her face. "I'm so sorry."

She caught his hand. "You don't need to be sorry. We're at war. And this is what happens." She moved closer to him. "Richard, I don't know what they're planning. If he really thinks we're assassins…and if he doesn't, well, it's still a prison camp. But we've got to bide our time carefully. I don't think… I'm not sure where we could actually get from here. The northeast side of the state is dangerous, you know. It's fifty-fifty whether a ship might be Yankee or Rebel. I think—"

She broke off. She saw that Finn, still shirtless, no blanket around his broad shoulders, was standing next to Doc MacKay, talking.

But he was watching her.

She lifted the dripping carpetbag. "I'll go to the spring…use it and be out, so that the men might have a chance."

Tara, unhindered, left the beach behind and headed for the cistern. When she reached the area, she began going through her bag, delighted to discover that, while the bag dripped, the lining of tight cotton duck had kept many of her possessions from being soaked. She delightedly laid out stockings, skirts, chemises and her greatcoat, and then happily stripped off what she'd been wearing.

After bathing in the pool, she found the driest of her belongings. She remembered she had left her shoes by the mangrove roots, so she would have to retrieve them. She was growing accustomed to the chill nip in the air, but now, the afternoon sun was strong as it began its descent and she felt clean and good.

She decided to leave her bag drying in the sun, and turned around to start her barefoot walk back to the camp. As she did so, she discovered that her path was blocked.

Finn Dunne. She didn't know how long he had been watching her. He was still in nothing but tight breeches that clung slick and wet to his shape. His shoulders now gleamed, and his drying hair was a toss over his forehead. She held still, watching him, unable to wonder what she would have felt for the man if they hadn't met as enemies. She was disturbed by the quickening sense she felt when he was near, and by the rampant thump that seemed to begin in her chest, her heart beating far too quickly.

Fear! she told herself dryly. *He* was *the enemy, and he seemed determined that she was a monster in truth.*

"My pardon. I didn't mean to intrude."

"I'm quite finished here."

"Ah."

"May I pass?"

"Certainly."

He didn't move for a moment; he watched her. Then he stepped aside with a sweeping bow. Palm trees seemed to rain down branches around them. When she stepped by him, she felt that she touched the heat of his chest. Of course, she did not, but she couldn't help an inner trembling as she passed him.

They were captives, she reminded herself. They could have been treated coldly, confined to a few feet of space. The Union men might even have restrained them uncomfortably.

She knew that he watched her as she walked away; she fought the temptation to look back.

And yet, puzzled, she did turn. Tall, and bronze in the sun, his shoulders broad and his muscled chest tapering to the waistband of his trousers, he was an appealing sight. She straightened her shoulders and stood tall.

"No ship has come," she said, frowning.

"No," he said.

"I would have thought…if a distress flare was sent into the night…"

"Curious, isn't it?" he asked.

She nodded.

"What do you think has happened?" he asked her.

She shook her head. "I don't know. I can't imagine. I'm not surprised that we've not seen another Rebel ship—the blockade is getting tighter daily. But…"

"Yes, there should have been a Union ship here by now," Finn said.

"Perhaps, by tonight."

"Perhaps. The men will keep the fires burning."

Tara finally turned again and started hurrying over the sand toward the beach. Richard was still working with Tremblay and Doc MacKay, unloading the precious salvage.

Billy was still watching over the fire, preparing the remnants of the boar with a few of the other men. She slipped by them, and hurried to the mangroves, anxious to find her shoes.

As she stooped to retrieve them, she froze.

There was a corpse in the water.

Horrified, she jumped back and nearly fell into the tangled roots.

She wanted to look away, but she could not. The man lay on his back, eyes staring up at the sky. Even though the gentle wash of the waves crashing against the mangrove roots lapped around him, the pool of blood at his throat still hovered there in a watery mist. He wore the remnants of a Union naval uniform, and his arms, legs and the length of his body looked as if it had been ripped to shreds by a beast.

Tara sat back, pressing her hand to her lips so that she would not cry out.

She turned and raced back to the camp. But there, she paused, not knowing who to tell. What she saw frightened her more than she had ever imagined. She had heard of such things, but...

Tara walked on by the camp, afraid of letting the men dwell on the fact that their situation could be blamed on her. She headed swiftly toward the cistern and the pool. She could hear splashing, and when she burst through the trees, she saw that Finn was relishing the cool clean water that washed away the salt of the sea. Water droplets flew into the sky as he rose from the pool, shaking his hair, and slicking his fingers across it to sluice out more of the water.

He spun to stare at her.

"Well, Miss Fox, this is surprise. I was rather of the impression that you evaded my company, rather than sought it out. However, of course, you are most welcome."

"You have to see...what I've seen," she said.

Perhaps he noted the ashen pallor of her face. He frowned.

"What's happened?" he asked, heading for the edge of the pool. Heedless of his state of nudity, he hurried out of the water, seeking the damp breeches he'd worn there. Instinctively, Tara thought to turn away, and still, seeing the taut muscle structure of his back and buttocks, she wondered if she hadn't come to him because of his power, and for reassurance.

"What—what is it?" he demanded, striding to her, setting his hands on her shoulders.

"A dead man," she whispered.

"One of Richard's men? None were lost aboard Tremblay's ship."

"A Union seaman. He's— You have to see," she whispered.

"Have you told the others?" he asked. "You need to take great care with what you tell the others."

"No...no, I've never seen anything like— You have to see the man..."

She was still so unnerved that she didn't think a thing of it when he took her hand and started walking.

"Where?" he asked.

"In the mangrove roots. I'd left my shoes earlier today. I went to find them."

"Agent Dunne!" Tremblay called, seeing them head back toward the tents. "Come, sir! Get yourself a coat or a jacket. It might well be a hellhole of heat here in the summer, but the winter night is coming on, and there's a fierce chill coming."

"Why, thanks... Miss Fox lost a trinket, a locket, by the shore today. I'll just take a look before we begin to lose the light, sir."

Finn didn't pause. They walked by the tent and the spit where the boar had cooked earlier, and where coffee brewed even now. Richard was there, seated on a log, and he looked up with concern as they walked by.

He stood. "Tara? A locket?"

"Just a little matter!" she said. "Richard, please, no harm will come to me."

He was still frowning as they hurried by. When they reached the first outcropping of mangroves, Tara hurried on ahead of Finn.

"This way...this way," she told him.

"What is it— Oh, Lord!"

She stood, balancing on a root. Finn had come behind her, barefoot and bare-chested still. He passed her, moving nimbly from root to root, until he could hunker down close to the body. Tara stood still, watching him.

He was silent, inspecting the body that was half in and half out of the water, appearing almost alive as it moved with the waves.

"Not a shark?" she whispered.

"No," he said grimly.

"Where did he come from?"

The sun was beginning to slip through the trees. Tara wasn't afraid of darkness, and yet, that night, with the dead man before her and the sky turning dark mauve, she felt a tremendous chill.

"He had to have been on a ship," she whispered.

"Indeed."

Finn stood, looking out on the horizon. He reached for an ankle sheath, which lay just beneath the fabric at his ankle, producing a long-bladed knife.

"Finn?" she asked.

She looked away then, aware of his intent. He hunkered down in the shallows, and she heard the swipe of his blade as he dispatched the man's head.

He tossed the head far out to the sea, and dragged the body and the torso out to be taken by the tide.

He walked back to Tara.

"What do you know about this?"

"Know? I know nothing!"

"You know what happened to the man, of course. It was a vampire attack."

She shook her head. "We've never had an attack... never, in Key West! I'm—I'm the only one of my kind there! Of course, my father was around years and years ago, but I never even met him. I've heard whispers about such things, other places. But I swear to you, never in Key West!"

"Well, Tara Fox, you've probably spent much of your life learning your own strength, and learning about your powers. And then you're not afraid, because you know there are only a few out there who would begin to know how to kill you. But here's something you should realize right now, and accept, and take to heart—you are a half-breed." He paused a minute. "I even know of others in your...family clan."

"You *know* them?" she asked, stunned and hopeful.

"I said that I know of them," he told her. "And right now, that's neither here nor there. There's a full-blooded vampire out there somewhere, and he's likely gearing up for a rampage. Your strength is going to be nothing against that of a full-blood. Tonight, you and your Richard will stay glued to my side until first break of morning's light. It's unlikely that a full-blood would attack after daybreak—darkness gives them their full strength. And if it comes to an attack, Tara..."

"An attack?" she whispered.

"An attack. We'll pray that their ranks are low, and I'm going to also pray right now that every word you've said is true. I'm going to have to teach you to use a few weapons that can be used against you, as well."

"And you!" she reminded him.

"Yes," he said, staring at her.

"Oh, don't think that I'm such a fool that I trust you as of yet—in any way, shape or form. However…"

"However?"

"If we don't survive this night, what would all the trust in the world even mean?"

Sheathing his knife, he walked past her, but then paused, and turned back to take her hand. "Come on, my naive beauty. You're about to learn some terrible truths."

CHAPTER SIX

GRIMLY, FINN STARTED WALKING back to the camp.

"Wait!" Tara cried, catching up and grabbing his arm to stop him. "I don't understand. You think that there's a vampire or a band of vampires out there on the water somewhere? I don't understand—why would they be here? There's really not much along these islands. What would they gain coming here?"

He paused, looking down at her. "Tara, most vampires want to survive in the world around them. They've learned how to fit into society. Then there are those, and there always will be, who want to exert their power and be monsters. The possibilities I see? Someone out there wants to start up their own killing clan, or maybe someone out there wants to sway the tide of the war, one way or another. We just discovered a dead man, an obvious vampire kill. Where *did* he come from? We believed that a ship would come, that Tremblay's flare was seen. It's quite likely that man came off the ship—and that rescue won't be coming at all now. But, obviously, some kind of chaos is planned. If it was a hunger kill, the man would have been decently dispatched, not ripped to shreds, as well as possibly coming back to life. You grew up on an island alone, knowing that there *were* others, but not who they were. It's possible for a new vampire to survive—if the person was decent while living, and has someone to guide him into being the new self he becomes. But the newly created undead, if you will, have a hunger, and that hunger can bring out the greatest cruelty, the greatest evil, if you will. Come on. We've got to get back to the camp. Darkness is coming."

He started walking again. "Finn."

"What?"

"How— I mean, what will you do? You can't just announce that we're half-breeds, and that evil vampires are coming. What would make anyone else believe that—that we're not just as evil?"

"I'm not making any announcements. I'm setting up some barriers, and we'll watch. We'll watch through the night."

She looked up at him with troubled eyes. He was startled to feel a tremendous surge of warmth sweep through him. She looked at him with *trusting* eyes.

He steeled himself and turned away quickly. War was quite one thing, and bitter and brutal at that. But the dead man caught in the mangrove roots added another dimension to the danger. Men wouldn't be shot, injured, captured or killed.

They would be consumed in a bloodbath.

He felt Tara hurrying behind him as he headed straight back to the camp. Looking to the sky, he could see that dusk was falling, and falling quickly.

He walked over to Tremblay. "I found the remains of a dead Union seaman, sir. I'm afraid that our rescue ship might have been attacked."

Tremblay seemed puzzled. "Most of the time, the blockade runners don't even carry guns. They don't really attack Union ships, just try to evade them."

"I don't think that they were attacked by a Confederate ship, per se. There's an unknown enemy at work here. Someone terribly brutal. The victim wasn't simply shot. He was torn apart. We need to take precautions against…whatever's out there."

Tremblay stood. "Attention! Bosun, call all men to the campfire. Agent Dunne, if you'll explain your findings to the men?"

Some of the seamen had been cleaning their rifles; others had been reading, doodling. One played a mournful harmonica.

They all gathered by the fire; he noted that Tara took a seat on a log by Richard. He didn't think that she'd had a chance to tell him anything, but Richard was watching him as if he knew exactly what he was going to say.

"We have to be on our highest guard tonight, seamen. Someone in the vicinity has committed an atrocious murder."

"Excuse me, sir!" Billy interrupted. He cleared his throat. "We're at war. Shooting the enemy isn't murder."

"This man wasn't shot," Finn explained.

He waited as a silence fell upon the men. He heard the fire crackle, and he began to speak again. "He wasn't shot, he wasn't the victim of an explosion and he didn't die by bayonet. We'll take shifts tonight—not just one man or two on guard. We'll split the detail. I don't know if we're looking for one man who might be perpetuating these crimes, or several. Recently, in Harpers Ferry, they had an outbreak of a…a disease, a form of rabies. The strain makes savage killers of those infected, so if you are attacked, you must make sure that the enemy is down. You've all seen bloodshed in this war, bodies torn and maimed. But if this enemy has been afflicted, as I suspect, we'll have to tend to the bodies quickly. Heads severed, hearts crushed, the whole of the body burned."

He heard someone muttering toward the rear. He attuned quickly to the whispered conversation, fully aware that he couldn't have the seamen thinking that he had been afflicted by a mental disease.

"Pinkerton men! They see spies in their coffee, and goblins in the sand!"

"I assure you," he said, his voice strong and rising well over that of the whisperer, "this is a real threat. You there, seaman." He pointed to the whisperer. "What's your name?"

The man stared at him, a dark flush over his face. "Lafferty, sir. Charles Lafferty."

"Mr. Lafferty, I hope that I'm wrong about this. I don't see goblins in the sand. The danger I'm describing is real, and I pray that your dismissal of my warning does not cost you your life."

"No, sir, of course not, sir. My apologies," Lafferty said. He looked hopefully to Tremblay, who stood to Finn's left. Tremblay nodded toward Finn, giving him the authority to continue.

"Sleep with your guns at your side, but know that bullets alone will not stop this enemy. Have your swords ready. Be ready to move in with bayonets, and always make sure that you strike true and hard—not the gut, but the heart, or to sever the throat. And when a man falls, do not expect him to stay down. The rabid possess unusual strength. Mr. Lafferty, perhaps you could see to it that the arms trunks are opened, and every man is assigned a cutlass, saber or sword and a gun—with a bayonet. I'll take watch with Captain Tremblay during supper. We'll hope for good light until then. Most likely, they will come in the darkness."

He heard the sound of the fire crackle again in the dead silence that followed his words.

"Billy? Men, see to your arms," he said.

They all began to move; Captain Tremblay shouted orders then, instructing Billy and Doc MacKay to make sure that each man had his rifle at his side, while others were ordered to dole out rum rations and prepare supper. Tremblay stood by Finn.

"What you speak of is some kind of monster, Agent Dunne."

"Men can become monsters," Finn said.

Tremblay looked at him hard. "What about the prisoners, Dunne? Do we arm them, too?"

"I'll keep watch of the prisoners," Finn assured him. "If it comes to it, we'll allow them to protect themselves."

Dr. MacKay walked over to stand by them. "What did you do with the dead man's body, Agent Dunne?"

"I removed the head, sir, and sent his remains into the current—fitting, Doctor, I believe, for a navy man."

"Have you ever had a patient with such a disease, Doctor?" Tremblay asked.

"I have not treated such a patient. But I have heard something about such illnesses."

"Rumor, sir? Or truth?" Tremblay asked.

"From men of good faith," MacKay said. "I'll do my best to see to it that everyone in our company understands that, in this battle, the enemy must be...dead."

MacKay walked back to the tent, pausing to talk with the Union men along the way.

Finn looked over to the log that lay near the fire; Tara and Richard were still there, now deep in conversation. He strode over to the two of them.

"Stay by me," he instructed.

"If there is an attack, do I get to defend myself?" Richard asked him.

"If there is an attack," Finn said.

That night, there was little conversation while dinner was prepared. There was fresh fish; while diving, some of the men had taken down a big grouper, and the meat was soon cooking while beans were ladled out of tin cans and rum rations went around.

Watching the night sky, Finn noted the pile of brush and tree limbs for the fire.

Not enough.

He rose. "We need more tinder. We've got to keep that fire going through the night." He looked down at Tara. "Stay close to MacKay while I'm gone. I have a feeling the good doctor has heard of this kind of event before."

Tara rose. "I should be helping. I should be doing something."

Richard stood at her side. "Certainly, I can be trusted to help forage about for more fire tinder."

Finn nodded. "Fine, we'll stay close to the camp. Even damp wood, if we have to take it. It will dry enough if set by the fire before it's needed. I'll tell Tremblay what we're doing."

Finn felt the intense need for everyone there to know exactly where everyone else was. He reported to Tremblay, telling the captain to keep an eagle eye on those around him, as well. As he walked away, he felt Billy watching him and he turned back.

"You won't be gone long?" Billy asked anxiously.

"Just to gather what we need," Finn told him.

Billy looked back at the camp, and then at Finn again. There was a look of longing in his eyes, as if he felt that he was being left behind, without defense.

Giving Billy a salute, he headed off, beckoning to Tara and Richard. They followed him into the interior, over the route they'd traveled so often already, breaking down foliage and tamping down the grass.

"We've about stripped the area right here," Richard said. "But there are some pines ahead that we haven't taken yet, good branches."

"I can start gathering the small branches here for kindling," Tara said.

"We stay together," Finn said.

She looked at him with exasperation. "I'm not going to try to escape."

"He doesn't think you're going to try to escape," Richard said. "He's worried about your life, actually."

"The better to discover the truth, of course, when we're brought to trial," Tara said lightly. "Fine."

Finn looked up. The sun seemed to take another shift down the horizon. "Let's hurry," he said.

They reached the pines. Richard and Finn set about breaking off some of the low branches while Tara scoured around on the ground. When Richard had a problem getting one limb to break, Tara came over and snapped it easily.

"Thank you," Richard said.

"My pleasure," Tara said, and walked past him, searching out more of the smaller sticks and branches to feed the fire while the heavier branches caught the flame.

"Oh!" Tara cried suddenly, jumping back.

"What?" Finn was instantly at her side. She looked at him with horror in her eyes.

"Another!" she breathed.

Finn stepped past her and hunkered down. The man had been wounded in the arm, the gut and the left leg. But touching his face and turning it, Finn found ripping bite marks around his neck. As he touched the dead man, he began to move, bolting up and reaching out blindly, teeth gnashing in a broken jaw.

Tara let out a gasp. Finn knew she'd never seen the making of this kind of undead. And this one was particularly horrible. In time, in his new "life," the man would discover that his wounds would heal.

Right now, they were gaping and horrible. His face a mask of the macabre, his eyes burned with the waking hunger and rage that was his rebirth.

Finn leaped to his feet, drawing his sword. The newly made vampire lunged for him, saliva dripping from his mouth. With one clean motion, he decapitated the monster. The force of his blow made a sickening sound.

"Holy Mother of God!" Richard breathed.

Finn turned. Both Richard and Tara were staring at him, wide-eyed, in horror.

TARA COULDN'T GET the picture of the dead man out of her mind. Especially the inhuman movements he made while coming back to life.

She had been taught something about her father's world, and she had thought that she knew what she was, knew her strengths, and could always handle herself in any situation. But tonight had taken her by surprise. She knew that she hadn't been *made* a vampire but been *born* one. She'd never imagined what it would be like to see someone who was *made* a vampire.

She'd always been so sure of her own power, and she had honed many of her abilities. She could move so that she couldn't be seen, she could cover great distances easily and she could certainly hold her own in a fight against any mortal man.

But she'd not imagined something just as strong as herself—existing in a state of raw hatred.

She shivered to think that, if she had not gotten Finn, if she had come upon the dead man alone, when the darkness was falling and he was awakening, she would have been taken by total surprise. She was unprepared and would have died as easily as any human.

They all sat again by the fire, watching. The night was wearing on, and they had shifted the guard. Neither Finn nor Richard intended to sleep, she thought. They had held their positions at the rear of the group, watching the inner island. Now, the bracken and trees that had sustained them seemed like an ominous shadow as the minutes passed by.

"Anything?"

Tara started as she heard the word spoken softly by Dr. MacKay. He had come from the tarp, and took a seat by her on the log, a brooding look on his face as he peered into the darkness.

"Nothing. The sun rises in another few hours," Tara said.

"A few hours can be a lifetime," MacKay said.

She nodded. "You've really heard of such a...disease before?"

"Not all that long ago. It ran rampant up at Harpers Ferry. The outbreak was quelled. You've never known about any such event?"

The way he studied her scared her. She prayed that he didn't suspect her of being a monster—nor the Gator assassin.

"I spent most of my life in Key West," she said. "I've traveled, of course. But...no, I've never heard about anything like this."

Finn moved over to her then, watching the sky.

"Shh!" he said.

He wasn't holding a gun; he carried a sword, and his fingers were tight on the grip.

She fell silent, trying to listen as he was listening.

"I hear nothing," MacKay said.

But then, what Finn was hearing became more evident. It was like the sound of wings, the air being beaten in the night, and a chattering sound.

"They're here! Everyone, up and at arms!" Finn shouted.

There was confusion beneath the tarp as men sprang up, grabbing their weapons. But even as Finn looked to the sky, Tara saw movement in the bushes.

"Finn!" she cried, and his eyes darted in the direction she indicated.

Richard moved forward, grabbing a burning log from the fire; she did the same. As the first of the corpses moved out toward the camp from the interior, Finn shouted to Richard, tossing him a rifle. Richard caught it grimly in one hand, and held the burning torch in another.

Four burst out from the brush, and the chattering sound seemed to be that of other, perhaps older and more experienced monsters appearing from somewhere—the water, out of the sky. Her mother had taught her well, and in time, vampires could become exceptionally good at appearing, disappearing and protecting themselves—and becoming killing machines. There were at least sixteen falling upon them. Screams of shock and surprise filled the air as men began to fight for their lives. Dr. MacKay snatched up a burning log from the fire, waving it ahead of himself. Tara saw Finn rush forward; with his strength, he was able to slash off the head of one and twirl to catch a second with the same sweep of his sword. One came at Richard, and he thrust out the burning torch. The thing caught fire, and began to burn, screaming with fury as it ran off down the beach. At her side, MacKay fumbled with his rifle as a hulking red-haired man in sailor's breeches and a cotton shirt came toward him. But the shot caught the thing in the foot, and didn't give it pause at all. Before the creature could descend on MacKay, Tara stepped forward, snatching the rifle and thrusting the bayonet with all her strength into the thing's heart.

It fell, clutching its throat. Finn jumped in front of her, hunkering down with his knife to dispatch the head.

"Here!"

Finn took the dead man's sword and tossed it to Tara. She managed to catch it deftly.

"Watch for the eyes, men! Watch for the eyes if there's any question! They seem to have a red glow in them, all in this bloodline of monsters!"

They turned to join the desperate fray now taking shape on the beach. Richard let out a cry, racing forward into it, his momentum allowing him to flatten one of the beings, and then savagely destroy it. Tara paused, felt something behind her and swung around.

He was tall and ruggedly built, without a wound showing. He wore no uniform, but had a waistcoat and shirt of some elegance. He didn't lunge at her without control, but paused, looking at her, and laughing. This was no new vampire, she thought.

"Ah, what a tempting morsel! A rose among the thorns, as they might say. Delicious…"

She pulled back her sword and aimed for his throat with all her might. He saw her intent just in time, and ducked; the sword caught his shoulder, ripping hard, and he bellowed in rage. Then he rushed toward her like a maddened bull.

Using her sword as a stake, she let him impale himself. But he was massive and strong, and though her sword hit home, catching him dead in the gut, his impetus brought him falling down on top of her. He straddled over her; her weapon caught in its torso, and once again he laughed. "Pretty, pretty, pretty creature! Fierce—lots of fire! I like that."

There was no way, being flat on the sand and strad-dled by the man, that she could draw it out. She gritted her teeth, trying to twist the sword more deeply through him. But her efforts didn't seem to have an effect on him. He leaned down toward her, bringing his face to hers.

"So tender, so naive…delicious," he whispered.

She felt the sand and grabbed a handful, throwing it into his eyes. As he cried out, he lifted a fist—

But the blow never landed. She winced and turned away, closing her eyes…and felt something hot spray on her arm.

His weight fell from her.

She opened her eyes. Finn was standing over her. The big man's head rolled to the side.

He reached down for her hand. *"The throat, go for the throat!"*

"I couldn't get to his throat!"

"He was old, experienced," Finn said. He spun around, slicing a creature coming his way, almost in half. But he didn't let it lie. He sliced off this head, as well.

"It's over," he said quietly.

Keeping her hand in his, he walked back the beach. Dr. MacKay had given up his weapons for his physi-cian's bag. Men were groaning, holding wounded arms.

Tara looked for Richard.

"He did himself quite proud," Finn said, walking slightly behind her.

She stopped. "Richard? What happ—?"

"Of course Richard. And he is alive and well. There," Finn said.

He pointed. She looked through the grotesque piles of bodies and heads, staggering men and wounded men, and she saw him. His shirt was drenched in blood.

"Richard!" she cried, rushing to him.

He caught her, hugging her close. "It's not my blood," he assured her.

Finn had followed her, and was looking at the remains of the battle. "Gather up the bodies—they should be burned. We'll assure ourselves that it's over."

"Wind is to the north-northeast," Dr. MacKay commented.

"Then we'll move them northward, and set the fire a distance from the camp," Finn said. He raised his voice to be heard by everyone. "Those who are able-bodied, gather the dead, head up the beach. And keep your eyes open."

Finn headed to gather wood and kindling from the campfire. Richard told Tara, "I'll help Finn."

"I'll come."

"MacKay needs help," Richard said, indicating the doctor.

She looked to the doctor. He seemed to be checking over every man carefully.

Tara had to wonder how he knew what he was looking for.

She came to his side, kneeling down by him where he sat with a man on the beach. It was Charles Lafferty, the man who had questioned Finn's warning of the assault.

He was bleeding from an arm wound. His eyes were dazed.

"There's bandaging in the bag," he told Tara. "Can you get me some...and that pail...? Bathing wounds with seawater will help." Then he turned to Lafferty, warning him, "It will hurt."

"I'm not going to lose the arm, am I?" Lafferty asked.

"Let's hope not. As long as there's no infection," MacKay told him.

Lafferty shook his head. "No...no, it was a sword wound, the bastard got me with his sword. Oh, holy hell, but the bastard was trying to bite me!" Lafferty said.

"He didn't manage to do so, did he?" Tara asked, unfolding the bandage.

Lafferty let out a yelp as the cold seawater washed out the wound.

"It was as if he was some kind of a cannibal. And he had one eye! He only had one damned eye left," Lafferty said. "But do you know the worst part?" he asked, looking at both of them. "I *knew* him. He was stationed at the fort and called out just three months ago for duty in Baltimore. I knew the bloody bastard! Pardon me, miss."

Tara gave a wincing smile at the absurd mannerism amid so much death. She'd wielded a sword right along with the men, and they were surrounded by carnage. And still Lafferty wanted to be polite.

"Get some sleep. There's an extra ration of rum for the wounded," said MacKay, finishing the bandage and rising.

Tara rose along with him.

"Any other wounds?" MacKay called out.

Captain Tremblay came walking down the beach; he silently caught the feet of a dead man, and started dragging him back along the sand. He looked old and exhausted, and there was blood dripping from his arm.

"Captain!" Tara called, rushing after him.

He paused and looked at her. "Ah, lass, I'm sorry for this. Sorry that one so young and tender should be here. You're well—unharmed?"

"I'm fine. But you're bleeding."

"It's nothing. A scratch," Tremblay said.

Down the beach, the fire being ignited suddenly snapped, shooting flames up into the sky. The smell of burning flesh permeated the air.

"Let Dr. MacKay bandage your arm, Captain, please," Tara said.

Finn and Richard were returning at an even pace.

"Agent Dunne!" Tara called. "The captain is wounded."

"See the doctor, Captain," Finn said, taking the body

the captain had been concerned with. "You can't let yourself fall prey to a wound."

Tremblay nodded. Wearily, he turned. He headed for one of the pallets beneath the tarp, and Tara and the doctor followed. MacKay cut away his shirtsleeve, and Tara gasped when she saw the deep slash in his upper arm.

"That's not a little flesh wound, sir," she said, unfolding the bandage while MacKay bathed the wound. MacKay didn't seem happy with seawater alone; he found a rum bottle and uncorked it, pouring some of the alcohol over Tremblay's arm.

"A waste of fine spirits, surely!" Tremblay protested.

"Ah, but good for all that ails such a wound, sir. Now, Captain, here's the bottle. Take down a good portion— I've got to stitch up that arm."

"I'm good at pain, MacKay."

"Then take a healthy swig so that you'll be good at sleep. The sun is nearly up, and we need our captain to have rest," Tara said.

Tremblay sighed and lifted the rum bottle, wincing as it burned down to his gullet. Tara assisted, preparing the needle and sutures, and when they were done, Mackay told her, "Some of us will have to get some sleep now, or this whole sad little party will be useless."

"I will close my eyes and rest," Tremblay said.

Tara rose. Down the beach, a group of the men stood, watching the fire.

She realized that she was exhausted.

"If the injured are all tended, then I will lie down, too," she told MacKay. He nodded. She asked him, "What were you looking for on the men?"

"I don't know what you're talking about," he said.

"You were searching them over—beyond their wounds."

He stared at her for a moment. "Bite marks, Miss Fox. Bite marks." He smiled grimly.

All she could do then was return his scrutiny, and nod. "Good night, then," she said.

Tara found her pallet and blanket and lay down. She was so tired, and yet, there was still commotion around her, and the sun was rising.

She closed her eyes. She heard conversation. The men were back from the mass cremation. Finn was assigning the current guard duty.

A moment later, she felt warmth at her side. Cracking her eyes, she saw that Finn had lain down at her left side.

And Richard was at her right.

Her protectors, she thought, before she did fall asleep for a bit.

WHEN SHE AWOKE, RICHARD still dozed at her side. The sun was steadily moving toward its apex.

But she could see that Finn had walked to the shoreline and stood there with Dr. MacKay and a few of the men, looking out at the horizon.

She quickly found her feet, made sure the blanket

still covered Richard and hurried down to the shore to join them.

"What is it?" she asked, coming to Finn's side.

He pointed. "There."

She looked out. Far on the horizon, she saw a ship. The sails were tattered, hanging limply. The main mast was broken near the top, and hanging precariously.

"She's a ghost ship," MacKay said.

"Among other things," Finn muttered.

"She'll just drift on by."

"She might. But we can't take that chance."

"There's no one at the helm!" Mackay insisted.

"Looks can be deceptive. She's more than a ghost ship, Doctor. I'm going to take a longboat out to her, and see if we can make sure that she is...abandoned. Those things came from somewhere last night, Dr. MacKay. I think that was our rescue ship. And I do believe that her crew is past help. No matter, we must search her out. And," he added, "when we make her seaworthy, she may still be our salvation."

CHAPTER SEVEN

FINN WAS CONCERNED. No one had slept until daybreak, which meant the day was well on by the time they'd all awakened. He chafed to get going, but MacKay had told him that the captain was asking for him, and that it was important that they talked.

Captain Tremblay's wound was causing him a great deal of trouble. Before he could set the course for the day, Finn knelt with Dr. MacKay by the captain's side, and felt the feverish touch of his skin. Dr. MacKay cooled his forehead with a cold cloth, and redressed the wound, Tara assisting from across the captain's prone body.

Tremblay seemed to be caught in his own dream-world, created, perhaps, by the fever. Beneath closed lids, his eyes made darting motions.

Then suddenly, the captain opened his eyes wide and stared straight at Finn. "You will watch out for my men, sir. You will watch out for my men!"

"Aye, Captain. But you're not going to die. You're going to get well," Finn assured him.

With an amazing strength, he suddenly gripped

Finn's arm. "You will not let me become one like *them*. You will not let it happen. Swear to me. Swear!"

Tara stroked a hand on his cheek. "You're not going to die, Captain. You can fight this."

"I am an old man," Tremblay said. "I feel my strength slipping far away. I do not fear death. I fear what I saw last night."

"You will never become one of them, Captain!" Tara assured him.

Finn watched her, noting the way she looked at the captain. She'd been his captive; his ship had been the one to run Richard's pride to a blazing death in fire and water. But Tremblay had treated her with courtesy, and she seemed to have acquired an honest affection for him. She looked at the captain now with tenderness, and her fingers touched upon the man's face with the brush of a feather.

She loved Richard, of course. That was so easy to see. And yet, the two did behave more as siblings than as...as lovers. It was, Finn had to admit, irritating to realize that he'd felt...yes, *jealousy,* regarding the man. Tara Fox was not easy to slip into a compartment in his mind. *Possible spy, assassin. Not to be thought of as a woman.*

Any creature, alive or dead, he mused, would find her appealing. Even that one creature last night, accustomed to seizing what women he chose—and murdering those who displeased him, bored him or were simply there when his hunger peaked—had known that she was different. She walked with pride and beauty; her eyes flashed with her passions, and though she knew fear, she knew as well to fight around it.

Finn found himself entranced, watching her, and suddenly wondering what it would be like when her eyes filled with tenderness and passion as she looked into the eyes of a lover. Though he'd been at war so long—his one guiding function to keep the president alive—he had thought about little else lately. There had been women; perhaps his very mix of blood made him attractive to the opposite sex, but he hadn't felt this strange torment of sexual longing that twisted at and tore into his emotions, as well.

He quickly drew his gaze from her and focused on the captain. There was no need to dwell on the future when they still had to persevere here. But if they did survive this...

Then what? She was his captive; she would be brought to trial—if they lived. He admired Richard, but Finn now found himself praying that neither he nor Tara was the Gator. But if not, then how had his information been so accurate, and how had Richard's *Peace* been setting to sea—*an armed blockade runner!*—when it had?

They were all captured here in a struggle now for life or death; if they didn't get ahead of the diseased they'd all perish; this was definitely a take-no-captives situation. Questions of national allegiance would all be moot.

"Captain, I will leave you in the hands of our good

doctor MacKay, and I will see to it that the ship out on the water is made safe. She will take us far from these waters, and we'll send a warning for those in the islands to take care. You will be fine. I will give orders and guidance to your men as if they were my own, and we will all fight our hardest to prevail."

Tremblay turned to look at Tara. "If I…succumb, you will do me the honor of death! Promise me that you will see to it that I don't flounder in a prison of death and destruction, that I may die in God's good graces, and stand before Him in heaven?"

"Dr. MacKay won't let you die," Tara said.

"Promise me!"

"We all vow such. But as you are an excellent officer of the Union, sir, we need you. We won't let you die," Finn said. Then he stood; it was time to get out to the ship.

He started walking toward the line of Union longboats. Tara came running behind him. "I'm going with you," she told him.

"You can't," he said, looking around at the campsite. This morning, every man seemed to be at work cleaning a rifle or honing a sword.

"I can be helpful," she said. "If someone does get at me, it won't matter. I am what I am—they can't *turn* me into anything."

"I want to take a party of six—two top deck all the while, and four to flush out the ship. What reason would I give to these men to take a lady aboard on such a mission? She is a monster? Please don't decapitate her be-cause she's a *different kind* of monster?"

"But *you're* a monster," she reminded him.

"A masculine monster, Tara. And I'm afraid that mat-ters among these men."

"But that's foolish." She pleaded, "There must be a way.... Please, you need to let me come. I can really help you—and you know that."

He looked at her, down into her eyes. He felt the sen-sation streak through him again that he wanted *more* of her.

That meant he should turn away, turn his wall into a brick wall.

Except that she was right. She had fought exception-ally well the night before.

"All right. Inform Richard. I'll leave MacKay to watch over the captain. We'll be three, then. I'll bring three more with me. Find Richard while I decide who is most able—and least wounded," Finn told her.

She nodded solemnly, and turned to do as he had bidden.

Finn looked around the camp. He thought about the second body they had found on the island last night. It was plausible that a tide had carried the body up to the mangroves. It was harder to construe how one might have wound up inland.

He'd seen the men as they'd worked, sailing the Union ship. He'd seen them all pitch together, setting up camp on the island. It was possible, though difficult to believe, that one of them was a traitor—or worse, a minion for a monster.

He looked after Tara, and then stared down at Captain Tremblay and Dr. MacKay. McKay rose, grim.

"You think that he was infected?" the doctor asked him quietly.

"I don't know. You'll have to watch over him, and the camp. But I doubt if anything will happen during the daylight hours. Someone got onto that rescue ship who shouldn't have been on it, or there has been someone among us all the while," Finn said. "Keep a sharp eye out while we're securing the ship. We'll bring her in and anchor her as swiftly as we can, and hopefully, be out of here by tomorrow."

"Any words of wisdom for me?" MacKay asked.

"Keep your sword at your side. Don't hesitate. Perhaps get a few of the men remaining to sharpen pine branches strong enough to pierce through muscle and sinew. And watch the captain."

The man nodded. "Godspeed, then. I will do my best here."

Leaving the doctor, Finn found Richard and Tara waiting at the longboats. Richard had a rifle over his shoulder, a sword in a scabbard. Tara had found a belt and sheath that would fit her, and she was ready, too.

Charles Lafferty was with them, his shoulder still bandaged, but he had a grim look on his face.

"Agent Dunne, I'm begging you, give me the chance

to accompany you, sir! I've learned what we're up against, and I'm ready for the fight."

Lafferty was a big man, and Finn had seen him wield a sword.

"Your arm is wounded."

"My left arm, sir. I can fight with my right, and do so well, I swear."

Finn nodded. "Lafferty, fine. You're in. You'll guard topside while we search below." He looked over the men who waited, some seeming as if they would like to be called. Others had the look of soldiers who would do their duty, but did not relish an actual confrontation.

"London, Grissom—are you up for the journey?" Finn asked. London was as solid as a steel drum. Grissom was not a big man, but Finn had seen the way he could move.

"Aye, sir," London assured him quickly.

"Aye," Grissom said more gravely.

Finn looked back at the camp. MacKay's arms were folded over his chest; he wasn't leaving his position by the captain.

"Then we're on our way. When the ship is secured, I'll send out a flare. Billy!" he called, searching the ranks for the seaman.

"Aye, sir!" Billy said, waving from the rear of the tent, near the fire.

"Someone on guard at all times. The good doctor MacKay is in command if the captain is incapacitated."

"Begging your pardon, sir," Grissom said.

"Yes?"

"The lady is coming with us? On such a mission—"

"I cannot leave her here, Grissom. Shall we go?"

He didn't wait for argument from the men but headed straight into the boat. The others moved in. Tara took a seat in the rear; Richard sat center, and picked up an oar. Grissom sat next to him, looked at him a moment and then picked up the other oar. Finn and Lafferty picked up the second set while London was near the rear.

When they reached the abandoned ship, Richard rose carefully. "I can nab that iron rod with a lasso," he suggested.

Finn knew he could leap the distance, and Tara most probably could as well, but it wouldn't do at the moment. "Aye, Richard."

"If this don't beat all," London said, grinning. "It's us and the Rebs today. Well, in my book, that sure beats fighting, for once!"

Richard was good, hitting his mark on the second try.

"I'll take it up first," Finn said.

He looped his arm around the rope and tested it; the hold was secure. He began his climb, careful as he reached the deck. Looking around, he saw no one at first, and then a body lying over the helm. He walked over to it quickly, jerking the man back.

This fellow had not been ravaged. Whoever had attacked the ship had been stealthy, had taken out the helmsman first. No blood hunger had caused this kill;

the man's throat had been slashed, probably from the rear, a quick slice from the left ear to the right. Blood pooled over the wheel, and down to the deck.

Leaving the corpse, he came back to the rail and looked down; Richard was on his way up. Finn reached down to assist. When he cleared the deck, Tara began her assent. She was quick and nimble, even encumbered with the sword. As she neared the rail, he and Richard crashed into each other in their attempt to help her over.

Richard gave way. Finn slipped his arms around Tara's shoulders, hiking her over and setting her down. He felt the brush of her body, and felt the reaction of his own. He stepped back quickly. "Lafferty, come on, we can give you leverage from here!"

London was the last up. When they were assembled on deck, they looked at the dead man at the helm.

"I know this ship, sir. I've sailed on her," London told him.

"How many decks?"

"Captain's cabin there, sir. One below, two officers' quarters portside and bunks starboard, and storage for food and supplies. Three below, you've got the cannon ports, and below that, ballast and more storage."

"There's no splitting up. No one goes anywhere alone. Richard, you and Lafferty topside. The rest of us will begin a sweep. Take the captain's quarters first, and dispatch anyone you find," Finn instructed.

Richard and Lafferty headed for the captain's quarters. While they made their way to the steps leading below, Finn watched the two. They worked well in tandem. Richard held back, ready with his sword. Lafferty kicked the door in.

"Dead captain!" Lafferty called.

"See to him," Finn said. "Head off, body in the water."

"Aye!" Lafferty replied.

Finn led the way down. The ship was laid out exactly as described. He paused, listening. There was nothing but the sound of the waves against the ship, and the movement of the two men overhead.

He motioned to London and Grissom, who began a thorough search through the trunks and barrels of salt, rum, dried beef and other food supplies. Walking ahead, he knew that Tara followed him. He paused as they came to the seamen's bunks. Blankets covered them. They glanced at one another, and started searching through the bunks.

"One here," Tara called, her voice tight.

He hurried over. A man lay in the bunk. His eyes were closed, his face unmolested. His torso was ripped from throat to groin. All that remained was a bloody mass.

Tara turned away. The body was so destroyed that Finn didn't think the man could make a return. Nonetheless, he drew his knife and decapitated the man. As he did so, he heard movement, and Tara let out a startled cry.

He turned; a man had burst out from the first of the

small officers' quarters; his eyes were blazing. Blood spattered his white shirt, but he showed no signs of injury. He was almost upon Tara. Finn spun with his knife ready, but his effort wasn't needed. Tara cried out again, both hands on the hilt of her sword as she brought it swinging high with true aim. She caught him dead in the neck and with such energy and power that the head went flying. For what seemed like a long moment the body stood, then fell at their feet.

Grissom and London came rushing over. London stared at the body, and then at the head, and then at Tara. "I will serve with you anytime, Miss Fox…"

"Take care. There may be more," Finn warned. He motioned to Tara, and they moved forward to look into the second officers' quarters. The man there was just beginning to rise. Finn strode over to him quickly.

The man's eyes had bulged open. He looked at Finn and started to jerk up, a cry of rage emitting from him, fangs all but bursting from his lips. Finn skewered him in the heart with his sword, withdrew the blade, stood back and slashed off the head. It rolled off the cot and onto the floor. There wasn't much blood—just the head, with eyes open, staring. Finn thought wearily that he had seen this sight too many times.

He turned. Tara was standing in the doorway, watching. There was both horror and pity in her eyes. "Is there never any hope?" she asked.

"Sometimes, if it's stopped," he told her briefly. He wanted to walk to her, hold her and shield her from the sight. It was what men did for women. But he could not; in truth, they were still enemies.

And she would not want comfort from him.

"You're done, you bloody bastard!" they heard from the corridor.

Hurrying from the second of the officers' quarters, they discovered that Grissom had found a man returning with thirst, and dispatched him—it appeared he had taken several blows with his sword to do so.

"How many more, do you think?" London asked, leaning hard by one of the swinging hammocks that made cots for the seamen.

"Not many—there can't be," Grissom said. "This ship wouldn't have had more than twenty or twenty-two men aboard. We killed twelve last night."

Twelve, two found dead on the island and four on the ship.

"Then we still have to account for more men," Finn said.

"There shouldn't have been anyone down at the cannons—the ship wasn't attacking," London said. "Or...maybe it was... Someone had to get aboard with the disease to do this."

"We'll finish here, and head down again. God knows, maybe someone ran down to the ballast hold," Finn said.

He led the way as they headed down again. Among the heavy cargo, including bricks, salt, sugar, rum and gunpowder, they found two more men.

There was little need to do much. They had been

ripped to shreds, and their throats had been so violated the heads were hanging on by a string. Finn ordered Grissom and London to deal with the bodies; he told Tara that they needed to head topside.

Richard, he reasoned, would be the best man to lead the wounded ship closer to the island where they could anchor, and make repairs in the morning.

He could have dealt with the bodies himself; despite her adeptness when dealing with the frenzied creatures as they came back to life, Finn couldn't help but want to protect Tara from the horror of such gruesome things.

He ushered her topside where Richard Anderson was keeping watch with Charles Lafferty. "Can you navigate her closer, Richard, and avoid the reefs?" he asked.

"That I can," Richard assured him. "The mains mast is cracked at the top, but we can unfurl the mizzenmast and bring up the main sail as much as possible. She's a steamer, too, if someone can fire her up."

"I'll get the steam going. Are we safe now?" Lafferty asked Finn.

"Aye. We're set to go. Grissom and London will see to it."

As he spoke, the men came up the steps to the deck, carrying grisly cargo. Again, Finn wanted to shield Tara; he could not. They walked by, the bodies wrapped in sheeting, but Tara was still watching, and her face was white.

Richard looked at Finn for a moment, and then passed by him, going to Tara. He took her in his arms.

Finn gritted his teeth, hating the fact that he longed to do the same.

"Grissom and London, see to her steam power. Richard, get her through the reefs, and we'll bring her in close enough to make use of her tomorrow."

THERE WAS A CHEER when they brought the Union ship in. Her name was actually *USS Freedom,* something Tara hadn't noticed upon their initial approach. Richard brought her safely to anchor beyond the reefs and to the sandbar that created such shallow passage at the beachhead and then took the longboat to shore.

Finn, of course, announced the situation they had discovered on board, and since it was getting dark again, plans were made to make the ship seaworthy for a longer voyage the next morning.

Tara noted that Dr. MacKay drew Finn aside quickly when they arrived, and that Finn listened to him gravely. She realized that they came to a conclusion, and that MacKay immediately went to work on something that he found in his doctor's bag of tourniquets, needles and syringes.

She approached Finn, wanting to know what was going on.

He looked at her and hesitated. "The captain is dying. And if he dies, he will change."

"We—we can't let him die," she said, shaking her head and looking into Finn's eyes. She almost took a step away from him; there was something in his steeled composure that made her tremble, and she realized that the world was incredibly strange. Just days ago, they had fought a sea battle, and the captain and Finn and all these men might have died—and to her, it would have just been the course of war. Survival against the enemy. But now, so quickly, the captain had grown dear to her.

And Finn had become a strange ally in a world she had experienced only on her own until now. She felt safe in his presence. She listened to the sound of his voice, and it washed over her, and touched her, just as that power in his eyes did. He was extraordinarily attractive, with his lean muscled build, and she found herself thinking about the shimmer of water on his naked bronzed shoulders and chest when they had dived. She wanted so badly to touch him, to be close to him. She realized that she fantasized about lying beside him, and allowing her fingers to play over his flesh. He knew what she was; he respected her abilities, and he understood her weaknesses, and somehow there was a balance there that made her not just feel that fluttering, that warm attraction, but admiration, as well. God forbid... she was fascinated with the man. She *liked* him.

But though he was now an odd ally, he was still the enemy.

Looking at her, Finn sighed deeply. "I can help," he told her quietly.

"How?"

"Blood transfusion."

"Blood *transfusion*? I've never heard of such a thing," Tara said, realizing that Finn's presence kept her from being horrified or afraid. No, she was just puzzled.

"Giving blood from one person to another. Actually, the first reported successful attempt from one human being to another was in 1818, and, no, it isn't common. But doctors *have* saved a few men in the Union army after amputations with such a procedure."

"How is it accomplished?" she asked.

"Dr. MacKay will certainly be better at the particulars than I am, but…quills are used to pierce the veins, and tubing, such as that used by embalmers. Dr. MacKay may well have what we need—the practice of embalming soldiers, when possible, has become more popular lately," Finn said. "I intend to give him some of my blood as it will fight against the infection. But… giving blood will weaken me, so you must be prepared to combat anything that might come by night."

She smiled at him. "I'm ready to stand in combat when our lives are threatened as they have been, but that's ridiculous. You are far more aware of what may come and how, and though I pride myself on being a quick learner, it's far more important that you maintain your strength."

"I can't really ask this of you."

"You're not asking. I'm volunteering."

HE WAS STRUCK AGAIN, as he was far too often, by her beauty. Oval face, hazel eyes and red hair, now streaming down her back like in the rich shades of the sunset all around them. Her mouth was generous, and he longed to run his thumb along her lips, and he had to catch himself from such thoughts again. They were speaking about the captain's life, and of transfusion, which had rarely been done.

But he had a feeling that even if MacKay did not have actual experience in the procedure himself he would do his best in faith.

Finn held still, feeling as if every muscle in his body tensed. He could feel his jaw lock. He didn't want to put this on her.

But it was true.

His strength was the more necessary. They didn't know if they had faced the end of the monster enemy or not.

"You know that it's the right thing to do, letting me be the donor," she said softly.

He still hesitated. Then he nodded slowly and spoke quietly. "All right. I don't like it, though, you know."

"I know. But it's the most logical solution," she told him. "Besides, in a short time, the captain has grown dear to me."

Ah, if he could but hear such words from her about himself!

"Let's see MacKay," he told her.

Together, they went to where MacKay still kept careful watch over the captain. When Finn looked at him, he shook his head.

"I fear that the end is near," MacKay mouthed to him.

"No, please, I need you to listen to me, and do the

best patient care you have ever done, for both patients," Finn said.

"Both patients?" MacKay said, frowning.

Finn explained that he'd seen blood transfusions before, and that Tara was young, and willing. Tara stood by his side, smiling. MacKay looked at her and said, "I've never performed such an operation before."

"But I have infinite faith in you," Tara told him.

"It's the only way to save the captain," Finn said flatly.

MacKay nodded slowly. "I have the equipment you mentioned."

"Then let's get to it. Before the situation becomes too dire," Finn said.

And so they began. Both MacKay and Tara listened as he gave instruction. MacKay was fine with Captain Tremblay, since Tremblay was unconscious; with Tara, MacKay seemed more worried.

"It's all right," Tara assured him.

MacKay looked at her a long time. Again, Finn had the feeling that MacKay knew much more than he would admit to.

"All right," he said.

Finn was surprised that it was Richard—among all the men there—that he called upon for help.

But, although they had begun this situation with a sea battle with Richard Anderson, he was the man he trusted most for assistance. Richard ordered Billy to start the men on mess, and Lafferty, London and Grissom were eager to get the evening meal going.

MacKay, as instructed, brought out clean quills. A pallet was set above the captain for Tara, and MacKay dug in his medical bag for the necessary tubing.

Tara winced slightly as the quill was stuck into her vein. She relaxed, though, as she saw her blood running through the tube and into the captain's veins.

Finn kept watch on the procedure.

And on the night.

But it seemed that they would be left in peace for the moment.

He scanned the sky, and he made sure that men were on watch.

The night wore on as the captain began to gain color again, and it appeared that he would live. Just as Tara was feeling the strain in earnest, the procedure was finished.

Tara was tired. Finn ordered her to lie on her pallet, and she smiled and did so. He lay next to her and asked anxiously, "You feel...all right?"

"Weak," she told him. "But I will be fine."

"And, I believe, the captain will live."

Her smile deepened. "He is a good man," she said. But then, her eyes continued to gaze into his. And she said, "You know something about my family. Please, tell me what you know. And you...how are you—what you are? I've been so far away from everything. Tell me, please?"

He paused, but her hazel eyes were on his. And there was no reason not to tell her what he knew.

"You have a brother," he said. "And your brother is a doctor. His name is Cody."

"I have a brother," she said with awe. "And his name is Cody. And he's a doctor!"

"And you have a sister," he said. "Her name is Megan."

"You know them?" she asked hopefully, feeling re-energized momentarily.

He shook his head. "I know *of* them," he said.

"How?" she whispered.

"Because they are the ones who quelled the rising in Harpers Ferry," he told her. "I was assigned elsewhere at the time, but when it was over, I heard about all that happened."

"I have a brother, and a sister!" She marveled. "So, of course, I'm assuming, they are children of my father."

"Yes."

"What about you?" she asked. She lay on her pallet, sunset hair spread beneath her, marbled and brilliant hazel eyes upon him. "Where do you come from?"

CHAPTER EIGHT

GRISSOM, LONDON, LAFFERTY and Richard were on watch. They had all exhibited a heightened sense of awareness since the night before, so Finn decided that he could dare ease off and trust in the intelligence of the others. Captain Tremblay was still falling in and out of sleep, gathering new strength, but in the morning, he'd be better off than when the night had begun. MacKay was watching him, and the world around them. Finn eased down to lie on an elbow as he spoke to Tara resting on her pallet.

"I can tell you something about you, first," Finn said, smiling at her. "Your brother was a Southern physician. He was almost killed, but he revived. I think people considered it something of a miracle. He was practicing medicine in New Orleans when an old general asked for his help out in Texas—where he'd been born. He went out there, became friends with the general and a sheriff, and they all came east when things started going awry in the Harpers Ferry area. That's about when he first met his sister, Megan." He smiled slightly. "I've wanted to meet Cody and Megan Fox, but circumstances haven't allowed for it. So, this is the story as I know it, and I believe it to be true. Your grandfather was taken and killed, but he didn't die, he changed. And there have been those who had seen him around the country ever since. When I heard your name, I told myself there were plenty of Foxes in the world, but then I'd realized your ability to disappear at will, and I had a pretty good feeling I knew exactly who you were."

"My father never married my mother," Tara told him. "But he did insist that I have his name, said it would be important in the future.... Will I be able to meet them? Are they friends with each other? Were they... Are their hearts with the North or the South?"

"Now? Neither. Like most of us, they see the travesty. Half the country is stripped and beaten. Great cities are burned-out ruins. They want the war over," Finn said.

"How do you know so much about them if you haven't met them?" Tara asked.

He smiled. "As I said, we keep missing one another. But we've been called to serve the same leader."

"And that is?"

"Lincoln."

She rolled on an elbow to face him as he spoke. The firelight burned gently over her face and hair, casting a glow of beauty on each. Her eyes were such an unusual hazel—although, among their kind, hazel was not a rare color. Still, hers seem to radiate in so many shades and hues.

"I wish I knew a way to make you believe. My passion has been to reach Abraham Lincoln, yes, but not to hurt him. There's something in my mind that's so real, I believe he has to know of it. I feel that he's spoken with me. And I keep trying to warn him that he has to be careful. I have this urge to be near him, so that I might cast myself between him and any danger," she told him. "Don't you see?" she asked urgently. "Most of us see that Atlanta was destroyed, and that Savannah had no hope but to surrender. Soon, there will be no young men in the South—they'll all be dead on the altar of sacrifice they once so nobly thought of as 'the cause.'"

She paused. "Finn, most thinking people in the South are bitter, and they know that the punishment the South will experience will be severe when this is all done. I know that you fear for Lincoln's life constantly— honestly, I do, too."

She was so earnest. He wanted to believe her.

Or forget the war. The endless years of bloodshed. The men who walked every city on crutches now, minus a leg, or with a pinned sleeve where a healthy arm should have been. There would always be monsters in the world, and when he had chosen to become a Pinkerton agent, he'd known he'd seek out monsters. But a war where families killed families, where sons died on their father's land, where brothers might die in one another's arms, went beyond all cruelty in the human mind.

He was startled when she reached out and touched him, her fingers just brushing his cheek.

She flushed. "I'm sorry—you seemed a million miles away for a moment," she told him.

A million miles away, and yet, I sense you here so acutely that it's painful, and still so seductive that I don't want to be anywhere else in the world.

"No, I'm here. I was just thinking about the war," he said.

"What about you?" she asked him.

"Pardon?"

"You. You are a half-breed, right?" She smiled as she asked the question.

He nodded. "My father was taken in an Indian fray in Illinois. My mother was determined to save his life. Through him, I was born with vampire blood, which is, of course, the same way you became this way. My mother did save my dad—thankfully, since that's why I am here now. Years later, however, they were both killed by a rogue band of vampires. I was a boy at the time. Later, I was introduced to Allan Pinkerton. He started off as a detective in Chicago when he was being fleeced and cheated. He began to grow the agency, and with the war, many of us were brought on to protect the president—and ferret out those who were trying to kill him. And, of course, as you can imagine, I am determined to fight those who make monsters of us all."

"Of course. How—how did they manage to kill your father?" she asked.

He looked away. He could still visualize the day as he told her the story. His father had become a champion of the people, protecting against any danger, including outlaws, murderers and thieves—those who preyed upon the farmers and ranchers on the frontier. When the vampires had descended upon their town, Andre Dunne had led the men out to meet them, and he'd brought them down, including their leader. But in his pitched sword battle with the leader, he'd lost his own life. Finn had been there to take part in the battle, even at the age of twelve. And when his father had lain dying, he had sent him back to care for his mother. Except that when he reached their house, he found that she had been murdered, probably before the battle had even begun. His rage and pain had nearly killed him—and almost set him upon a path of nothing but murder. But his uncle had arrived, and told him he'd die himself if he didn't learn control—and his own power. And that he needed to head into a field of higher learning so that he could best understand the world, and all the dangers within it. And so, he had gone with his uncle to grow up in Chicago, and there he had met Pinkerton, and first heard of Abraham Lincoln.

"I'm so sorry, Finn," she said softly. Again, the tone of her voice was sincere. Her hazel eyes gazed upon him with glittering compassion.

"It was a long time ago now," he told her.

"You knew them both. You obviously loved them. I believe that my father is out there somewhere. I hope that I can find him and meet him. My mother believed in him. She understood that he needed to keep moving on. She said that their time together was brief, but that she'd have rather been with him for a short time than with any other man for a lifetime. She loved him very much. And, of course, we were in Key West. Not that there aren't those there who believe themselves to be the height of society, but still..." She smiled. "We are isolated, and we have a population from all over the Caribbean, so it's easier to live and let live."

"And here we are," Finn murmured.

He lay back on the pallet. It was so good to be close to her. To rest. And yet, they weren't out of danger. They still didn't know exactly where the danger to the island had begun. A rogue vampire aboard the Union ship when it had left Key West? Or something out on the water?

And there was still the matter of discovering the identity of Gator.

He turned to look at Tara again, but her eyes had closed. She was sleeping. It was the sleep of one who needed the healing of time.

He rose and walked over to Captain Tremblay's pallet. Dr. MacKay sat at the captain's side, honing his sword.

"How is he doing?" Finn asked.

MacKay nodded. "Well. His color is returning, his pulse is strong. He has made a complete turnabout."

Finn walked out back, where Richard and Billy were keeping watch by the fire. All seemed quiet. Richard asked him, "Tara?"

"She is fine, sleeping," Finn told him.

Richard nodded.

Finn headed out to the front of the camp, and saw that Grissom and Lafferty were keeping watch on the sea.

"Anything?" Finn asked.

"The night is quiet," Lafferty told him.

He returned to the pallet next to Tara's. He eased himself down, and knew that he was exhausted, too. He had to trust in the others for a few hours. Feeling the heat of her body so close to his, he basked in the warmth, and slept.

THE STRANGE VISION CAME to Tara again that night.

She should have thought of it as a dream, but it wasn't a dream. It was as if a part of her traveled, and was, in truth, walking the corridors of the White House.

She stood in the room. Lincoln was at his desk. He looked up and smiled at her. "Welcome, my dear."

"It's good to see you, sir," she told him.

He was working with a number of papers on his desk. "I take heart. I still watch the casualty lists come in daily. But now I am working on my second inaugural address." He hesitated, looking at her. "I fear for my dear Mary. She had another séance in the Red Room last night. She feels the pain of fighting her own family so deeply. And she cannot bear the loss of our Willie… so many thoughts and dilemmas weigh down upon us all. And, of course, you are here to warn me again that I must take care of myself."

"You are needed."

He smiled. "It is good of you to say so. I have such

strange dreams. Of course, this is one of them, because here you are, and yet, you are not. I don't know you, but I feel that I will."

"Yes, I want to be near you, sir. I want to protect you."

He smiled. "Now, girl, a slender beauty such as yourself, longing to protect a worn-out man who has aged twenty years in four. You give me faith, and that is something that I have fought to maintain throughout the hard and bitter years. I will see you soon?"

"God willing," Tara assured him.

She felt as if she was drawn backward through a field of mist.

And then she was on her pallet on the little island.

She blinked, awakening slowly. She could hear birds chirping. Beyond the tarp, she could see palm fronds gently weaving in the breeze.

She turned to her right, and smiled. Richard, ever faithful, was beside her.

She turned to her left and flushed; she had been sleeping curled against Finn's back. She moved quickly, which startled him; he grabbed her arm suddenly as he looked at her.

"I'm sorry!" she whispered.

He flushed, as well. "No, no, I'm sorry. I don't usually sleep so deeply."

He rose then, and she followed him. He walked out to the beach and looked out to the sea; the ship still awaited them.

Tremblay was up; he was staring out at the ship with a spyglass.

"Time to get moving, eh?" Tremblay asked Finn. "We've gotten the enemy off the ship, so I've been told?"

"So we believe, but this morning we'll again take care," Finn said.

"Aye, as you say. So, I shall have you move out with the same men who have now learned the most. We'll get pulleys and levers going to reload, and our ship's carpenter instructing us all as to repairing the broken mast. It's time, indeed, that we head out!"

"Apparently, sir, you are feeling chipper this morning?" Finn asked.

Tremblay smiled. "Thanks to you all," he said. He looked at Tara with the affection a man would show a daughter. "Thanks to *you,* so Dr. MacKay tells me. Child, you've saved my life. I am in your debt."

Tara dropped a little curtsy to him. "Captain, it was my pleasure."

"And you have suffered no ill effects?" he asked her.

"None whatsoever, sir. Despite our situation last night, I slept deeply."

"Well, good, then," Tremblay said. "I must say, it's like magic! I feel far more hale and hearty than I have in years. So, onward to the day's work. We'll fix our meal, and get moving. That mast will take most of the day, and I'm grateful most of my men are like monkeys.

We'll head north, Agent Dunne, and get you where you need to be."

Finn hesitated. "We can't head north, not directly," he said. "A few of these men must return to Fort Zachary Taylor. Someone must be there to warn the people of Key West, and to see that they're armed against those inflicted with the disease. I believe we've got the majority of the poor souls, but we don't know how the infection came about."

"Ah, that's a grave situation, Agent Dunne," Tremblay said. "The men at the fort will not take kindly to the citizens with their Southern sympathies being heavily armed."

"If you describe the situation—you and Lafferty, Captain—the people will believe you," Finn said.

Tara spoke up. "The people on the island are not going to rise up and kill the soldiers. Perhaps once..." she said, her voice trailing away. "Sir, you can't let this infection get to Key West."

Tremblay rubbed his cheek and looked at Finn. "Aye, it will but cost us another day."

"A meal—and on to the ship," Finn said.

He took Tara's arm, leading her over to the fire. There was oatmeal; she was touched to see that the men had prepared hers with care, dexterously making sure no bugs had come to rest in the portion being offered her. She drank coffee, talking with Billy. The captain had announced to the men that they had to go back to

Key West and Billy was relieved. "I've so many friends there. They are completely unprepared."

Tara thought about Seminole Pete. "Seminole Pete will know if there's a strange shift in the wind—the arrival of something that isn't quite human."

"How will he know—until after half the island is consumed?" Billy asked.

Tara shook her head. "He just knows things. There is no explanation."

She saw that Finn was beckoning to her. "I believe I'm with the crew to head back to the ship first," she told Billy.

"You should not be," he muttered, looking at Finn.

"Don't worry, Billy," she told him. "I grew up with Seminole Pete, remember? Some of his instincts rubbed off on me!"

She left the young sailor looking after her, and hurried to catch up with Finn, Richard, Lafferty, Grissom and London. They headed to the ship, where it was much easier to board, as they had left the ladder down last night. They repeated the efforts they had gone through the morning before, and after a thorough search of the ship, they found no bodies—alive, dead or in between.

From the deck, Finn shot off a flare, letting the others know that they could begin the laborious duty of returning their goods to the ship and breaking down the camp. The remaining longboats began their journey out beyond the reefs to the ship at anchor, and pulleys and

winches were set and the boarding began. Billy seemed
pleased as he came aboard, having collected a large
supply of coconuts. He grinned and told her, "Since I
came to Florida, I discovered the sweet meat of the coconut. Delicious. And add some of the milk with lime
to your portion of rum, and it's quite a treat."

Lafferty, hauling the coconuts up, laughed. "Ah, well,
our pretty girlie drink for our young lady, Billy Seabold.
A man takes his rum as he takes his rum," he said.

"Well, the lime does a lot to stop the scurvy," Dr.
MacKay said. "It's just a seaman's rum punch with a
bit of greater sweetness. I'll be happy to try one, Billy."

As the day went on, Tara discovered that she could
be the greatest help by shimmying up the mast with
London, who was the ship's carpenter. London was
adept with wood and nails, and she was quite comfortable with heights. In a matter of hours, he'd repaired the
masts enough to set sail if the steam failed them, though
London had also repaired the steam engine before they'd
even begun their work on the sails and masts.

The work went on throughout the day. And finally,
just as the sun lowered in the sky, the crew let out a
cry of pleasure and triumph; they were ready to weigh
anchor. The night had picked up a steady breeze, and
Tremblay decided to combine his sail and his steam
power; it would take them a night to return to Key West.
There, they would likely be assigned another ship, as
this one needed yet greater repairs.

As they left the island behind, Tara stood at the bow,

watching. She felt Finn's presence as he came up to stand beside her. For several long moments, they stood in silence.

"I never thought that everything I felt and knew about my own life could change in a matter of days on an island," she said at last.

He was quiet.

She turned to look at him. "And despite the fact that I've basically been slaying real dragons with you, Agent Dunne, you're going to take me back to Washington. I'm still under arrest, and I'll go to trial. Richard, as well."

He didn't answer right away. She was surprised when he did. "How do we even really know what's in the heart or mind of someone else? There are many out there who believe that killing Abraham Lincoln would make them a hero. There are Northern widows, fatherless children and others who despise him. He has political opponents who believe we should have let the South go. But," he said, turning to stare at her, "I must say that over the past few days I've come to believe that neither you nor Richard would kill a man in cold blood. But the point is, somewhere in your mind, you must know something, Richard must know something. You're both Southern patriots—haven't you heard anything?"

"I don't know anything about this Gator," she said.

"We have a man who was arrested at the capital. He was lurking around the White House, and when a soldier called to him, he ran. Once captured, he was found to have a correspondence from Gator, who meant to get arms to the north of the state of Florida, and then travel on to the North to gain access to weapons. *Sic simper tyrannis*—'thus always to tyrants.' The threat to the president is clear, and since the one man was captured essentially watching the president for his schedule and habits, it's taken as a very real threat." He hesitated. "Blockade runners don't often run with arms— Richard's ship was armed."

There was no argument for that. "Richard is not an assassin," she said. "And I am not, either. And most of the blockade runners out of our area have been captured—and many have been killed. I honestly don't know who this person might be."

"They were definitely coming out of Key West," he said.

Tara leaned over the hull and felt the wind blowing through her hair. She turned and looked at him. "Have you ever considered the possibility that it's not a Rebel or a Confederate sympathizer that wants to kill Lincoln? We were on that island together—I know that even given a certain amount of freedom, you were watching Richard and me all the while. Whatever happened on that island was perpetuated by someone else."

"We both know that the island was attacked by a vampire, yes," he said.

"And maybe your Gator is a vampire. You had no trouble suspecting *me*. And, as you said, we both know what I am."

He was quiet. He turned away, leaning against the

rail. "It might have been the old monster, the one who nearly killed you. Yes, I gave that some thought."

"Then, in your heart, you know that we're not guilty."

"I still have to take you to D.C.," he said quietly.

She let out a breath of frustration, and she was surprised when he caught her by the shoulders, turning her to face him. "Don't you see? Blockaders caught ultimately go to a prisoner-of-war camp. Usually, they are not dealt with harshly, Tara."

"What do you know about the prisoner-of-war camps?" she asked him.

"They're better in the North than in the South. When a government can't feed its troops, it can't feed its prisoners, and the North still has a solid supply mechanism in place. But here's what you don't understand—Richard fired on us. He brought down a federal ship. The punishment could be…well, much worse. He's not a soldier, is he?"

"No," she said.

He was still holding her, staring down into her eyes with a dark gaze that caused her to tremble. He wasn't flush against her body, but he might as well have been. She could feel the tension and pulse within him so strongly that she simply longed to fall against him, and take whatever time they had. Of course, he would push her away, and so she made no move.

"When we reach the fort, they'll want to charge Richard—he fired on and sank a Union ship. The men on this ship will fight for him, I have no doubt. On land, he was armed and fought a mutual enemy, and didn't try to escape. I'm sure he'd never attempt an escape when you were still with us, but that's something we don't need to say. You will be held at the fort, however, until we set sail again."

She nodded. "Richard does not deserve harsh punishment!"

"A prisoner-of-war camp is where every blockade runner goes when captured. First he'll be questioned, so that will take some time. And by then, God help us, the war may be over."

"Ahem!"

They both turned, unaware that they had been watched for the past several minutes. A number of the crew members were there, including Captain Tremblay, Richard, Billy, Lafferty and London.

"Miss Fox! We've your cabin ready for you!" Captain Tremblay said.

"My cabin?"

"Come along, my dear," the captain said. He stepped forward and took her by the arm. Finn shrugged, grinning, as curious as she.

She was surprised when she was escorted to the captain's quarters on the main deck. The men had cleaned it, found fresh linens and set it up with fresh water at the washstand, a number of books on the side table and a vase of flowers.

She looked at Captain Tremblay and then around at the others. "This is lovely, so lovely, and I'm so appreciative, but I can't take this from you, Captain Tremblay."

"I insist," he told her. "I wouldn't be alive if it weren't for you, my dear. This is where I'd like you to be. Please, grant an old man a simple request and accept this hospitality."

Finn stood back, behind the others, a subtle smile still curling his lips.

"Well, then, I…I thank you!" she said.

Captain Tremblay's smile faltered. "We will fight for you—and Mr. Anderson—when we reach the fort. But I cannot promise you will have such acceptable accommodations there."

She lowered her head, nodding.

She wasn't worried for herself; she was worried for Richard.

Even if they hanged her, she would survive. Richard wouldn't.

"I accept this hospitality, sir, with my greatest thanks." She went to each of the men, kissing them on the cheeks and thanking them.

And then, one by one, they left, Richard and Finn hovering at the end.

"Some comfort for a night," Richard said, giving her a hug. She looked past him to Finn, who was still silent, and then looked at Richard.

"Where will you be?" she asked him huskily.

"When not on guard tonight? I will sleep like a lamb

in one of the bunk cots below. Good night, my dear sister," he told her.

He started to leave; she drew him back.

"Richard—"

"I'm not afraid of tomorrow, Tara," he said. "I have known the risks throughout the war. I am not guilty of any conspiracy, and I am certain that will be proven. My dear, General Mosby was incarcerated at Old Capitol, where we will no doubt wind up. If men such as Mosby were held there, it is an apt place for me to be."

Tara was startled when Richard walked toward Finn. And to her amazement, the two men embraced briefly, as friends.

Richard turned and grinned at her, and continued out.

"You didn't know about this?" she asked Finn.

"No. The men did it all on their own," he said.

"It's all quite lovely. But where will Captain Tremblay sleep?"

"He'll take one of the officer's quarters below."

She turned and looked around at the handsomely appointed cabin. There was no sign that a man had been killed here recently.

"I'm still not sure I will rest so well," she said softly.

"There's more to come," he told her.

"What do you mean?"

"You explained it yourself. There is still someone out there. We won a battle on the island, then we came to the ship and removed the...dead. But there's still no explanation for how this all came about. You'll need to rest now. I have a feeling that this cloud will be following us."

"We killed so many," she murmured.

"Ah, yes. But in my experience, such commanders send in their minions to be exterminated while they watch and wait for the optimal moment to carry out the true mission. What frightens me most is the possibility that the monster is among us. Someone so old and experienced that he wears a coat of humanity with incredible ease. One would never think of you as a half-breed, except that I learned what you could do. So far, this person is acting the role of humanity so well that not even I can recognize him."

"Or," she suggested, "someone has been following us."

"Yes, or someone has been following us."

They stood an arm's length from one another. Tara again felt the almost overwhelming desire to walk to him, to touch him at last, explore the contours of his face and feel the vitality of his body next to hers.

She stood still, instead.

"For tonight," he told her, "rest."

She nodded, but before Finn could leave, there was a tap at the door. Billy Seabold was there. "Come along! Come along. We've fashioned something of a sumptuous meal. Lafferty is on the harmonica and we're celebrating!"

"What are we celebrating?" Tara asked him.

"Why, life—and a return to civilization!" Billy said. "Miss Fox, if I may?"

Tara accepted his arm. On deck, she found that Lafferty was indeed on his mouthbox, and Billy had created his concoction of rum and coconut and lime. Even those who had mocked his feminine drink were imbibing it. London and Grissom were dancing together, London wearing a mop top and pretending to be Grissom's lady.

"Perhaps a real lady will dance with me?" Billy suggested.

"My pleasure!" Tara assured him.

And so she started out with Billy. As she accepted his hand, Tara noted that there were two men up in the crow's nest, keeping watch. The crew might be celebrating, but they were not fools. Captain Tremblay stood at the bow, watching over the water and the night.

Tara danced, accepted one of Billy's drinks and the fish and beans they had prepared for dinner. She danced again with Richard, and then, at the end, with Finn. As she moved in his arms, she felt the way that his eyes touched her, and she wondered how she had ever thought him austere and hard, but then, she knew that was what he must be for his position.

They didn't talk. They looked at each other, and she felt his hands, and she longed for more.

But eventually, the celebration came to an end, the mess cleaned up and guard duty doled out.

Finn escorted her back to the captain's quarters.

"Sleep," he told her.

She grinned, looking away. "You know that I really rest best by day."

"Of course. I'm equally aware that you've learned to adjust to those around you, and take rest where you can."

"What about you?"

"I'm on guard duty first. I will sleep later."

He hesitated. His head was close to hers. She thought that his lips would touch her mouth.

He lingered there for just a moment.

And then he stepped back. "Good night, Miss Fox."

CHAPTER NINE

THE DREAM OF THE VISION came again, soon after she lay her head on the pillow.

She wasn't with Lincoln in the White House. She rode in his carriage with him as they traveled through the mall.

"One day," he said, "there will be many buildings here. The American people will create museums to rival those around the world. We're young, a fledgling nation. But united again, we will grow strong, and on our principles, we will stand against the world."

"You believe that, sir. That the nation will heal the great rift."

He was silent for a minute. "There will always be those who seek revenge. There will always be those men who see themselves above others. But this great nation has been forged on the backs of pioneers and great thinkers. Oh, I'm not a blind man. I have seen the way that I am lampooned in the papers. But I think holding fast does not so much influence today as it does tomorrow. Look at the world around us, Tara. War is as old as man. But we are the new world—we are an ocean away from the old world. We must cling to one another to be a bastion against the old world."

"You believe the war is coming to an end."

He smiled. She had so seldom seen him smile. "Yes, I believe this."

His smiled faded.

"What is it?" she asked him.

"I have had a dream," he told her.

"What is the dream?"

"I awake. I hear tears. I am in the White House. I come along the corridors, and there are so many tears. I see no one, but I can hear the soft sound of crying. And at last I come to the East Room, and when I'm there, I see a catafalque. And I ask someone, 'Who has died to cause this sorrow?' They tell me, 'The president is dead.'"

Tara was silent. Then she said, "That is only a dream, sir. I have come to tell you so many times that as much as you feel you must be a man of the people, you must take great care, as well. I believe, as you do, sir, in the goodness of humanity. But as you have said, there are always those who will seek revenge."

"Don't fear for me. I am surrounded by friends, and those who guard me."

"But you must let them be with you at all times, sir."

"The war is drawing to an end."

"*Especially* because the war is drawing to an end. There will still be great and horrible battles, sir. And mostly, those who blame you, North and South, for the deaths of their loved ones."

"Look at the mall, Tara. One day, there will be a great museum here—"

"No, no, you can't think about the museum right now, sir! You must worry about your safety. Don't you see? You are having the dream because you are in danger!"

She tried to reach the president; she couldn't. Suddenly, someone was holding her back. She began to struggle and kick, and then her eyes flew open. "No, no, let me go! Don't you understand? I have to reach him! I—"

"Tara! It's a nightmare!"

The room was lit by only the pale glow of a lamp. The candle within it had almost burned to the end. But in that soft illumination, she saw Finn's face before her. She saw the curious red glint in his dark eyes, and the dark concern that knotted his features. She was cold where he did not touch her. She was afraid. Afraid enough to forget all logic.

She threw her arms around him, trembling as he held her.

He didn't push her away; his arms encircled her. His fingers stroked soothingly over her hair and down her back.

"It was a nightmare," he told her.

"It's not a nightmare," she told him. "It's… I'm with him. Somehow, I'm actually with him."

"Him?"

"Lincoln. President Lincoln. I was with him in his carriage, and he was telling me about a dream…he had a dream about his own death. He saw himself in the White House, people were crying, and when he asked about the commotion, he was told that the president was dead."

Finn eased himself back from her. "No," he said, and the sound of his voice was harsh.

"I have to reach him!" she whispered.

He was silent, and then pulled her against him again. "All of us fear for him, Tara. All of us who admire and love him. But you're having a dream, and nothing more."

"I wish I believed that," she said.

He pulled away to look into her eyes. "It's a dream. You know, by the very fact that I am here, that we take every threat very seriously, and will stop at nothing to see that he is safe. Tara, I will find Gator. No matter what it takes, I'll find Gator."

"You'll find Gator," she whispered. "You'll find others. You'll stop the people in the crowd when he is speaking, and you'll find those who offer the kind of threat that *you* see. But this has been a long and bitter war, and some people don't see. They don't believe that evil—with supernatural power—is out there."

His fingers ran down the length of her hair again and was silent for some time. "I'll see that you're able to meet him," he told her at last. "And you'll know that you've been dreaming."

She lowered her head. "Really? You believe me?"

"Yes, Tara, I believe in you. Now—"

He started to pull away. "Don't leave me," she said.

"Tara, I can't stay like this…with you," he told her.

She was silent for a moment, looking at him.

"But what if I don't want you to go?" she asked softly.

"Tara…"

She slipped her arms around his neck, meeting his eyes. "I don't mind being compromised. And I know that I'm your prisoner, and that you risk compromising yourself. I will not try to escape you. I don't wish to escape you. I am innocent—as is Richard—of any attempt to enjoin in a conspiracy."

He groaned softly. "But I must still take you to Washington."

"Indeed, you must." She smiled. "You've promised me that I will meet the president, after all."

She touched his face, something she felt she had longed to do forever. Her fingers stroked his cheek. He caught her hand. "Tara, I don't take advantage of—"

"Ah, but Agent Dunne, I believe I am the one taking advantage of you."

He caught her hand, met her eyes and eased them both back upon the captain's bunk. For a moment, he stared into her eyes.

And then he kissed her.

His mouth was gentle, and then firm. His lips teased upon hers, and then formed hard upon them. When his tongue slipped into her mouth, she felt as if an exquisite heat burst forth within her. He played there long with his lips and tongue, kissing her in a way that ignited longing in her limbs—indeed, in every fiber of her existence. She returned the kiss, eager to learn, and more eager to satisfy. His mouth broke from hers at last; they were both breathless as they stared at each other. He nearly ripped his jacket and shirt from his body, and she remembered when she had first seen and admired his naked chest, when they had been diving, and the sun had glittered down upon him.

She pressed her lips to his throat, and his chest, and she felt the shuddering within the man. His finger fell upon the buttons of her dress, and she relished the touch of his hand against her naked flesh. Even as they disrobed in a tangle of clothing, she felt his kiss, and his hands. And when they lay naked and panting together, she was aware of the corded strength in his limbs and torso, and the fire that just being so close together seemed to burn within her. Again, he kissed her, and then she felt his lips as they began to ease down the length of her body. His touch, gentle and like a feather brush against her throat, the lightest graze of his teeth against her, the caress of his mouth on her breasts. And then her abdomen, her kneecaps, her thighs. She lay stunned and still at the sensations that arose within her, and then she swallowed down a cry as his hands gripped her hips and his kisses roamed even more intimately and she felt something like an explosion. She gasped, catching his shoulders, rising against him, drawing him back to her while she trembled as she found his mouth again, and feverishly rode her kisses over his shoulders and chest.

He pressed her back to the bunk again, his eyes on hers as he moved himself easily between her thighs, and came into her with a slow, sure thrust that took the greatest care. And then, when she felt the force of him, he began to move, so easily at first, his eyes never leaving hers. She stared back at him, entranced, and then she felt the growing wonder once again, and instinct took over and she began to move, too. She gasped, and eased her mouth to his chest again, and felt the hunger begin anew, something that made her body react in a way as old as time. She arched and clung to him, finding a rhythm that brought her gliding with him as gracefully as the dance, and as haphazardly as the roll of the ship upon the waves. Shimmering ecstasy spun and swirled before her. Even as they melded together, she seemed to forget everything in life except for the need, and the man entangled with her. Then there was an explosion within her, and she felt as if the world had rippled with fireworks, and there could be nothing wrong in heaven, or even in hell if she was there with him. She felt his extreme tension, something so taut it seemed like molten fire, and then he eased himself against her, drawing her to him.

They lay in silence for long moments, and she relished the way that he held her. Tara caught her breath, and felt the cool night air wash over her, easing the burn in her body. She wondered if she was mad, or if she had simply given in to something she had craved so much, and told herself that the consequences, whatever they might be, had been worth something so desired. She wondered at his thoughts as she lay against him, and so she turned to him then, seeking out his eyes.

"I meant what I said—I would not compromise you in any way," she said softly. "I will remain your prisoner, and I will answer to any court. I will make no attempts to escape you."

"I know," he said quietly.

He rolled over on an elbow, looking down at her. He touched her face and said, "You have been on my mind since that day at Gettysburg. I couldn't bear, for one, that you had escaped me. Pride, you see. But beyond that, something about you haunted me. And when I caught you on the island, I knew, of course, *what* you were, and I was stunned that I had you back in my life, no matter the circumstances. And though I fought it in my own mind, I was jealous of Richard, thinking that you loved him."

"I do love him."

"It was hard for me to imagine such a brother," he said softly.

"But he is my brother, really," she said, smiling.

"I know that now. And I know, as well, that you are like me, that you are like your family. And I have seen how you dream of Lincoln and fear for him. I believe in you. And still, the die is cast."

She reached up and touched his hair. She knew that his loyalty and his commitment to his work was part of what drew her to him. What made her admire him, and want him so very much. "I wouldn't have it any other way. I will face any charges. I would stop Gator myself, in any way that I could."

"I see rough times ahead," he said.

"Whatever they are, I will not regret...*you*," she told him.

He pulled her into his arms again. They held fast, close for a moment, and then she felt again the incredible sensation of his sleek nudity, and the moment of comfort became something else again, quickly. She was strong, and she rolled atop him, caught his hands, leaned down and kissed him, and the kiss deepened. Then, again, in the night, as the ship sailed ever closer to the Union garrison, she forgot the future. She began fluttering her kisses against him; she teased, and he allowed her to do so until he took control, pulling her strongly against him. She was one with him again, and the world seemed to escalate all around her. She was heedless of it all, wanting only him.

CAPTAIN CALLOWAY SAT behind his desk in his command office at Fort Zachary Taylor, staring at the men before him with incredulity plastered upon his worn face.

"Let me see if I have this straight, gentlemen," he said. "You went after a blockade runner, lost a ship, but then caught the blockade runner, and found another Union ship with monsters aboard? I believe that you both might be in serious need of long leaves!" He stood at the last, staring at them.

"Captain Calloway!" Finn said. "I assure that we are of sound mind. This is something I know about because the capital was recently made aware of the disease that claims and kills men—but makes each victim a machine of death in himself. Harpers Ferry was just so plagued in the midst of war. It is a very real threat."

"We returned here to warn you of this threat," Tremblay said. "We might have continued on, sir, but we feared for the men at the fort, and for the citizens of the island."

"The Rebel-loving horde!" Calloway said, sniffing his dismissal of the danger. "We have had the organization of troop movement to the north from here in the days that you have been gone. General Newton received information that the Confederate, General Milton—son of the state's governor—was reinforcing troops to the west of the state. We are down in numbers here, and I cannot be worried about the fates of men and women who would *spit* on my men if given the chance. Especially for some such ridiculous report about *diseased men* attacking."

Tremblay walked forward and slammed a fist on Calloway's desk. "I have long served the Union with my passion and my life. And you will listen to me *now, sir!* I saw these beings in action. They set upon my men with the fury. We found all aboard the Union ship I then commanded *dead*. Or in the final throes of dying of the disease. You must understand this. The danger could be coming here."

"We are a sound fort. We can withstand the rabble on the island, and we can withstand any assault by sea," Calloway said.

Finn hesitated. "No, you won't be able to withstand it, sir, because you won't know when it's coming, and you may not know when it's here. It's like a disease, sir. One man gets it, and then others are inflicted. And it could happen within the walls of the fort without your ever realizing it's begun."

"This is insanity!" Calloway said.

"I swear to you that it is not. Ask any man who was with us on our ill-fated voyage," Tremblay said.

Calloway sat again, staring at them. "I admit to being stunned, gentlemen. What would you have me do? You caught a blockade runner—one who fired at you and sank a Union vessel! The captain of that runner must face trial—since he made war on us, he should be hanged!"

"No, sir. He should not," Tremblay said stoutly. "When we were besieged, he fought with us. And he saved many of my men, no doubt."

"And he is still *my* prisoner, under special authority of the Pinkerton Agency," Finn said, staring at the captain.

Calloway tried to return the stare; he looked away.

"So, Agent Dunne, you still intend to take these prisoners to Washington. You believe one of them to be your Gator? Perhaps we could solve your dilemma now with a hanging."

"No. Captain, I'm not in the business of killing men. My goal is information, to lead me to those who aren't just at war, but those who believe that murder might well be a sanctioned part of war. That's not what the president wants. Lincoln is now planning for the day when we are one people again. When the North does win the war—which is inevitable—he wants to heal the land. The point of peace is that men will stop killing other men. I have to ferret out the truth regarding Gator. I don't believe that Richard Anderson is Gator, nor do I believe that the young woman, Tara Fox, is involved in any kind of espionage. I do believe that, perhaps, somewhere in their minds, they may have information that will help me to ferret out Gator. They may not even realize that they heard something somewhere, and it may come to them at some point."

Calloway threw up his hands. "So, Tremblay, what do you say? What would you have me do now?"

"Give me another ship," Tremblay told him.

"And warn the men. I need to speak with the civilian authorities on the island, as well—warn them about what may happen," Finn said.

"Captain Calloway, my good man!" Tremblay said, indignant. "The mission could have been completed. We had an injured ship on hand, but—"

"There should be an inquiry into this!" Calloway bellowed, looking from Finn to Tremblay.

Finn looked at Tremblay and they both shrugged. "Indeed, there should be an inquiry. Call the men in here, sir. Call every last man."

Calloway stared at him. "You may be a Pinkerton, sir, and you may be chosen by the president himself, but you're talking like a madman. I will bring them all in!"

"Please do so," Finn said.

"Gentlemen, if you will get out of my office?"

Finn and Tremblay looked at each other again, and exited as instructed. They walked out to the sally port and stood there waiting. A young officer passed them by, obviously headed off to summon the others who had been on the ship.

"No one believes," Captain Tremblay said.

"Until they are faced with the truth. And, of course, survive it," Finn said.

"And yet, you've known," Tremblay said, watching him.

"I told you, there have been other outbreaks," Finn said.

"But there's something special about you, Agent Dunne, isn't there? And something special about that young woman who saved my life, also."

Finn shrugged, looking away. "We know what can happen, that's all. Tara heard the tales when she was young."

He started; there was a hue and cry near them. He saw that someone had come across the walkway, and was seeking entry.

Walking to the gate, he saw a tall Indian man in a calico shirt and blue denim breeches talking to the guard.

He strained to hear what was being said.

"I have come for Tara Fox!" the large man said loudly. "You are holding a civilian, and you have no right to do so. I will take the girl home, and see that she is safe! And there is more, if you will be men and not military men, not Northern or Southern. There is a danger that awaits, and I can help prepare you for it!"

"Seminole Pete," one of the men on guard murmured.

"Let him in! Let him see the commander!" another said. "It's Pete. He'll stand there until he's heard, and before you know it, we'll have a whole contingent of Key West citizens disrupting all in the barracks!"

The gears began to grind; the gate was opening.

Finn sensed someone behind him; it was Richard. He knew that before he turned around; he had become attuned to the man.

But Richard wasn't looking at him; he stared at the tall, stoic Indian who had come.

"Pete!" Richard cried, stepping forward to embrace the man.

"Richard." Seminole Pete greeted him in return. "Tara—where is Tara? I heard that you two were here, confined, but I see you—"

"We are prisoners, Pete, but I was just summoned before the fort's commander to give credence to the story that we returned to tell. Tara is fine. And—"

Richard had seen Finn standing there, and was about to introduce Finn and Tremblay to Seminole Pete, Finn thought, but a young officer interrupted Richard. "Sir! I am to return you to your cell!"

Pete had a grip on Richard's arm, and was about to challenge the officers. Finn stepped in quickly. "There is no harm being done your friends, Pete."

"This is Finn Dunne, Pete," Richard said. "He will tell you what happened. You need to see the commander here when they bring you in. Let him know that the people must be warned, and that the fort shouldn't be alarmed if they arm themselves in their homes, that their target isn't the fort or the Union."

Richard looked at Finn, and he knew he was being implored to see that no harm came to Seminole Pete.

"Pete, if you'll spend a few moments with Captain Tremblay and me while you wait?" Finn asked.

Pete nodded; his face gave away no emotion. His tall, stalwart body remained stiff. His posture was that of a ramrod.

Finn gave Pete a hasty summary of events, starting from the sea battle until their return to the fort. Pete listened; he winced when he heard that Richard's ship had exploded, and that the crew had gone down, and his jaw tightened when Finn described the attack on the island.

"You think it will come here?" Pete asked him. "I had only heard rumor this morning. People were talking about the return, and about an attack on the island that was not Seminole, not white. Not human."

"We don't know," Tremblay said. He sounded indignant as he added, "However, we returned here to bring warning of the menace, to tell people how the enemy must be killed to—to stay dead. And that fool does not want to listen to me." He hesitated, looking at Pete. "You believe what we are saying?"

"My people have been aware forever that there are many enemies a man may find on earth—some are flesh and blood, some are in the mind and some are true monsters," Pete said. "I believe your story. I will tell the commander that I have heard of such attacks before, and that he must listen or he will have the people on the island in revolt. And that if the disease becomes an epidemic, no fortress walls can protect him."

Charles Lafferty exited the commander's office, and came toward them. "He's asked to see the Seminole." He nodded toward Pete. "We've all told him what happened. He seems to think that we're victims of some form of malady—a hallucinogen in the island's fruit!"

"Agent Dunne, don't you have the authority to demand that he pay heed?" Captain Tremblay asked.

"I am not military, Captain," Finn said. "He has no power over me, and I can demand my prisoners, but I can't command the man to believe what he won't."

"I will speak," Pete said. He lowered his head to them, and then turned and headed for the commander's office. He stood well above most men, and his long, straight black hair only amplified his height and his size.

"Pray God, he can make Calloway have some sense!" Tremblay said.

The tension in the little group waiting seemed to grow. It was hard to imagine, of course, that the fort could be taken by any small group of men—or even monsters. The thick walls rose for three stories. It was cut off from the mainland, save for the walkway. The fort was exceptionally advantageous, surrounded by water on three sides, and its strength had been fortified by the building of the east and west martello towers on the mainland. The fort was well supplied with cannons; the Rodman and Columbiad cannons had a range of three miles.

Seminole Pete was in with Captain Calloway for what seemed like a long time.

And then the two men emerged.

"Agent Dunne, I will summon all I can to the inner grounds so you may give them a presentation on what to watch for and how to combat this enemy—should it arrive among us. We will be prepared. It's better to prepare for the preposterous, as I have been led to believe, than fall prey to it. Tremblay, if you will summon your seamen, sir, I will see to those on duty here at the fort!"

It seemed odd, standing beneath the bright Florida sun on a day when the winter's chill seemed to break, when it was almost hot standing beneath the brilliant blue sky, trying to explain what might occur, what men should watch out for—and how they must be on guard for danger from outside the fort—and from within. He was sure that most of the men watched him with the same disbelief as Captain Calloway had done, but others listened to him with grave attention.

Hopefully, in the end, enough listened. They might not believe, but if enough listened, they might have a fighting chance.

When the men were dismissed, Captain Tremblay came to him. "So, sir, I have been given leave to take another ship. Do we stay, and hope to help if action occurs? Or do we set sail as quickly as possible? Apparently, though Calloway longed to dismiss our tale, his orders regarding you were stanch—you were to have all assistance, a decree that apparently came to him straight from the secretary of war, Mr. Stanton."

Finn smiled. Thank God that Stanton, among others, believed heartily in the manifold dangers to the president.

"We'll bide two nights, and take our leave," Finn told him. "I don't know whether the danger will come here—or if it will follow us. One way or the other, we will stay and watch tonight, and tomorrow night, and then we will once again sail northward."

TARA KNEW THAT RICHARD was in a rough prison cell with other men who had been taken for various reasons. Some were blockade runners as well, and a few were dissidents from the island. A few were drunkards who liked to talk too freely, and torment the Union soldiers when they were on duty in the town.

Her own "prison" was not so rugged; she had been

locked in a room just steps up from the yard. She was kept above barracks due to the men of the fort, and she had heard their speculation and whispers the night before. Some of them longed to climb the steps, just to be near her. Some of them laughed crudely and spoke about being closer. For the most part, though, they were young men far from home, and longing just for gentle companionship.

She had been offered no hardship; indeed, she'd been brought a real bath, with hot water. The young aide who had been in charge of her incarceration had been pleased to tell her that they managed to make the "facilities" work with the outgoing tide. She had a comfortable bed, and pillows, and her bag had been searched but then brought to her. There were a few books on a dressing table, and she was supplied generously with fresh water and plenty to eat.

But it was frightening to be kept away from the others. Try as she might, she heard nothing but what the men said in the chambers below her, and they usually spoke as boys. She couldn't hear anything regarding Richard, nor her own status.

Finally, she heard a commotion when the men hurried out to the yard, and she could hear Finn's voice, though she couldn't follow all his words. When he finished speaking, the sun began to set, and she found herself waiting, and then pacing, and then again trying to listen to the men beneath her as they spoke in their quarters.

Some laughed.

Monsters, indeed!

Well, bring them on.

Others seemed to be urging at least some caution regarding the threat.

An officer entered to quiet the men, and call some of them to the walls for guard duty; soon after, it seemed that the rest below her fell silent, either keeping their thoughts to themselves, or weary from the day's work.

At length, she heard the chain rattle outside her room. She walked quickly toward the door, and then hesitated, something inside her warning her to take care.

As the door opened, she saw it was only one of the enlisted men, standing there with a food tray. "Evening, miss," he said. But he looked over his shoulder, as if afraid.

Instinctively, Tara drew him into the room and thrust him behind her. The panic that touched his face made her bring a finger to her lips, shushing him.

She waited, and thought that she had been wrong, that she had misread the soldier's expression.

And then another man stepped into the doorway.

The stranger was in uniform. Union naval uniform. But there was something about him that wasn't quite right. It was the way he moved, perhaps, or the strange angle of his head.

She had never seen him before.

Another moment revealed a still-healing scar on his throat. At one time this man had been dead.

She had no weapons; there was nothing to grab.

But the man didn't expect trouble. She didn't know him, and he didn't know *her*.

"Ah, lassie, it's time for you to come out now. The commander has asked to see you, yes, that he has! Come to me, girl. I won't be hurting you!" He started to laugh, and she saw the saliva glistening on his teeth, which were becoming fangs.

She thrust the poor seaman forced to do the monster's bidding far behind her, and set a hand on the bedpost. The seaman would see her, of course, but she had no choice. When the monster took a step toward her, she tightened her grip on the bedpost.

The changed *thing* stared at her.

"I'll enjoy every minute of this, the lead up to the taste of your sweet fragrant flesh...."

CHAPTER TEN

PETE STOOD WITH FINN high upon the wall. From that vantage point, they could see below to the yard, onward to the town and south to the sea.

Finn pointed to the inner yard, and the level of rooms up a short flight of steps. "You must rest assured that Tara is well. They are offering her no discomfort. Calloway is not a bad man. Most men cannot be convinced that such an unearthly danger exists, especially men who have fought the years he has. So many of the captains and commanders are old warhorses from the Mexican War, and the enemies they know are guns or cannons, or they've seen men die of yellow fever and dysentery and other horrible diseases. Death is all too final for them. They can't imagine a disease that causes the once-dead to ravage and murder with heedless delight."

"Except for Tremblay," Pete said, looking at him.

Finn nodded.

"Tara saved his life."

"Yes."

"You let her."

Finn nodded. "Tara is still…learning. It was her choice, Pete."

"She is like my child."

"I know."

Finn was surprised to realize that he was feeling like an errant suitor; he didn't have to explain himself. And yet, he felt that he should. "There was not really a choice, but what there was, Tara made it." He inhaled. "I would do whatever it took to save her, Pete."

The Indian turned away. He was a strong man; in the dim lights from the fort and the sky, his face seemed etched in character. Finn found himself touched by emotions he hadn't felt in years. He wondered what Tara's young life had been like, and he was glad that she'd had such a man to watch over her—even if her own strength far excelled his by the very nature of the being he tried so hard to protect.

"I swear, I would never harm her," he added, and he heard the tremor and the passion in his own voice.

One night…

Just one night. And it was changing him. He had to take care, because he needed the single-mindedness he had maintained throughout the war, and he needed to remember that his quest was greater than either of them.

But even as he looked at Pete, he felt an odd shift in the air.

Pete, somehow attuned to things that other men refused to see, looked at Finn. "There's a change in the wind," he said.

Tara.

TARA HAD GONE THROUGH her life knowing what she was. She knew human ways more than anything, however. She had not imagined the truth of what she might have been, or what her father might have been.

This man—newly turned, she thought—had a ravenous, crazed hunger in his eyes. He spoke, he moved, but he was…off. Finn said that some survived and learned to be crafty, to take care and live and move in the world. But not this one. Someone was behind everything that was happening here, someone so adept at what he had become that he didn't look anything like one, with fangs visible, saliva dripping, eyes burning with insanity.

"Let's play, pretty girl. Let's play!" he said.

Behind her, the seaman who had brought her supper tray was sniveling in terror.

She tightened her grip on the bedpost, hoping that her strength would not fail her at this moment.

The man watched her, and took a step closer.

She grasped the bedpost and jerked at it, using all her strength. The wood came clear, a nail protruding off the knobbed side of the post.

The undead man gave pause.

She didn't.

She swung the bedpost, knocking it against his head with all her might. He stumbled back, and she stepped forward and thrust her makeshift weapon into his chest.

She set her weight against it, and impaled him, creating a massive hole in his torso.

"Holy Mary, mother of God!" the terrified man behind her yelped.

Again, Tara slammed the post harder into the creature now flailing on the floor. He went still, eyes open, but the gleaming flame dissipated. He was truly dead at last, at peace, she could only hope.

She turned to the seaman. "Get up. Sound the alarm. The fort is under attack!"

He didn't move.

"Seaman! *Get up.* Our lives remain in the balance!"

He still stared at the dead man, shaking and stunned. Tara reached out a hand to him, and he looked at her with uncertainty.

"Please, man! The battle we're about to engage in may be far more horrendous than any you have seen at war."

He looked into her eyes, nodded, grasped her hand, and rose.

FINN WAS ON THE WALL when he heard the cry to arms.

He realized that he was heedless of who might be watching as he tore across the grounds and up the steps to the rows of rooms and barracks there. Pete ran behind him, though he could not keep up.

Finn paused when he reached the landing. Men were running in from all directions. They were armed with their swords, as instructed, but they surrounded *Tara.*

"She's killed one o' us!" a man cried, pointing at her, and the men seemed ready to advance on her.

Just as Tara was about to speak, another stepped forward. "No—no. It's Irving Watson, and *he* threatened my life, forcing me to open the door to her chambers. He weren't Irving no more, I can tell you that for sure!" the second man said. "She saved my life, she did, and how she did it I do not know, except that God Himself intervened, and that's all I'll ever say!"

The men seemed convinced by the plea, but before further action could be taken a commotion down in the yard rang loud. Finn turned.

"It's happening," he said. He looked at the man on the ground, and saw that he had been armed with a rifle and saber. He drew the saber from the man's sheath and tossed it to Tara.

"I'm going for the prisoners!" she cried. "Richard… he, the others, they'll have no defense."

They rushed down the stairs.

In the parade ground, Finn quickly saw that two haggard men had fallen some of the other soldiers, who, forewarned, kept their distance and managed to behead both of the enemy.

From the cells where the prisoners were kept, there came a scream as if Satan had squeezed a banshee. Finn turned quickly, following Tara, both racing to the stairs faster than most men could fathom.

Tara beat him there and was wrestling with the bolt

on the iron door leading to the prison cells when he caught up.

"Let me," Finn said.

She stepped back. He moved forward, glanced behind him and shoved the door in, breaking the bolt.

Richard was doing his best to keep the three infected men in the cells from attacking the others, but one already lay on the ground, gurgling as blood bubbled from his throat. Richard was using the leg off the single small stand in the room to battle off the two prisoners who had turned. He was holding his own, but he was pinned atop the pallet that had once served as someone's bed.

Finn rushed in, sword at the ready, decapitating the man nearest the blockade runner. Richard gave him a nod of gratitude, and Finn turned to the next being in the room. When he had finished off the last attacker, he turned to see that Captain Calloway had rushed into the prison cell, as well. Looking at the man, he said without pomp, "Sir, as you can see now, the truth is just as we have warned."

Calloway looked ill. "They were my men who died tonight, and these fellows were simple prisoners we had taken in. One had hurled tomatoes at my men, and now he is on the floor, in a pool of blood. This can't be real. Disease makes a man sick. It makes him weak."

The commander's voice died. For a moment, Finn just watched as disbelief turned into a sick truth within Calloway's mind.

"Captain Calloway, a rabid dog is dying. But as he

dies, he becomes vicious and will attack against any odds."

Calloway swallowed hard, staring at Finn. "So, you have seen this before."

"Yes. And you must be prepared to deal with this situation. I've known of such outbreaks in the past, as does the government, which gives me authority to dispatch it. I believe that most likely there is one individual who has hidden his contraction of the disease and perpetuates this chaos. He thrives on the death—and the blood. This will not end until the host is brought down—that individual who kills and creates death and mayhem for his amusement, or to reach a goal. You *must* be prepared to deal with it—as I have instructed you."

Calloway nodded, still watching him as he did so. "As you have warned, Agent Dunne, so we are already preparing."

"The mayor must be warned, too," Pete said, standing behind him. "Now."

Calloway nodded again.

"I'll go with you," Finn told the Seminole.

He looked across the cell. Richard was still panting from his exertion, and holding Tara against him. Something bittersweet twisted in his heart. He had her in a way that Richard never would; Richard had her youth, her history and her loyalty. He held something that Finn never could.

"Let's go," he said to Pete.

"I'll send men with you," Calloway told him.

"No," Pete said. "We will best manage this mission alone—not military."

"Bring horses," Calloway commanded. He turned and looked at the dead men on the ground, and at the other prisoners who were huddled against the floors or walls, terrified.

"If your home is on these islands, go there. Protect your families."

Some of the men scurried out. One, and landless man, remained behind, wishing to join the fight.

Calloway would have to handle the problems in the fort. Finn looked at Tara. Her eyes met his with under-standing. He was fairly certain they had quelled the danger in the fort for the night, but she knew she had to keep guard, and he knew that she was up to the task.

He turned and left with Pete. Outside, horses were ready for them. He and Pete mounted up; the gate was opened, and they rode across the island, seeking the ci-vilian authority.

Crossing the causeway, Finn found himself looking back at the fort. The high walls rose in the night, and the water and the moat surrounded the fort; the guns stood tall and dark and ominous up on the ramparts.

They rode through the night. The island was a mix of paths and dirt roads, and there were simple homes in the shotgun style; in summer, the front and rear doors would be open—so that a shotgun's bullet could pass clear through—allowing for the ocean breezes to cool down the inhabitants. There were enormous mansions, built by wealth made off the business of salvage. Barns were scattered here and there. Dogs barked, and the whinny of horses could be heard as they moved along. Pete knew the way.

The mayor's house was a handsome edifice, elegantly built with trim in mahogany, brought in from the Caribbean. A boy rushed out to take the horses, and the pair hurried up the wooden porch steps. Someone was playing a piano from a salon highlighted by elegant bay windows. They were stopped by a manservant in the doorway.

"We must see the mayor," Pete said.

"My name is Phineas Dunne, Pinkerton, and we have urgent business with the mayor."

"What is the ruckus?" someone demanded from the salon before the servant could reply.

A middle-aged man suddenly filled the entryway. He looked at the two of them with indignant query.

"We have come to warn of an attack," Pete said.

The man looked at them, his brows rising higher. He almost smiled. "An attack? By whom? The people have long claimed to be on the side of the State of Florida first and foremost. The Union sits hard in the fort. We tend to go about life here, Pete, and you know that well. Now, you're interrupting my niece's parlor piece, and she's a shy girl—"

"This is an attack by neither North nor South, sir," Finn explained. "You will not be prepared for the strange horde that has inflicted the fort, and which may well take to the people of Key West. These sick men, they do not die, but awaken to feed on others."

"Feeding?" the mayor demanded.

"This is not an idle warning," Pete said.

"You must see that the people are prepared. There must be safety for them," Finn said.

"Danger? What is this danger?" the mayor demanded.

"Please, can you sound the alarm?" Pete asked.

"You've just said that the fort was diseased. What would you have me do? Bring Southern citizens to bide in a Union fort, where this 'disease' has already run rampant?"

"Bring them to the church," Finn said.

"This is preposterous!" the mayor said. "Is this some plan to harass the citizens yet further?"

"Neither of us is part of the Union military," Finn told him.

An attractive woman came to stand at the man's side. She appeared slightly pale. "What will it hurt, to be safe? Edward, please. Sound the alarm. Bring the citizens to the church. We'll let these men have their say."

"Preposterous. Utterly preposterous!" the mayor said. "This is Key West! We've had scalawags and pirates, and every form or brigand in between. Union and Southern. But a disease in which the stricken rise and kill...such madness. Will the Union soldiers laugh at us, and say, 'Ah, the citizens of Key West are but simpletons!'"

"It is no laughing matter to any man within the fort," Finn told him.

"You are responsible for the citizens," the woman said quietly.

The mayor was silent. He inhaled. "The commander at the fort knows of this?"

"Once again, we've come from the fort," Pete said. He stood solidly before the mayor. "I am a citizen of Key West. I've seen this. Call the people."

The mayor looked to his valet. "Get to the rectory. The father is away on business, but wake his curate, young Father Timothy. Have him sound the church bells. See that all are summoned to meet at the church."

The valet looked at them all with wide eyes. He nodded and hurried out.

"Gather our family and friends," the mayor said to his wife.

"I'll move on to speak with the curate," Finn told Pete. "You see that his family reaches the church safely."

The Seminole nodded. Finn hurried to the street. As he did so, he noticed that the wind suddenly picked up from the northwest. It was a chill wind, and he remembered a long time ago when his mother would shiver at times, looking at the sky. *A chill wind. A wicked chill wind comes, one that will do no good. Always take care in such a wind, my love.*

He could almost hear her words aloud as he stood there.

Quickly, he mounted his horse, wishing he had Piebald, who knew the slightest inflection of his voice, the least movement of his thighs. But he did not. He began to rue the fact that he allowed Tara to remain at the fort. He was now feeling the responsibility of the civilians weigh down upon him, and he wanted her near.

Distances were short on the island, and so he was at the church in record time, and he saw that the mayor's valet had run quickly. The rectory was on the side street, and as Finn dismounted, he noted the two men standing on the steps of the rectory. The young priest was standing in a long white nightdress, listening to the valet try to explain.

Finn went quickly along the path and up the few steps to the porch. "Father Timothy, dress quickly. I will see that the bells are rung. Gather everyone to the church."

The fellow looked at him. He was no more than twenty or twenty-one years of age with a head full of tousled brown hair. He frowned, but stared at Finn a long time. "I believe my faith will be tested tonight."

Finn nodded grimly. "How do I reach the belfry?"

"My name is Tito, sir. I will see to the alarm," the mayor's man said. "I dared not speak, but I have seen such horror before. In Haiti. I saw many die. I saw survivors weep, and burn those they killed. I will sound the alarm."

"I must dress," Father Timothy said.

"I will wait for you," Finn told him gravely.

When the priest was adorned in his clerical robes and a large cross made of silver, he joined Finn in the parlor and they started across to the church, listening to the peal of the bells.

Even as the priest let them into the church by the side door, citizens began to arrive. Some had come with nothing. Some carried carpetbags or blankets, and one man had a large bottle of rum. The local physician had come with his bag.

"Are we finally besieged?" one anxious fisherman asked first, running down the aisle to the priest.

"If you'll take seats in the pews for now, people, this gentleman will explain the situation."

The mayor had arrived, and he walked down the aisle with bustling authority.

"We are living in a time of war, though sometimes it feels that the bloody battlefields are far from us," he announced, glancing at the priest and at Finn. "Agent Dunne is going to tell us what we're up against."

"Agent Dunne?" someone demanded. "What kind of an agent is he?"

"I'm with the Pinkerton agency."

"Yankee spies!" someone else shouted.

Finn raised a hand. "I'm not here on either side of the great schism. I'm here in the name of humanity."

"Spy!"

"Mayor, why are we listening to the enemy?" another demanded.

"Have you forgotten that there are enemies out there other than your brothers?" a voice demanded, rising hard and high.

Finn looked down the far end of the aisle to see it was Pete, now walking down to join him, outwardly calm but with a forceful tone.

"This man has come, risking himself and what he holds to his heart, to warn you. Strangers! To teach you. You see my face, and you'll remember that our people went to war, and your children died, and my children died. And then the war waned to a close, and the hatred remained. Now, you look at faces just like your own. You look at your own blood, and you call your friend your enemy. Forget the color of my skin, or the blue of an enemy uniform. The foe we face tonight is like no other that you have met, and there is no code of warfare, no decency, no captives, and the sweet and innocent are taken just as the warrior is taken. Listen to this man!"

As he stopped speaking, an eerie shriek came from the skies, out of the night. The sound of birds' wings, thousands of them, flapping in the night, seemed to sweep over the church.

"Get everyone in! Everyone!" Finn cried. "Hurry!"

He ran down the aisle to the main entry, throwing the doors open. Townspeople were still coming. Some had paused to look at the sky, trying to make sense of the beating of the wings in the night and the screech that had sounded like something from hell.

Finn raced outside, shouting, "Get in, get in!"

Looking up, it appeared that there was a large bird in the sky, creating a darker shadow in the deep blue-black of the night. It moved, just as would a bird in flight.

"Hurry!" he shouted, sweeping up a little girl and running ahead, urging her parents to follow.

People drew closer, aware of the shadow in the sky. Finn didn't want a panic, but he did want them moving as quickly as possible. He saw that Pete had dashed around to the side, hurrying people around the grave of an old sea commander. Running back in and down the aisle, he found Father Timothy speaking reassuringly and ushering people into seats.

"Line the inside walls and especially the doors with holy water," he told the holy man.

Father Timothy looked at him, wide-eyed. "You're— you're serious."

"As death. Do it, Father, please."

He went back out. For some families, it was harder. A few had brought buggies, others had ridden, but some were still straggling down the street.

A man stood next to him as if dumbfounded, staring at the figure of a woman who was moving slowly along the side road.

"Marybelle!" he breathed.

Finn took a good look at her, frowning.

"Marybelle!" the man shouted. He started to run toward her.

Finn grabbed his arm. "Who is that?" he demanded.

The man looked at him, blue eyes not really seeing, his gray bearded face working into a picture of astonishment.

"My wife...my wife..." the man said, his voice choking on tears. "We tried to save her…but she died the night before last. We buried her this morning. But, oh, God, but she's alive!" He started toward the woman.

"No!" Finn cried. He raced after the man, catching him just before they reached her.

"Marybelle!" he cried as Finn tackled him.

Marybelle was covered in dirt; her arms and head seemed to be at an old angle. She let out a screech of fury and pounced toward them. Finn thrust the man out of the way. The reborn woman fell on him with tremendous strength. She tossed her head back; her canine teeth grew, wet and glistening. She made a lunge for Finn's throat.

Throwing her aside, he leaped upon her, reaching to his ankle holster for his knife. As he raised the knife above Marybelle, her distraught husband cried out again. "No, no!" He knocked Finn over, and the vampire jumped up with another horrible banshee scream, charging for her grieving husband once again.

"No, man, you've got to let her go!" Finn cried. He managed to push the man just before his wife embraced him, mouth open, fangs now fully developed and inches from his throat.

Finn was up. He wrenched the woman back by the shoulders and spun her around. When she came for him, he was ready this time, catching her from ear to ear with the knife in his hand. She fell to the ground, shaking up and down in sweeping spasms.

"My God, my God, she was dead...but she was alive...."

"She's dead, and at peace now. Get into the church!" Finn told him.

Another family group was coming from the south. Finn rushed to them, hurrying them along. When he got them in, he looked out upon a darkened street. No one else seemed to be coming.

"Listen!" Finn cried out. "It's a disease that can make the dead appear to walk. They're not your loved ones! Come into the church, stay away from the windows. Wait it out here until daylight. The only way they can be killed is if the heart is destroyed, or if the head is *fully* removed. You may think again that the dead have risen. They have not—they are tainted, they are sick."

"They are like puppets, playing to their own hunger, and a puppet master," Seminole Pete, standing stoically by him, said. "Listen to me—you know me. You know that I do not lie!"

They heard the loud sound of wings in the air again, screeches and screams, as if they were about to be attacked by all the harpies of ancient Greece.

For a moment, everyone in the church stood still. Then children clung to their mothers, and men sat in fear, listening.

The sound came again. And when it seemed the wings were deafening, the sound stopped.

"In the trees," someone murmured.

"They're out there," Father Timothy said.

A thump sounded, and then another.

And then another.

All was silent again.

Father Timothy started down the aisle, toward the front. He paused by Finn.

"You've sprinkled the holy water all along the walls?" Finn asked softly.

"Yes." He looked at Finn. "They're out there, aren't they?"

"Yes."

"What are they? Spawn from hell?"

Finn didn't answer. "Please…listen," was all he said.

As they did so, they heard someone out in the night, someone hailing them.

"Hello? Hello? Where is everyone? Hello! Father Timothy?"

Father Timothy started for the door. Finn caught his arm.

Timothy looked at him. "That's Jasper Hawkins. Him and his wife, probably, and his little girl and boy. They're from the far south side of the island, have a farm over there. We have to open the door to them."

Before Finn could answer, they heard a scream.

"Help! Oh, my God, help!"

A dozen men rose.

"We can't sit here like this! We'll take them on, damn it!" one man roared.

"No! Stay here. I'll get them in. Do not leave the

church. Father Timothy, get these pews broken up. You need stakes. Yes—stakes! Get to it, all of you!"

The sound of the scream came again.

Finn drew his sword and went out to meet the undead.

CHAPTER ELEVEN

WAITING FOR PETE AND FINN to return seemed to take an eternity. The entire fort was edgy and on guard.

Captain Calloway seemed willing to accept what advice Tara had to give him, and everyone remained together in a group. One person could turn another, but in a group, someone would certainly notice such a thing, and therefore all were called to muster—and the living and the dead were all accounted for.

Calloway didn't argue the removal of the heads. The killed would be decapitated and thrown into the sea.

While men were busy at their tasks, they heard the town's church bells begin to peal.

The sound made a horrible force in Tara's heart. She was afraid when she heard them, even when she knew they were only a warning.

Richard stood with her in the parade ground, listening.

"Sounds like a death knell."

Captain Tremblay walked up to stand by them. "Or a dinner bell..." he said quietly.

She shook her head. "Finn is calling them to the church. It's the safest place."

"The fort would be the safest place, wouldn't it?" Tremblay asked.

"I don't think so," Tara said. She looked at Tremblay. He was watching the walls of the fort, but he knew, because he had seen with his own eyes, that evil could slip behind the high walls with little effort. "Besides, there might not have been enough time."

"What's that?" Richard asked and pointed up.

Looking up, they could see a formation in the sky.

"Birds? In such a flock? At night?" Tremblay asked speculatively.

Tara shook her head. She looked at Richard. "I have to go."

"Are you insane?"

"No…I'm the only one who can really help."

"Finn knows what he's doing. You said so yourself," he argued.

Tara was surprised when she felt Tremblay's hand on her shoulder. "She may be right."

"She's not," Richard argued. "Tara—"

A strange screeching filled the sky.

Tara walked a few steps from them. She clenched her hands into fists at her sides and gnawed hard on her lower lip.

"He's going to need help," she said.

"I can arrange for some men—" Tremblay began.

"No, keep the men here together. We have to hope that whatever monster came among us tonight is now busy with the hordes beyond the walls. I have to go alone."

"And you're going to just walk out, past Captain Calloway?" Tremblay asked.

"No," she admitted, looking at Richard.

"Don't ask her, and you'll be happier," Richard said. He caught her by the shoulders. "You're not invulnerable," he reminded her. "You are…who you are, but you've never been in a real battle before…before the island."

"I'll be careful, Richard, I swear."

He hugged her to him. She felt him trembling. "I'd stop you if I could," he told her.

"I know. I'm glad you can't."

Tremblay interrupted. "We shall hold down this fort, young lady. See what you can do for the people now." He wrinkled his face in a grimace. "I've been spit at a time or two around here, but that's no reason to make the citizens face this!"

She smiled, gave him a kiss on the cheek and slipped away.

She might still be learning about battle, but as a child she had learned to test her abilities. Sometimes, of course, this had infuriated her mother, but she still had to know what her unique talents were.

Eyeing the fortress, she decided on the far wall, where the shadows were deepest to escape undetected.

Certain that no one had seen her scale the wall, she

began to run, and she let the breeze carry her along. She could still hear the church bells peeling.

And she could still hear the horrible sound of the screeching on the air.

And the screams that naturally seemed to follow that sound.

A STRANGE HUSH QUELLED the noises of the night as Finn stepped outside the church. The creatures, possibly longing to play with their prey, had gone silent. A little distance off, they stood together like a massive, wing-shaped shadow, blocking the way into the church.

Finn stood still, watching.

He saw the man who must be Jasper Hawkins looking into the eyes of the creature before him. Hawkins had his arms around his two children, a little boy of about nine and a girl not much more than six, and he held them protectively against his body. His wife clung to his shoulder, her eyes enormous. Jasper had gotten his breeches on and had thrown on an open shirt; his wife and daughter were still in bleached cotton nightdresses. They all seemed to glow white beneath the moon.

Finn viewed the horde of vampires that had taken sight on the people of Key West that night like a pack of wolves. The one facing Jasper Hawkins was a young man dressed in a fine waistcoat and jacket. One, of which Finn could only think of as a lady of the night, had her skirt hiked up and her bodice stretched low and tight over ample breasts. She was licking her lips. The two were surrounded by four others—an old woman, and three who looked like old salts. Two were in Union uniforms, while the other wore the insignia of a Confederate artillery officer.

Where had they come from? Finn wondered. There was always a leader in such a group, and he was certain that the leader wasn't among them. To have amassed this group of people, care had been taken, the leader keeping them under control. This night, he thought, was part of that control. Whatever monster was pulling the puppet strings wanted to fulfill an agenda, not just create mayhem and murder in the dark.

Finn felt himself move forward like the darkness itself, placing himself between the Hawkins family and the young dandy.

He heard Hawkins gasp and his wife choke back a scream. Finn so startled the dandy vampire creature that he took a step back, but then paused, grinning. "Ah, the feast grows more delectable!" he murmured. "My friends, shall we dine?"

One of the oldest war tactics: take down the head of the beast first. Finn swiftly raised his sword and swiped cleanly. The dandy's head crashed against the roots of an old sea grape. The body stood a moment and crashed to the ground.

Hawkins's wife didn't try to choke back her scream.

Even through that horrible sound, Finn detected the guttural chattering that could begin among a horde of vampires, the newly created especially, and he knew they'd pounce immediately.

They tried to move on him en masse. He spun with the sword, using a hard backward push to cast the old woman out of his way as he pierced the throat of one of the Union officers. He had to wrench at his sword to get it back from the man's collarbone, costing him precious seconds. The Confederate reached for Hawkins's young wife, and Finn found himself forced to allow his sword to fall while he used his fists to ward off the Confederate.

"Get to the church!" he warned the family. "Get to the church."

Hawkins gave his wife a shove. "Run!" He swept up his daughter, prodding his son.

Finn wanted to stay with the family; one of the things could easily slip away and rip into the fleeing group while he was hard-pressed with the remaining monsters. But even as he feared trying to divide his attention, he felt a presence at his back.

Tara.

"Finn, the family...I'm good here. Go!"

On the one hand, he'd told her to remain at the fort.

On the other hand, he was grateful as all hell that she had come.

Finn reached down for his sword and tore after the turned soldiers, now nearly upon the family. He caught up with the Union officer first, bringing him down with a double-handed swing of his weapon. He caught the

Confederate soldier just as the thing's fingers grasped into the little girl's dress. He ripped through the man, wrested his sword free and struck again.

Then he dared to turn.

Tara was holding her own just fine. The old woman had risen; her jaw was so wide open it appeared dislocated as she made snapping advances in Tara's direction. But Tara stood tough, and as the old woman approached, she swung, and the woman died so swiftly she might have met the blade of a guillotine.

Finn rushed back to Tara's side as the Hawkins family raced into the church. Dispatching the last two monsters there, they swung around and headed for the church themselves.

Finn barely had time to see it coming—another sweep of shadows, blocking them just when they would have reached the doorway to the church. The one was an enormous Negro man, and the other, a mammoth fellow who would have excellently graced any painting of the Viking days.

Finn nodded to Tara, and they split apart.

This new round of the enemy had not come unarmed; as Finn raised his sword, the Viking came at him with a cavalry saber. The giant black man with rippling muscles took a step toward Tara. His weapon was a massive machete.

For a moment, Finn's heart sank. The weapon was heavy, and she was so small.

But when the Viking swung, Finn lifted his sword to

parry the blow, and for some seconds they were locked together, neither giving ground. Finn willed his strength to the fore and shoved hard against the bigger man. When the creature fell back and swung again, Finn leaped to the side, the blow went through the air, further sending him off balance. Finn responded with a sharp blow to the jaw. His head was not dislodged, but he did stagger, trying to right himself. Finn jumped onto the porch and from there onto the man's back, wielding his knife and killing him from behind. The head fell.

Finn crashed to the ground with the body but rolled clear quickly and rose.

Tara was being forced back against a banyan. Using the tree to her benefit, she slid to the right when the monster's massive weapon came down. The blade struck into the tree. As the giant tried to wedge it free, Tara swung with both hands, slicing through half his neck. Finn rushed forward, finished the job, grabbed her by the arm and went racing into the church.

Father Timothy was at the door; he opened it and dragged them both in, and then slammed it in their wake.

Shaking, Finn looked at Tara. "I told you to stay at the fort!"

"You're lucky I did not!"

"You could have been killed!"

"And you could have been killed!" she countered.

"Excuse me, *we* may well have been killed if she didn't come," Jasper Hawkins said, looking from one of them to the other. He recognized Tara and spoke to her. "Tara? Tara Fox?"

"Yes, Jasper," she said quietly.

He stared at her speculatively, but his wife rushed forward, hugging her. "Tara, oh, dear girl, I don't know where you got the strength, but thank you!" She turned to Finn. "I don't know you, sir, but I thank you, as well!"

"Are they coming again?" Father Timothy interrupted, looking at Finn.

"How *do* you know so much about them?" Mrs. Hawkins asked.

"I've seen them in other war zones," Finn said. "Most recently we encountered them up northeastward on another island."

"But we are on *islands*—we should be safe here," a woman said softly.

Father Timothy cleared his throat. "How do we combat them—if there are more?"

Finn took a deep breath and looked around. Tara was staring at him, a rueful little twisted smile on her face; she was glad he was the one getting the questions.

He cleared his throat. "It's like a disease."

"Oh, my God!" the mayor's wife cried softly. "Do you mean…if they touch us, we turn into *that* and then…die, or have to have our heads chopped off, or—"

Her voice was starting to rise hysterically, so Finn cut her off quickly. "No, no, you can survive a scratch or a…bite. But you have to watch for the infection. Our captain and another of our men were wounded, but survived. Above all, you have to do everything possible to keep the wounded alive. If there's a fever, cool it down. If there's an open wound, keep it clean. Use rum, use anything that you have. The disease takes hold when the person appears to have died."

There was a clamor of fear in the church. Finn raised a hand. "You can learn to defend and protect yourselves. Ladies, too." He looked at Father Timothy. "Sir, we need holy water. Lots of it. And we need whatever vials you can find, any vessels will do. This will slow them down. Swords remove the head, but you can also kill the creatures with stakes. We can start to make stakes out of the pews. Remember to aim for the heart with them. Destroying the heart means destroying the creature."

"Stakes," someone said.

"Are these creatures like…bloodsucking vampires? Something out of old legend?" Hawkins asked, staring at Finn with disbelief.

Finn answered carefully. "All legend has a core of truth to it. The legends surely came from this horrible disease, and yes, once the creatures come back, they thrive on blood."

"Demons! Demons from hell!" Mrs. Hawkins shouted.

Finn looked at her, still cautious in his speech. "*Evil* things do come from hell."

"You're saying that holy water can kill them," Father Timothy pointed out.

"Holy water will hold them back—if you get them in

the face, you can blind them. They know this and will fear it, if they are true evil ones. However, there have been cases where those who come back are *not* evil, and can withstand the hunger for death and blood, and then the church and the holy water do no ill."

He didn't know what effect he was having on the people. He wanted to scare them, but not to immediately attack Tara should they find out about her, or him. "But, sadly, most often, when created by an evil puppet master, as *you* have suggested," Finn said, looking at Seminole Pete, "they will never have had the opportunity to learn goodness. You can't risk mercy when there is a wolf-pack-hunting single-mindedness among a group. I know that all of you long to see your loved ones come back. But…you must defend yourselves. Take grave care. Watch for a tinge of red in or around the eyes, and don't be taken in by the longing we all have to see our dead loved ones alive and in our arms again."

There was silence for a minute. Everyone was contemplating what he'd said, and listening for the sound of wings.

"Will they come by day?" Father Timothy asked.

"By day, those who are new to come back are usually extremely weak, and the daylight hurts them. They come by night," Finn said.

Father Timothy said, "Men! Fashion stakes of the pews. I will bless more water. Come, we will work as a community tonight. Whether we sympathize with the North or the South, we will remember tonight that we are all God's creatures in this church, and we will work together!"

Father Timothy might have been young, but he seemed to know that he needed to be the one to guide his flock. That meant being God's warrior and, as such, strong this night.

Finn gave the man a nod, and Father Timothy stepped over the befuddled mayor and all authority to assert his own.

Finn walked over to Tara, who was standing with Pete.

She looked concerned. Finn knew that she was worried about these people; this was her home. He noticed many speaking to her, and he had a feeling that even before tonight she was admired and loved by many more of her neighbors than she might have thought.

"There have been more mysterious deaths, some have told me," she said to him. "That means...well, there may be more about to come back to life in the cemetery."

"The graveyard here seems to be in one piece," Finn replied.

Pete stepped in. "There's a cemetery in the middle of the island, on the highest ground. Years ago, a storm swept through, and the bodies buried closer to the south beach area popped out of the ground, and caskets and corpses floated down the main street and rose into the trees. That's where all the interments they're talking about took place."

Finn looked at Tara. "And you want to go to the cemetery."

"I have to, Finn."

He could stop her. He did have the strength, and the authority. He was sure that Captain Tremblay and Richard had wanted to stop her coming here, too.

"Tara—"

"It's nearing dawn, Finn. We can leave Pete here. If the people stay in the church, they will be safe, and Pete and Father Timothy and the mayor will see that they don't leave. Please, we have to stop this. I'll never be able to leave the island if I'm not certain that the people are going to be all right."

"Tara, don't you see? We'll not have a guarantee, no matter what," he said gently.

She shook her head. "They'll fight those they don't know—those they don't see as their loved ones. You know as well as I do how seductive the newly changed can be. Please, Finn, we have to do what we can *before* their own deceased make it here."

Pete looked at Finn gravely. "She's right—they can recognize an enemy, but they will fall prey to loved ones."

Finn groaned softly and started to walk away.

"Finn!" she cried.

He turned back. "Yes, yes, we're going. I'm going to tell Father Timothy our suicidal plan."

FINN WHISTLED WHEN they left the church.

Tara looked at him curiously.

He paused in the churchyard, looking around. "I'm forgetting my borrowed horse is not Piebald," he told her, with a wry grin.

"The horses ran. They're smarter than humans," she said.

"So we walk."

"I know the way," she assured him.

They started inland, moving swiftly. As they did so, they watched the sky, but no shadows fell around them. There was no beat of wings in the air.

She wanted to speak to him, to reach out in some way. But theirs was an awkward relationship, so fraught with instinctive desire, and torn apart by circumstances. They were enemies, and they were allies.

"Thank you," she told him.

He smiled tightly at her side. "For? Destroying Richard's ship and taking you both captive?"

"For knowing when your enemy isn't your enemy. And for tonight, for the people of my island."

He nodded. "No one wants the death of anyone. Yes, the armies will continue to rip each other apart, and God knows how many more men will die. But...we can stop some of this bloodshed, if nothing else."

She nodded, lowering her head. "I was afraid, at first, that you would turn me down, thinking it best that I remained here, and plagued you no more about President Lincoln. But I had forgotten, of course, that I'm your prisoner."

He was silent, which puzzled her.

"You did come to find Gator," she reminded him.

He hesitated, and she pulled back, catching his hand. "What?" she asked him.

He watched the sky, and listened, not ready for an instant to neglect the danger of their situation. Then he looked at her.

"I'm wondering..." he started, with an impenetrable look on his face. "I can't help but think that this...attack came after we captured you and Richard on the island."

She stiffened. "I assure you, I was no part of any of this, and Richard is—Richard is a man. A good man, but just a man."

"I'm not accusing you again," he said quietly.

"Then?"

"What if we should have headed straight north? What if, by coming here, we actually put these people in danger?" he asked.

"I don't know what you mean. What would have happened tonight if we hadn't been here? We couldn't have caused what happened—we weren't here for the strange deaths over the past few days."

"I'm wondering if it wasn't all part of a plan...."

She remained puzzled. "But...*whose* plan?"

He took a deep breath, studying the sky once again. "Finn, please?"

He looked at her, and despite the fact that they needed to be so very wary of everything around them, she couldn't help but feel a tremor of warmth, and realize again just how much she admired him, and cared for him. His eyes, with their unusual cast of crimson, were so striking amid his dark features. He stood so tall and strong against all odds, and his actions were as powerful as his appearance and his abilities. She thought that he was truly a man of honor, and she was grateful that he had come to believe in her, and in Richard and Pete and others because of her.

"There may well be a traitor among our ranks," he said.

"You mean…"

"Yes, I mean someone within the Union ranks who is, in truth, a Southern sympathizer, and as a sympathizer, mistakenly believes that President Lincoln should be killed. God knows, our beliefs and our loyalties can twist our thinking. Those who supposedly love and fear God the most are prone to kill in His name, when surely God looks down in horror."

"Who?" she asked.

"Duck!" he told her suddenly.

She felt a whir pass her by, and she turned, and she saw that while he had been ever vigilant, she herself had failed at the task. She had nearly been knocked over by the arrival of a shadow, someone moving swiftly in the night. Someone now standing just ten feet away, on the path that would lead them into the cemetery.

A child.

She felt her heart lurch. It was a little girl with long golden hair and huge blue eyes. She carried a large stuffed doll, and as she looked at them, she stuck her thumb in her mouth.

Then she smiled, and said with a pout, "I want to play."

Tara looked at Finn.

"She's a sweet innocent girl no more!" he warned her.

"But—"

The little girl suddenly started to laugh. She dropped her thumb and her doll and looked at Tara with her eyes bright. "I'm hungry! So hungry!"

Lifting off the ground with the breeze, the small form moved to stand directly in front of Tara. Tara was still stunned, struck by the age of the little girl.

"Hungry!"

She grabbed Tara's skirt.

Finn ripped the child away, throwing her on the ground and pinioned her with his sword. The child began to thrash and spasm, her teeth gnashing as she stared at them, her mouth opening, fangs elongating.

"Finn, please, swiftly!" Tara pleaded.

He obliged her, withdrawing the sword, and—Tara looked away—quickly severing the neck.

Finn gripped her by the shoulders. "You can't fall prey to appearances! You must be strong!" he told her.

She nodded, but still, it was impossible to believe that a child could become such a monster.

"Let's hurry," he said.

They walked swiftly to the gates. The moon was falling, and in the next minutes daylight would come.

They entered through the wrought-iron gates and were greeted by whitewashed aboveground crypts, in-ground burials, weeping angels and downcast cherubs. A large brick tomb sat among those that were white and opalescent in the waving moonlight. All seemed to be quiet.

"Perhaps we were all wrong," Tara whispered.

"It's a big cemetery," Finn commented grimly. "So many vaults…"

They started walking along the main pathway. Wildflowers and weeds grew among the graves, even in winter. Lone trees stood here and there, casting great shadows in the strange light that meant the coming end of darkness, the dawning of day.

"There," Tara murmured.

"Where?"

"The large oak over there…I thought I saw something."

"Let's go."

As he spoke, Finn almost stumbled. Tara caught his arm, but he had righted himself.

"What is it?" she asked.

"An open grave."

He hunkered down, and she lowered herself beside him. She could see that the earth had spewed out, as if from some inward eruption. At closer inspection, they could see that the coffin within had been shattered, as well.

A plain wooden marker stood at the head of the grave, reading: "Lieutenant Abraham Winters, First Florida Volunteers. While the enemy could not make his great heart shatter, so did the coming of fever. God's will. May he rest in peace."

Finn rose, looking around. Tara held still, biting her lower lip.

"Tara?"

"I knew him," she said softly. "I played with him... here, as a child."

"Tara, he is no longer the man you knew."

Finn caught her hand and dragged her to her feet. He whispered close to her ear. "There are more.... The shadow you saw...it's there again, but if you'll look, there is more than one. You must be ready. You mustn't hesitate."

She nodded.

He kept her hand. He drew her along with him, and she didn't understand where he was leading her until she realized he'd gone to one of the aboveground vaults where the coffins were in rows, one atop the other. The seals around the graves were tight.

He'd chosen a place where they could have their backs to the solid wall created by the graves.

He had barely gotten them there before the first shriek came.

She looked. The great shadow by the tree was moving; several of the newly changed advanced toward them. A young girl of perhaps seventeen, an older man and another young man. Then she saw Abe Winters, a handsome young man in his militia outfit; he'd been buried with his sword, but kept it sheathed, as of yet. None of the others was armed.

The newly dead seldom knew that they should be.

"Tara! Why, Tara Fox, it's so good to see you," Abe began. "The war was hard and long.... I was injured and they sent me home to heal. It's so good to see you, so very good. I was homesick...and I'm home, and you're here!"

He looked at her as he always had. His hat rode jaunty over his brow and his thick honey-colored waves of hair. His smile was the smile he had always had. She couldn't help it; she found herself listening to the tone of his voice.

"Tara, no!"

Finn stepped forward just as Abe Winters led the group toward them. Abe saw the danger as Finn produced his sword, but too late. Her old friend went down. The others hesitated, pausing again to stare.

Then the young woman let forth a guttural, chattering sound of fury and sprang. Tara fell back against the wall of sarcophagi and raised her own sword quickly. She caught the girl in the throat and, though sickened, managed to draw back and strike again. It wasn't a clean sweep. The woman fell down, choking and screaming, and the sound was terrible, but Tara gritted her teeth and swung and swung again.

Again a moment of stillness as the others stared, processing what had happened. They turned to run.

"We can't let them go, Tara, come on!"

Finn gave chase. It was horrible as he caught the old man from the rear, but his strike was swift and sure, and the thing went down.

Tara ran behind to follow. But there was nothing for her to do. Finn had swiftly caught up with the others, and hastily finished them off.

She stood in the cemetery, shaking. He came back to her, taking her by the shoulders, and pulling her against him. "It's all right. You were fine, and you'll *be* fine. And you were right—the people would have fallen to their own loved ones if these undead had reached the church. We all want miracles. We all want those we've lost to come back from the dead."

"Not like that!" she whispered.

"Not like that."

As he spoke, the moon disappeared. The cemetery suddenly was lightened by streaks of mauve and crimson. The first hint of the sun was sending tendrils up into the eastern sky.

"We can go back," he said. "We can let the people go home for the day."

"And then?"

"And then, we'll bide another night. But, if I'm right, all will be calm."

"Calm," she repeated, searching out his eyes.

"Because I believe that the evil will be waiting now. Waiting to set sail with us."

CHAPTER TWELVE

WITH THE SUN RISING and a brilliant day on the horizon, Pete returned to the fort to report on the night's events. Neither Finn nor Tara went back with him.

The Hawkins family had made a bed of coats and blankets, so they were able to catch a few hours of sleep. During the day, the people returned to their homes, all to gather food and clothing for the following night they would spend in the church.

Tara had known it was inevitable that she'd dream of Lincoln again. She was standing in the center of the mall in Washington, D.C., watching as masons worked on one of the new buildings for the Smithsonian. While she stood there she saw the scurry of people in the capital—wounded soldiers limping, mothers with children, volunteers bringing amputees out to the mall for some sun and politicians going past in their buggies or carriages. Schoolchildren ran across the grass, waving their bound books at their sides.

She saw a poster on a tree advertising a musical benefit for injured soldiers, and another announcing a play. A young boy in the street was hawking newspapers. Life went on, in spite of war; only the canvas it was played upon seemed different. To the one end of the mall, she could see the Capitol building—at the other end, the White House. Scaffolding rose around the Washington Monument.

She felt a hand on her shoulder, and she turned. President Lincoln was there. "Beautiful day, my dear. Beautiful day."

"It's cold."

"Yes, it's cold. Cold as the grave."

"Where is your escort, sir?"

"Oh, I'm sure there is someone about, watching me. Shall we walk?"

She strolled along at his side.

"Mary had another séance last night. She said that Willie came and spoke to her. I fear that she misses the child so much that it is causing her to become unbalanced. I'm afraid for my poor Mary."

"What about you, sir? Have you attended the séances?"

He nodded. "Not as many as Mary…but I have listened to the mediums, and the soothsayers, and mostly, I have listened to my own heart, and my own mind."

He stopped and looked at her, holding her shoulders. "None of us can bear the weight of losing a loved one. We all want our loved ones back. But what God has taken belongs to God, and none of us may return from the grave."

She shivered again, thinking of the corpses that had risen in the cemetery.

And she felt a deeper tremor.

Lincoln was wrong. Sometimes, things do come back.

She couldn't say that to the president. Not to a man who had lost children—one during his term as the president—and not when he carried the weight of nearly six hundred thousand deaths upon his shoulders.

"Oh, sir! I know what you are up against. I know the enemy we fight, the many enemies we fight. Your child Willie certainly belongs to God now, and I believe that there is a very different day, and different place, where we will see our loved ones as God intended we should all meet again."

He looked at her. "Don't let me come back. When the call comes, let me go and be with him."

"It won't be for a long, long time," she told him.

"I know what I saw in my dream."

He pointed to scaffolding on the "castle," the first building to house the Smithsonian Museum. Others were rising around it now. "This is a museum for the American people. All the American people. And the dream of the Union is something that can never die. It's something that will always change, as it was set forth by the great men who argued, debated, befriended and loathed one another. Even as they wrote the Declaration of Independence, individual men had a say, and they were not all popular, or beloved. Washington spent a winter at Valley Forge, and all hope seemed lost, but somehow they prevailed when all odds were against us.

We are destined to grow, and continually be a melting pot, and one day, equality will mean *all* men, not men of a certain color or nationality. That will live. Rest assured, that will live."

His voice seemed to fade as he spoke. When she turned to face him, he was gone, and there seemed to be dark clouds and black-winged shadows down the mall.

"Tara!"

She woke to the soft-spoken whisper of her name, and saw that Finn was by her.

"You were dreaming again."

"I was with him. We were walking on the mall."

He started to pull away. She grabbed his arm. "Finn, I believe he is in danger."

"I know that he is in danger," Finn said. "He is always in danger."

"He said that he—he doesn't want to come back. He wants to see Willie in heaven."

"In time, let's pray that we all meet in heaven—indeed, that there is a heaven."

She sat up and looked around. The church was empty, except for Father Timothy, who was at the altar praying over water, with a young acolyte by his side.

There was no one to pay them any heed.

"Finn, how did you come to be...what you are?"

"I was born this way, the same as you," he told her.

"But what about others? You said that I have a sister and a brother," she said.

He nodded. "I told you, I know *of* them. I don't know them."

"And you believe that…they're not evil."

He smiled and assured her, "Not evil at all."

"But our father…what do they know about him? Men often think that women are foolish, that they give their hearts to men who play them falsely. But you didn't know my mother. She would have never loved someone evil."

He hesitated. "There are cases where someone is turned—completely turned—and yet, they have still been saved."

"We…we dispatched children last night, Finn."

"Because, at the point we met them, there was no hope."

"So you can believe that my father isn't evil?"

He brushed his fingers gently against her face. "My father was not evil," he told her. "But when he changed, he was with his father, and they'd been on a hunting expedition into the Dakotas. They were with an elderly Sioux man, Jim Whitefeather. When the attack came, Jim tried to protect and warn them—*he* had vampire blood in him. My father told me the worst of it was that they recognized one of the turned as a farmer who'd owned the property near his father's, and they weren't under attack because the monsters were hungry, but because the neighbor wanted my father's property. My grandfather was ripped to shreds. My father was killed, or nearly killed—I'll never know the total truth of that now—but Jim Whitefeather knew how to save him and how to guide him. If there's someone there…if a life can be saved, brought back with the blood of another vampire before death, then the person's life can go on as it did before. When death comes, only those who are very lucky—those who have a guide—stand a chance of retaining their sense of humanity. I've seen where a father hesitates, though, when seeing his own child. But unless someone has learned to control the desperate need for blood, that someone will go after sister, brother, wife, lover—child."

Tara put out a hand and touched his face. "You've seen so much that's so horrible."

He caught her hand, holding it against his cheek, and he smiled. "I wasn't alive yet when my father was changed, obviously. I've seen the horrible—we've all seen the horrible. But what you always have to remember is that this disease, as we call it, is no respecter of children, the good or the innocent, once they wake with no one and feel the hunger. It's as if you come out of a deep sleep, and for a few minutes, you remember your loved ones…but then the need is a burning inside, and it blocks out all humanity. When my father came out of the sleep, Jim was there. He had shot a buck, and he was able to feed my father before the hunger took full hold. He talked him down, talked him through it. Jim had seen things before, and he knew what to do."

"But later…he couldn't save your parents?"

"Jim was very old," he told her. "He reckoned that he

was about fifty when he had been changed. He could remember the continent before any Spaniard, French, Englishman—any white man. When his last wife died, he went to the hills alone. He told us all goodbye, and to pray for his soul, because he believed that he had one, and that the Buffalo Woman had walked with him all of his life, and he'd meet the Great Father. He felt he'd spent his time on earth, and he went out and willed himself to die. I was young when I accompanied my father into the hills and found Jim. My father saw that all his tribal rites were carried out, and I believe that he did find peace. And I learned from my father, who was able to lead me from the time I was born."

"My father could still be out there—and be decent, wherever he is?" she asked.

Finn looked away for a moment. "I know of your brother and sister, because we have mutual friends in Washington—good friends who know about *us,* and who know that they need us to combat the outbreaks when they occur."

He stood suddenly; she, too, heard the sound of hoofbeats.

Father Timothy paused in his rite, looking at Finn. Finn waved to him and headed to the main door of the church.

Tara followed Finn.

Captain Tremblay had ridden back with Pete. When they stepped outside, Tara saw that the day was truly striking; the sun rose high, the sky was crystal blue, the air was cool and the breeze that blew in from the ocean was sweet. It had rained sometime before, and it seemed that the world was fresh-bathed, almost as if the sky had known that the land needed to be cleansed from the night before.

Captain Tremblay and Pete dismounted and Tremblay lifted a hand in greeting as Finn walked out to him. "The mayor is coming, with some of the other town councilmen," Tremblay said.

Finn nodded. "Was there any more trouble last night at the fort?"

"It was quiet, but all are now on guard. And that, of course, is what we must discuss with the mayor." Tremblay looked at Tara and hesitated. "Most of the Union forces have gone northwestward. The Cow Cavalry is expected to make advances on Union troops near Fort Myers and in the Tampa Bay area. There will be no reinforcements at the fort now. Every man and woman here—Union and Confederate, military and civilian—must be prepared to defend and fight together. Especially because, if I've understood you correctly, you are still eager to reach the North with all haste."

Finn nodded. "Yes. And I believe that while there may still be pockets of danger here, once we're gone, they will be minor. The intelligence behind these attacks, I feel, will follow us."

"*Is* there intelligence behind such attacks?" Tremblay asked.

Tara couldn't help but speak up. "Is there intelligence behind any war?" she asked.

Tremblay looked at her, shook his head sadly. "We fought for the Union, young lady. Your side fought for an intangible *cause,* and in this, I honestly believe that God was on our side."

"States' rights," she said.

"But no one has a right to own another human being," Tremblay said.

"Or to kill off native peoples, assuming them all savages—"

Finn lifted a hand. "We have no control over either for the moment, Tara, Captain. We need to leave these people safe. Let's go in."

Inside the church, Father Timothy was waiting for them. Tara noted that only a few pews remained. There was a large stack of stakes now piled up near the baptismal font, and Father Timothy had gathered old medicinal and alcohol bottles, and they, too, were amassed in rows near the pile of stakes. Many people had left jackets, coats and blankets; they would be returning by nightfall.

"I have prepared as best I can," Father Timothy told them.

"Excellent. Before dusk, have the church bells ring," Captain Tremblay said.

The door opened again. The mayor had arrived with a contingent of councilmen. He paused in front of Captain Tremblay.

Captain Tremblay offered him his hand.

The mayor took it and they shook. "This must never, never go into the records. God knows, we might both be written down as traitors."

"This is just a battle of men. There will be no logs written," Captain Tremblay agreed. "Those people who are not here may not understand, and history might well make fools and renegades of us all." He hesitated, looking over the mayor's head to Finn. "We'll stay tonight. We'll watch well, tamp down any last offenders. Then, tomorrow, I must set sail. We'll pray that both Union troops and Key West's citizens will join together, and combat a common enemy, for once remembering that we are actually brothers, though we may be brothers at odds."

The mayor shook Tremblay's hand again. He stepped back, saluting him. "I will have the citizens armed and ready. We will keep guard here at the church, while you maintain the fort."

"We will be here tonight, as well," Finn assured the mayor, shaking his hand, as well.

The mayor looked past him to Tara. "Miss Fox, our gratitude," he said. He smiled suddenly. "Forgive those of us in this town who were rude to your mother, or ever treated you as anything but our finest citizen. Pete, our gratitude."

Tara nodded. She'd never seen anyone treat her mother with disrespect, but she knew well that many citizens had whispered about her behind her back, and that she had always been looked upon as an oddity.

Tara smiled at the mayor. "I'll be back," she told him. "This is my home."

"It is your home, our home," he said, looking at Pete. "And when you return, we'll all rebuild together."

He left, followed by the councilmen, who all noted how the church was prepared as they departed.

The mayor paused before leaving. "Father Timothy!" he called.

"Sir?"

"We are grateful," the mayor said and left.

Father Timothy looked after him.

"How odd," he said.

"What's odd?" Captain Tremblay asked him.

"It seems after all this time, we *do* know how to make peace," Father Timothy said. "If you will excuse me, I believe I could do with a few hours' rest."

Smiling, Captain Tremblay left.

"I'm going to see if there's anything here that we didn't notice last night," Finn said.

"I'm coming with you!" Tara told him.

Pete said to Tara, "You take the horse I rode from the fort. I'll be home. Join me when you are hungry." He looked at Finn. "Both of you."

They bid goodbye to Father Timothy together, but out in the churchyard, Finn hesitated.

"There aren't many graves here. They were mostly moved to the Key West cemetery," Tara said.

"Yes, but I want to make sure that nothing has been disturbed. Other than the obvious."

But nothing had been disturbed, and the citizens of Key West had already removed the diseased that had been slain the night before.

"It's all right, isn't it?" Tara asked him.

He nodded slowly. "Yes, it's all right."

"Where should we head first?"

He shrugged. "It's your town."

"And it's beautiful, especially in winter!" she told him, smiling.

"Let's mount up, shall we?" he suggested. They walked around the side of the church, and found the gelding Finn had ridden and the mare that Pete had used when he'd returned with Captain Tremblay. The gelding hadn't broken free and taken flight during the attack the night before. Finn was quiet, thinking that they needed to be grateful that they were prepared, and the fight hadn't been elongated, that none of the diseased had attacked the horse.

Finn patted the mare's long sleek neck as Tara mounted. She was quiet, looking northward.

"We talk about the war coming to an end, but Florida has a militia still fighting, you know. They call them the Cow Cavalry, because they protect the beef used to feed so many of our soldiers. The Union men sailed from here to do battle with them."

Finn looked up at her. "We can't stop the war," he told her.

She nodded. "I know."

Finn mounted as well, and they rode along. She pointed out some of the trees, and the bursts of colors, and she explained how many of the streets had been named for the founders, such as Simonton, and Duval, of course, was for Florida's first civilian territorial governor, William Duval. "Angela and Margaret Streets had been named for his daughters, and that it was like a frontier, and not a frontier, of course, because of all the money that had come in through the salvage business. Eaton, of course, was named for John Eaton, President Jackson's secretary of war, until politics undid him. He was the second territorial governor, but I also believe he owned property down here when they were naming the streets." She paused, looking at him. "And, yes, there are about four hundred slaves here, though with the Union fort having been held so long, and the Emancipation Proclamation, most are now escaped, or free. But even before the war, Finn, there were about one hundred and fifty free African men who lived and worked here, and our whole population is just about two-thousand and two hundred, and you saw so many of the people last night. Our mariners come from everywhere on the East Coast and they're Italian, French, Spanish, from the islands...."

He laughed as they rode, reaching over with a hand, taking hers. The simple touch seemed to shoot sparks of fire throughout her, and she flushed, remembering now, by the light of day, how sweet it had been to feel his intimate touch. She looked away quickly, not wanting to give away how she longed for a time when they were just together, the two of them, and she wondered if such an event could ever take place again. Assuming they both survived, they would reach Washington, and whether he believed in her or not, there was still Richard's captivity to consider, and the war, and the bitterness.

But Finn was unaware of her thoughts, and he spoke with amusement and courtesy. "This is a beautiful place, Miss Fox, and I pray that no more harm comes to your island."

She sucked in her breath suddenly, wishing the same fortune.

Upon reaching the west martello fort, soldiers halted them. Here, there were only a few men, but they were protected by strong walls, and they were wary at the appearance of visitors. Like Fort Zachary Taylor, it was still under construction, but supplies ran daily on the railroad between fortifications.

Finn showed his badge to the young officer who approached them. They were allowed entrance and spoke to the young lieutenant who had been apprised of the situation. They went out to start searching the grounds, and the graveyard. The graves were located toward the beach, and there had been little here before the fort had gone under construction. As they walked out, Tara noticed that an old woman bent over one of the graves that looked freshly dug. But it was no ordinary grave: a heavy piece of coral had been set at the head of it, and there were crosses constructed from palms and bits of wood around it.

Tara went down on her knees by the woman, whom she recognized. Elsi Hatare—and she had come with her husband, Henri, from Haiti, years ago, when Tara had been just a child.

"Elsi," she said, setting a hand on the old woman's. "Is this a grave for one of your family members?"

Elsi looked at her and nodded, great sorrow held in the rheumy gray of her eyes. "Henri," she told her. "Two nights past. He died of a fever and flu."

"I'm so sorry, Elsi."

Elsi continued to look at her. "You've come because you fear the day.... There is no need. We have tended to these graves. In the islands, we know that the dead don't always rest well." She paused, looking up at Finn. She crossed herself, and spit on the ground. She looked at Tara again. "He is with you?"

"Yes. This is Finn Dunne. I'm so sorry about Henri, Elsi."

"I know you are, Miss Tara. I know you. But I don't know *him*," she said, staring at Finn again.

"Finn has not come to do trouble here, Elsi," Tara assured her. She tried to think of something to say that would convince the perceptive old woman. "Pete is his friend, too. He is here to help."

Elsi sniffed, and arranged another cross on the grave. "Well, Pete, he knows. But something came to the island. Something evil blew on the wind, just night's back. And they were here among us last night."

"Didn't you hear the church bells?"

Elsi offered her a smile at last. "It's a good church, Miss Tara. The pastors there, they are good people. But we have our own church." She lowered her voice, assuring herself that the soldiers were standing far enough back. "We call it Catholic, for the white folk. It is more than that. Richer, with the culture of the Caribbean. You understand, right?"

"If you are protected and safe," Tara said, "that is what matters."

Elsi nodded. "You needn't fear. We tended to my husband, and to all the dead and dying here."

Tara said again, "I'm so sorry, Elsi. Henri was a very fine man." She stood, offering a hand down to the woman. "May I help you?"

"No, Miss Tara. I will bide here, with Henri."

"Please, Elsi—"

"I will watch for the dusk," she said with finality.

Tara nodded and stepped back. Finn appeared indignant, but he didn't speak. Tara walked back to the soldiers. "It's all right. Elsi and many of her friends are from Haiti. They have their own means of defense, and I believe you are all safer here, because of her."

"I'd not have believed…" one of the soldiers murmured.

"I'll see to it that she eats," the other said awkwardly. "She's been here all day."

"She will appreciate your generosity," Tara told him. She and Finn returned to their horses.

"She didn't like me!"

Tara laughed. "Ah, well, she knows what you are."

"Then she should know..."

"You're a stranger," she told him. And she smiled again. "You're a stranger, and a Yankee. Everyone here doesn't understand that neither means *bad* yet!"

He lowered his head, hiding a half smile. "I don't believe that she was worried about me for *those* reasons."

She had to smile at that. "Elsi has always *known* many things. The island girls and women always went to her for palm readings. And, of course, reading tea leaves. She could always warn the men of a storm that was brewing, or a ship floundering. At first, only the freemen living in the sparsely settled areas believed her. Eventually, good fishermen, who would show up bright and early for church every Sunday, began to consult with her, too."

She was startled when he reached over and caught her arm.

"What is it?"

"Let's go back," he said.

"Where?"

"To see Elsi."

She was surprised, but she nodded. "If you wish."

The soldiers were concerned with their return to the fort, but Finn quickly assured them they had just come to talk to the widow again.

Finn went back over to Elsi and Tara followed. Her eyes were closed and she was praying. Finn went down to his knees at her side. He waited, patiently. She didn't open her eyes for a long while.

Tara knelt down next to Finn. At last, Elsi opened her eyes and looked at Finn. "What is that you want to know, half-breed?"

"Elsi…" He hesitated a minute, as if he might have worried himself that he was a fool for believing so easily in an island mystic. "My name is Finn. Finn Dunne."

"You're with the soldiers," Elsi said.

He nodded. "But I'm not in the military, Elsi. I'm a detective."

She studied him for a long moment. She waved a hand in the air. "It's been coming. I've felt it. I've felt the evil coming, and I've known that—even when men speak softly in their homes, knowing that war will end—there has been something wrong here. Now it is here. Now it has come in force. It has grown and waited, and there's been such a bitterness beneath the beauty and brilliance of the winter skies. Is that what you're *detecting,* sir?"

"Elsi, I think that the evil is deeply hidden. And I believe that it's following me."

"Give me your hands."

Finn stretched his arms out, so they extended over the grave.

Elsi took his hands and closed her eyes again. She rocked slightly, humming. She smiled before she opened her eyes. "You have too much pride and arrogance, young man. You have strength, but you rely too much on it. Still, you have honor, as well. And I can feel your heart. You will fight what you see as the good fight. But don't forget, others believe in the honor of their fight, too. What is here is different. A power that you don't see, and don't know. The evil doesn't *follow* you, but it is going where you will go. You are trying to block it, and the evil sees. The evil sees so much more than you know."

Elsi still had his hands. She held them tightly.

He nodded gravely. "Elsi, when we leave, will the people on the island be safe?"

She nodded gravely. "But you know that!" she told him softly.

"Thank you, Elsi."

She didn't release his hands. "You may help me up now. Already the day grows short. I hear the whisper of darkness on the wind. You, go, too. Take care, young man. You have a good heart. I pray you will survive."

Finn helped her to her feet. She paused, looking at Tara.

"No one can stop you from what you seek," she told her softly. "But the evil will try. You must take care. And hurry. Go to your church. It's winter, and the sun is deceptive. The blue is catching the sun's rays in pastels—we've not much time."

Head high, she left them.

And even as she did so, Tara saw that she was right. The sun was falling into the western sky.

Another night was coming.

CHAPTER THIRTEEN

FINN WAS QUIET, PENSIVE, as they rode.

"Many people think that the séance craze—that the mediums and fortune-tellers are all fakers just trying to prey upon the bereaved for the money," Tara said.

He looked over at her and smiled. "And many people believe that dreams are nothing more than our thoughts and our fears doing battle in the night."

"But you believe in the future being foretold?"

"I'm not sure. I know that there are those around us—like Pete—who have an instinct and know when someone is…different. *I* can usually tell when someone is different, even when they were those who had been helped, like my father. I can't understand it, because I'm so afraid that it is someone who is with us—or who was at least on that island."

"You found nothing unusual about the men when you sailed, or when we came to the island?"

He cast her a glance, his brow arched and a rueful smile on his lips. "When we sailed, I was seeking a blockade runner, not an unworldly being. And on the island, I was hoping that we were discovered and res-cued by a Union ship rather than a Southern. And as to Elsi, yes, I believe that she has a power to recognize the world around her. Can she really see into the future? Nothing but the future will tell."

He reined in for a moment, looking up at the sky.

"Home?" she asked him.

"*Your* home," he told her.

"You'll need to be careful, you know."

"And why is that?"

"I've been among your people," she told him. "And now, you are among mine."

"I think the fortune-teller likes me now," he said, still smiling.

"But you must admit, you should be careful, perhaps even extremely courteous to me. You are among *my* people. They will defend my honor."

"Tonight, they're all one," he said, chuckling at her light tone. "And I do believe that I've been extremely courteous, except perhaps when we first met. But then, when we met in Gettysburg, you were frightfully rude."

"You wanted to arrest me—for wanting to give the president a *scarf.*"

"And if *you* were charged with protecting him, wouldn't you have come after anyone who was so eager to get so close?"

"I like to think I'd be a better judge of character."

"It's a pity we can't all judge character so swiftly as you. Which way?"

"Toward Whitehead," she told him.

They rode together. Roosters and other livestock

ambled about, but there were no children out on the road, and the few businessmen and passersby they encountered acknowledged them grimly, and hurried about their business in the waning daylight hours.

They reached Pete's tavern, and their home. It was a large whitewashed structure, built some forty years earlier. Front steps led to an entry hall. To the left was a staircase that led to the rooms above, and to the right, through an arched doorway, was the tavern. As they entered, Pete came hurrying out, a large satchel swung over his shoulder.

"Provisions," he said. "We need to leave quite soon. Agent Dunne, if you'd see to getting these tied on to one of the satchels?"

"Yes. Is there more?"

"One more. Coffee and kerosene heaters, and some fresh-baked biscuits for those who stay awake to keep watch. I'll get the rest," Pete said.

"I'm going to grab a few things from my room," Tara said, and hurried upstairs.

She decided that she could afford the time to swiftly wash up. She poured water from the ewer at the washstand and scrubbed her face, and then hastily changed her clothing. There was a knock at her door and she opened it. Finn was standing there.

He smiled. "You look—"

"Yes?" she asked, surprised that the question was a little breathless.

"Clean," he said enviously.

"Oh, yes, well. Clean. Thank you."

He laughed, reached out and touched her cheek, and suddenly drew her to him, holding her in a way that was oddly tender and gentle, almost as if she were fragile, and yet, he did it with a great strength. She didn't breathe; being with him, touching him, could stir so many emotions—passion such as she had never imagined, and then this, something she had felt so seldom in her life. *Cherished.*

"I can't imagine that you've gone through life without a slew of compliments, my dear Miss Fox. You look clean. And lovely. Glorious, actually. The sun setting against the color of your hair creates a dazzling halo greater than that cast by any heavenly body alone. Your eyes are those of the mesmerist, of every siren known to man in the length of the history of the world. And your face! Ah, like that of Helen of Troy, you could sink a thousand ships. Ah, my love, excuse the last— we've both seen a few too many sunken ships," he said, moving away and meeting her eyes.

"You're mocking me," she said.

"Never," he told her, stroking hair from her face. "There were times today, far from cemeteries and soldiers, when I could imagine that there was no war, that we faced no unholy enemy. I thought what it would be like to live in this strange paradise with the sway of the tree branches and the scent of the ocean in the air. I've seen the seafarers and fishermen, seen all the colors of the people, heard their accents and their languages, and I know why you find this to be such a unique and special home. I would never mock you. It's that my own words trip me up and I'm thrown back into reality, where all we can do is pray for an end to this war, and for safety from this unholy enemy."

She looked at him, marveling that someone she had once thought so brutally single-minded and austere could have such dreams of a different world—and touch her as he did.

"Tara! Finn!"

Pete's voice broke into her thoughts, reminding her of the world they did live in. Finn caught her hand.

"We must go," Pete said.

"It's dusk," Finn said huskily. "The sun is going down. I should have sent Pete up to get you before."

"Why didn't you?" she asked.

He grinned. "I wanted to see your home, your wonderful abode. And it's a beautiful old house, a fine tavern, and your room… That's a picture of your mother, isn't it?" he asked, pointing to the dresser.

She nodded, feeling a tightening in her throat. Lorna Douglas Fox had been stunning in life, more so because she had such a sweet and gentle smile. The warmth in that smile had been caught in the one poor photograph that had been taken of her just before the war had begun.

"She was lovely, too," Finn said. "Let's go—before Pete thinks I'm up to no good."

"He's my friend, not my father," she said.

Finn laughed. "He may not be your father, but I believe he'd kill any man for you. And Richard may not be your blood brother, but I believe that he'd do the same. You're a very lucky young woman in those who love you—father, brother, friend or other. They do so with a passion."

Taking her hand, they walked quickly down the stairs. Pete was waiting for them on the porch, holding the door open.

As ever, his strong features were stoic and impassive. She knew that Pete had decided that whoever—whatever—Finn might be, he was a man to be respected. She was glad. He wasn't her father, but he meant so much to her.

A second large satchel was now attached to the saddle of the mare, but they were just blocks from the church, so none of them mounted the horses. Pete looked at the sky as they walked along the streets.

The air was crisp and cool; the breeze was coming in from the northwest, and it seemed as if it were something so clean, it couldn't possibly allow for a whisper of evil upon the night.

A block from the church, Pete stopped, and signaled for the two of them to do the same. The gelding he led neighed, pushing against Pete's back, as if even the horse knew they needed to reach their destination.

But Pete set a hand on the gelding's nose. "I nearly forgot. There is a drink for you both in the satchel the mare carries. You've been facing a great deal each night. You need to keep up your strength."

Finn thanked him and found the two canteens that Pete had prepared. He watched them steadily as they each swallowed down the contents.

"Now," he said, "you're ready for the night."

The church bells were ringing, and the streets were filled with the stragglers who had not made it in earlier. They arrived with the strangest solemnity. People greeted the three of them with a grim welcome. They were courteous, as if it was a Sunday morning and they were all heading into the Anglican mass. And, yet, of course, it was because the skies had gone silent. Even the wildlife and the trees listened, and waited. Father Timothy had aged overnight, so it seemed. He was grave, and strong, and ready to greet his flock. The church had only a couple pews remaining, so most found places on the floor, and sat in family groups. Many had brought their suppers with them, most were willing to share.

Father Timothy spoke to his flock, and gave a blessing that night. He thanked God for bringing them through the darkness and the shadow of death the night before, and asked that He guard over all in His house, the church, that night. That He watch over the island of Key West—all of His children, no matter the great divide ripping apart the country. Everyone answered with a solemn, "Amen."

Finn sat with his back to the wall. His eyes were half-closed as he listened.

"Finn?" Tara asked.

He opened his eyes and looked at her. He smiled, caught her hand and squeezed it.

"What were you thinking?" she asked him.

"That there's hope."

He didn't mean just for the night, Tara realized.

The hours passed. Mrs. Hawkins came by, slightly shy, but determined to offer them some of the biscuits and chicken she had brought. She was eager to please, to do something for the people who had saved her life, and she, Pete and Finn gratefully accepted. Pete set up his portable kerosene stove and brewed coffee, and the men who would be on guard first came to drink it.

Children lay on pallets of blankets and clothing set up by their parents and the church. Some played with dice and jacks, some read and a few of the men played cards. Tonight, no simple pleasures were considered to be sins.

Finn was restless; every few hours, he spoke to the men standing at the windows, and when there was a disturbance outside—the raucous cry of a dozen roosters and the squeal of a pig—he took his sword and went out to investigate. Gone for several long minutes, which seemed like eons, when he returned, he noted that a horse had broken free, frightened the rooster and the rooster had attacked the pig.

Somewhere along the line, Tara drifted to sleep.

When she did so, she was far away from the church. She found herself in an elegant dining room, seated across the table from President Lincoln. Mary was there, at his other side, and she could see that two men were standing by the door, watching inward, their eyes never leaving the crowd or the other diners. There were soldiers milling around at the bar; they chatted, enjoying a drink and the music of a single violinist who played softly from a small corner stage.

But they were all aware of her.

"It's amazing what war does for some," President Lincoln said, carefully cutting off a piece of meat. "This fine capitol was nearly as small a city as your Key West, my dear—all but empty during the summer months when the heat is liquid and the mosquitoes infest. But come the war it's become mammoth, with hotels and restaurants doing a booming business, as you see. The Willard does exceptionally well. It is one of my favorite places to dine. One day, I'm sure, I will bring you here."

He was speaking to her. Mary Lincoln didn't seem to hear him. She was concentrating on a wayward pea that was escaping her fork.

"It's a beautiful restaurant," Tara said. "But—"

"Ah!" Lincoln said, and he set his fork down. "You're worried about me again. I *must* go out. I am leading these people, and I have led so many to death. What do I say to the mother who lost her son fighting this great battle if I don't take a few risks myself—the risk of telling them how sorry I am for their losses? Excuse me…"

One of the officers who had been milling at the bar came to the table, bending down to speak softly to the president. Lincoln listened gravely.

The officer excused himself to Mary and left the table.

"Mr. Lincoln, good news, I pray?" Mary asked him.

He nodded. "Even my good news is sad news, I fear. Our troops were attacked in Florida by the Cow Cavalry there. Our positions were not taken, so that is fortunate, of course." He smiled, squeezed her hand and paid heed to a waiter hovering by him. "I would, indeed, sir, enjoy more coffee. Thank you." The waiter hurried away.

"February turns to March. As the year comes closer to spring and the snows melt, so the armies will move in force. Again, I will go to sleep each night seeing an army of dead soldiers walk before me, and I will pray that in death they do not despise me. That in the end, when I meet them in heaven, I will be able to say, 'Forgive me, that I called upon you for your life, but look at the great nation you created.' And even then, I know, when I am called to my rest, I will meet the Confederate boys, and the generals—some of them old friends from different days—and I will have to explain that I believed, in my heart, that slavery is an abomination, and that we could not continue to expand our nation and make beasts of our African brothers. I will tell them that I know that they died for honor, be that honor mistaken, and that in God's eyes, all men are truly equal."

"What's that, dear?" Mary Lincoln asked. Her attention seemed to be elsewhere; perhaps she still thought of the son she had lost during the war, and lived in her own realm of pain.

"I was thinking that this fowl we are dining on is quite fine, Mrs. Lincoln," the president said. "And I wish that I knew that our men in the field ate so well."

"Stand your course, Mr. Lincoln, stand your course," Tara said.

"Rest assured, my child, this evening all is well. As you can see," he added, coming closer to Tara and whispering as if they were conspirators in a joke, "the door is guarded by two gentlemen from the Pinkerton agency, and there are lieutenants and officers abounding at the bar. I am praying that this is the spring of good hope for the nation. One nation, under God. Indivisible, as it's said."

He leaned closer to her again. "There can be sweet life and better times ahead. Look at my poor Mary. Some think that she is unbalanced, and God help me, the death of our little Willie certainly made us both so. But there could be no better wife. Her family members fight for the South, and she stands by my side, supporting me with her whole heart. Be kind to her when you meet—those around me can't always see clearly. She is my support. We lean on each other." He eased back. "All is well this night," he told her.

The restaurant, with its sounds of chatter, clinking silverware and the soft strains of the violin began to grow dim.

After some moments of unbodied colors and sound, Tara awoke.

When she did so, she saw that light was coming through the church windows in a splendid palette of pinks and yellows and oranges and golds.

She blinked and realized that she had been sleeping on Finn's shoulder, and that he was looking at the colors of the sun himself.

Father Timothy was at the door. He opened it, and the light burst brilliantly into the church.

"It's morning, and all is well. We have passed through the night. Hallelujah!" Father Timothy said. "What a beautiful day."

It *was* a beautiful day. All the more so because the night had been uneventful.

Finn felt all the better when they'd left the church and gotten the tub out over at Pete's tavern, and he'd had a good freshwater bath. He'd readied himself hurriedly despite the longing to savor the water, and he'd headed out to speak with Captain Calloway and Captain Tremblay at the fort, regarding their sailing plans, while leaving Tara to gather a few more belongings, and indulge in a bath herself.

Tara was enjoying her last time with Pete before heading north, uncertain of when she would return. Richard had been escorted to Pete's tavern to say his own goodbyes. Had Finn sovereign power over the situation, he would have seen to it that Richard was released. But he didn't; no real ill would come to the man.

He would be imprisoned for the remainder of the war, but Finn could arrange things so that he was kept in Washington, D.C., where he and others could see to his welfare.

Adding to his hopeful mood, Finn believed what the elderly Haitian woman had told him. Once they left, the island would be safe. At least, as safe as it was before.

The evil was waiting. And the evil would set sail with them.

Still, despite that fact, there was always the possibility that a diseased person had escaped their notice, and so he stood with Father Timothy again, going over everything that the people needed to know—how they must look out for anyone who fell sick, and how they must deal with the dead in the next weeks, even in the case of an accident witnessed by a dozen persons. He knew he repeated himself, but he had to make things clear to Father Timothy.

Father Timothy listened.

And when he was done, Father Timothy said, "You've taught me and our people well, Agent Dunne. We will do all you say. Pete will be here, my mainstay who knows and understands. The war continues, so I doubt that the soldiers and the civilians will maintain a real friendship, but they touched hands when the need arose. We are all, as I've said, children under God."

Father Timothy seemed to have his flock well in hand. Finn bid him farewell and headed to Seminole Pete's to collect Tara and Richard.

Tara hugged Pete for a long time. Pete and Richard solemnly shook hands.

"Until we meet again," Richard said.

"The Great Father will watch over you," Pete assured him.

They embraced.

Pete looked at Finn. "Protect her well."

"With my life," he promised.

Pete nodded.

They all mounted up and returned to the fort. The men were assembled—all those who had previously sailed with them and two new seamen, Andrew Fletcher and Bjorn Gustafson. Bjorn had landed in the United States Navy within a year of arriving in the United States. Andrew Fletcher hailed from Tennessee, but believed passionately in the Union—and in the abolishment of slavery. Finn was glad to have them along.

It was still early morning when the tenders sailed out to the new ship they would take north, the *USS Freedom,* a three-mast steam clipper. She was equipped with twelve guns, and ready to take on a fight.

The supplies were loaded; barrels were filled with salted beef, fish and pork, beans, potatoes, limes and fresh produce from the island. There were barrels of rum, sugar and fresh water, canvas sacks of fresh coconuts, and fishing poles. They were also well supplied with munitions, matches and gunpowder—just in case they should be lured into battle.

Finn made a point of speaking with every member

of the crew, largely to see if he might sense which one might be a traitor. Captain Tremblay now knew of his suspicions, and Finn had impressed upon him that while they were at sea, they had to discover the truth of each man in the command.

Finn wanted to believe that the vampire who had caused the infection had died in the many battles that had taken place—on the deserted island, and Key West.

But he knew that it wasn't true. And even if he did, he couldn't possibly take that kind of a risk.

And so, an order had been proclaimed: no man was to do anything without two other men nearby. It would be groups of threes, always. They were not even to sleep alone; even on a quiet night, there would be three awake watching over the bunks while three slept. With Captain Tremblay enforcing it, the men didn't question the order.

Dr. MacKay listened quietly, arms crossed over his shoulders, grave as these boarding orders were given. "And I had thought," he said wryly, once the men were dismissed and sent to stations, "that it was difficult being called upon to perform amputations on the battlefield. I'd not thought it possible to face something worse."

"It could be precaution for nothing," Finn said.

MacKay looked at him with skeptical eyes. "Perhaps. But I, like the others, intend to be nowhere unless it is in a group of three. What I don't understand, Pinkerton agent, is how you haven't fathomed who this person is. You seemed to have a grasp on the disease earlier. You've guided us in the way to survive its threat."

Finn didn't want to tell him that the creature causing the problems was probably extremely old—perhaps hundreds of years old—and a full-blooded vampire. He didn't think it would help the doctor's concern to know that they were up against a combatant likely much stronger than Finn himself.

Fortunately, as a Pinkerton, he knew enough to be confident that strength alone didn't win fights. Much more important was an agility of tactics, and the intelligence to wield strategy. He hoped this meant that *he* held the advantage.

"Perhaps the instigator is dead!" the old doctor said.

"Perhaps," Finn replied. "But we don't know that."

Further questions from MacKay would be put off; the captain was shouting orders and men were hoisting the sails. A cool, crisp winter's breeze meant that they were going to catch the wind. Richard Anderson worked the sails with the other men, and none seemed to be displeased that their prisoner was such an excellent seaman.

The *USS Freedom* had once been the *Mary Jane,* carrying passengers on transatlantic voyages. She had been overhauled to become a warship, but she still offered certain amenities not found on other ships, such as grand or master cabins both stern and midship on the top deck. One, of course, had been granted to the only woman aboard.

As they got under sail, Finn walked along toward the cabin door. He knocked, and Tara threw the door open. He entered and closed the door behind him, leaning against it.

"I'm not beholden to the 'three together anywhere at any time' rule?" Tara asked him.

"Not so long as you're in your cabin. With the door locked, of course," he said.

She smiled at him, but her face grew solemn. "Do you still think that he's among us?"

"I'm afraid so."

"But one slip, one mistake, and this creature infects one man, and then another and then—"

He set his fingers gently on her lips. "We couldn't leave a man behind, not when there is a civilian population on Key West."

"I know. Thank you."

"It wasn't just for you. I think that the man is a traitor—he hasn't been caught or noted because he's been biding his time. He's known about the Union movement, and he managed to get the correspondence to the man we're holding in Washington, and made it *appear* that he was a Confederate blockade runner."

Tara walked to the cabin's elegant little windows. Drapes closed securely to keep out the sun—and the view of the sailors working on the ship. But Tara drew them aside.

"Richard is out there," she said worriedly.

"And Richard is intelligent and wary," Finn assured her.

"You should let him go," Tara said softly.

"I can't, and you know it. You're technically my prisoner still, yourself, but it definitely appears that neither of you is Gator, and therefore, as a blockade runner, Richard is Captain Tremblay's prisoner."

"He's *fought next to you*."

Finn took a deep breath. "Tara, it's nearly spring. God help us, but this war can't last much longer. He'll be safer in prison."

She bit her lip, and didn't reply, looking out the window.

He felt awkward. "Well, 'tis bright sunlight, and there's a day to be sailed."

"Of course," she murmured stiffly.

He wanted to walk to the window. He wanted to draw her to him, and God help him, he wanted to make love again, feel the life of her beneath him, and the passion and moments of beauty that seemed to make breathing worthwhile.

It didn't seem at all appropriate while he could hear the men scurrying about, Captain Tremblay's orders on the air and the shouts of compliance and organization.

"I'll come back," he told her softly.

"Ah, well, I'm not one to sit in a cabin all day, you know. I'll come out soon, as well," she said, still looking out at the action.

He hesitated. She looked beautiful as she gazed out the window, her eyes bright as they caught the sunlight, her hair gleaming red and gold and her chin held high.

He longed to walk over to her, just to touch her shoulders. He wished he knew her thoughts, and he wished that she would turn to him and just smile.

"What if there's more than one man?" she whispered.

"There's one, just one. Of that, I'm certain. One very old, very accomplished and very calculating...monster. But if the men hold to the rule, if he tries to act again, we'll know immediately."

"And if he doesn't?"

"He will," Finn told her. "He will, of that I'm certain. And I will be ready for him."

CHAPTER FOURTEEN

DESPITE FINN'S CERTAINTY that they sailed with a traitor, their first day at sea proved to be uneventful. The wind kept up, so they didn't have to rely on steam. The sky remained bright and blue, Richard's expertise on the waters allowing them a shorter route through the islands, shoals and reefs than Captain Tremblay might have dared on his own.

Richard stood by the captain at the helm, pointing out their location, and Tremblay nodded gravely, and complimented him on his knowledge of the sea.

Finn asked him curiously, "What will you do, Richard, when the war ends?"

Richard smiled. "Get a new ship, first. I plan to be a merchant again, and sail the seas where I choose, and when I choose. And hopefully buy a home in Key West. There is a house on Whitehead, not far from Pete's place, that I plan to purchase, and each time I return from the sea, I will go there. I will love that I have such a home, among the banyans, and am able to awaken each morning to feel the sun and smell the sea air. And you?" he asked Finn in return.

"Strange. I barely remember a time when there was

peace. I imagine I will stay with the Pinkerton agency, and go where I am sent."

"Maybe it will end soon," Richard said quietly. He looked at Finn. "There has been a rumor that President Davis and President Lincoln have corresponded. There has been talk of a peace conference between the two leaders."

"I know that it was in the planning stage when I left Washington. But I don't know how far the plans went."

"I need to pray that conference takes place, don't I?"

Finn was quiet. "I will see that you are treated fairly. I believe you know that."

"Aye, I do."

"Richard! Mr. Anderson, sir!" Tremblay yelled from the helm. "Tell me, how close do I dare to hug the coastline here?"

Richard went to stand by Tremblay again, pointing out features of the land—and a ragged shoal that they needed to avoid.

Finn went to work among the men. Some tended the sails; some sat about at their leisure, and some were taking the precious time to sleep, all in groups of three or more.

He talked to the men, and there was an amiable air amongst them all. There were no clues as to their adversary to be found there. While the day began with a certain tension, by the afternoon, the comfort of the men seemed to be growing.

By nightfall, a sense of camaraderie had arisen

among the crew, and a sense of well-being settled over the ship. Rum rations and the evening meal were enjoyed, but as they moved through the velvet darkness of night, Finn maintained a constant watch. He didn't worry about Tara; she had stayed on deck during the day, reading in the sunlight and the breeze, talking with Dr. MacKay and the captain, or Richard and himself while they ate their evening meal.

As they eased through the night, Finn suggested that Tara go ahead and get some sleep. But she looked at him and told him, "I'll rest by morning, as I'm assuming you will."

Morning came. At the first light of dawn, Finn was both relieved and disappointed. He had been so certain something would happen, something that would at last unmask the traitor among them, that he began to fear that Tara might well be right: the monster would hide in the guise of peaceful patriotism until they reached D.C.

To get close to the president.

Captain Tremblay came from a few hours' sleep to stand watch over the day and the helm. MacKay, who had also slept, joined him. At that point, Finn thought that he dared sleep.

"I'll find Richard," he told Tara. "And I'll have him keep watch over you."

She looked at him with her beautiful hazel eyes and smiled, taking his hand. "You will not," she told him.

"Tara, we're aboard ship, and your cabin is in plain view, and—"

"And this is not like any other ship, and I don't care whether people speculate, or what they have to say, though I doubt that these men will think ill of me. We have been through too much together. Not that I haven't been the object of scorn or ridicule at any other point in my life. I am suddenly respected for my ability to stand my own ground and slay a common enemy. I have no illusions that society will change, but you're not leaving me alone."

He smiled. "I'll warn Richard that we are resting."

Tara went to her cabin. Finn found Richard near Tremblay; he had been describing some of the dangers of the northern Florida coast. Drawing him aside, Finn warned him to shout out like a banshee if there should be any trouble.

Richard looked at him gravely. "You'll be with Tara?"

He nodded. He was surprised when Richard lowered his head, his smile deepening.

"She'll be safe," Finn said.

Richard looked at him. "Yes."

"I mean her no harm."

"I don't believe that harm is what you intend," Richard said. "Of course, I suppose I should say here that, if you were to hurt her in any way, no matter what your strength, no matter that I'm a prisoner and you hold the power, I would find a way to call you out—to challenge you, kill you or die in the effort."

"I mean her no harm," Finn repeated.

"So, I guess at this point my question is, just what are your intentions?" Richard challenged him.

From what he knew of Tara's friendship with the man, Finn shouldn't have been startled by the question, but he was. And for a moment, he wasn't sure what to say. "At the moment? My intentions are survival, and ferreting out the man I came to find."

"And when this is all accomplished?"

"When it's over," Finn said softly, "well, that will depend on Tara." He took a deep breath, and realized that he did know his intentions. "Tara began her voyage with you because of her dreams regarding President Lincoln. I intend to introduce the two of them. I believe that two of her father's children—two more like her—are still in Washington, D.C. I intend to find them for her, and see that they are able to meet. And then...then, as I've said, it's up to Tara."

"Am I to assume that means your intentions are honorable?" Richard asked.

Finn hadn't thought out the future; the present had been far too pressing.

But Richard's words forced him to put his life into perspective. No, they forced him to think about his feelings for Tara, and they were actually easy to discern. "I have never met anyone before who could seduce me from any direct goal, who could look at me and distract me from the business at hand."

Richard laughed, and Finn was taken aback.

"You're going to have to do much better than that, Agent Dunne," Richard told him. "Are you going to tell Tara that she's a lovely distraction?"

Finn was amazed to feel a flush of color come to his cheeks.

"No, of course not!"

"Then?"

"Let's survive, then we'll think of pretty words," Finn said. He gritted his teeth, aware that Richard was chuckling as he walked away.

He tapped on Tara's cabin door. She bid him to come in.

The cabin was dark. His eyes adjusted almost instantly and he saw her stretched out on the bunk beneath the covers. She leaned upon an elbow and patted the side of the bed. "That took a bit of time."

He walked over to the bunk and sat down awkwardly.

"What is it?" she asked him. He found himself mesmerized by the hazel brilliance of her eyes, shining even in the poor light that made its way through the draperies covering the little cabin windows. It was dawn's light, touched by a shadowed palette of colors, and her hair gleamed sleek and entrancing.

"I have just had a lecture that's given me a bit of pause," he told her.

She laughed. "Richard?"

"Indeed," he said, and he felt a throaty rasp in his voice.

She eased up, and he realized that she had stripped

naked. When she slipped her arms around him, he was instantly aware of her bare flesh against him, and he burned inwardly.

"Richard is my friend, and my brother," she said softly. "But he is not my keeper."

He wanted to speak again, but he couldn't. Her lips teased his ear with liquid heat, and he drew her harder against him, finding her mouth. Her kiss at first was a tease, a featherlight touch against his lips, and then it seemed that she was fused to him, and his tongue was in her mouth and each second of time passing seemed to ignite something harder and more urgent and desperate within him. They eased down to the bed together and the caress of his lips and tongue moved down the length of her silken nakedness. He knew that one thing was true; he had never felt like this, never felt about a woman as he did Tara.

He tried to tell himself that the act of making love was a natural one and craved by those who were living and able, but he knew that this was different. He wasn't sure if this was because they were essentially the same, but he knew somewhere inside that it had nothing to do with their bloodlines, that it had everything to do with her as a woman. Her flesh was different, so sleek and soft. Her eyes were different with their hazel fire. Her hair was like tendrils of flame that had taken root within him. And there were those things that tore at his heart—the loyalty until death she showed those she loved, the desperation to save a man she had never met, her vision on the world and those around her. She had seeped inside of him, not just into his natural needs and desires, but into his mind and his soul.

Then he thought no more.

She smelled of sweet cleanliness and of herself; her flesh eased and moved against him, and each light brush was like a pinpoint of lightning and fire. He rose, anxious to rid himself of boots and hose and clothing, and desperate to lie down beside her again with the length of him feeling the vibrant energy within her limbs, the erotic feel of her bare breasts and the twine of her limbs. She kissed him in turn, and moved along his length, the press of her mouth on him like bolts of fire ripping down his flesh. She tormented him, lips here and there and everywhere, teasing around his growing erection, centering upon him until he thought that the world would explode.

And then he could bear no more. He swept her high against him, met the copper glow of her eyes and rolled with her upon the bed. She gave him a gaze of triumph and wonder, and he smiled, kissed her lips. When she would have welcomed him with open arms and limbs, he kissed her again, and ran his kisses down her length. He heard a muffled cry escape her and felt the tug of her fingers in his hair, and his mouth found hers again as he thrust into her at last. They looked into each other's eyes as they slowly melded into one, and then began to move with hunger and urgency until there was nothing but the two of them and the erotic and carnal ecstasy of

soaring toward the point of climax when the world itself
exploded with a burst of light so shocking they might
have been drowned in the light of the sun.

Shuddering, shaken by spasms of aftermath, he eased
down beside her, and he could hear their hearts, like
thunder, almost in beat, and the ragged expulsion of
their breath. The cabin came back into view, the damp
sheets clung to their flesh and he drew her close, lest
she feel the chill that seeped in, now that the explosive
fire of their movement had ceased.

He lay in silence, and she moved against him, rising
slightly on an elbow to search out his eyes. He touched
her face, and he smiled slowly, admiring the line of her
jaw and, as ever, the exquisite green and gold and fire
within her eyes.

"Richard actually likes you, you know," she told him.

He eased to his back, and heard a slight edge to his
voice. "And I actually admire your Mr. Anderson, but
I'd just as soon not be discussing him here."

She didn't take affront at his tone. She studied him
gravely. "I don't know what Richard said to you. But
whatever it was, remember that it didn't come from me.
We're here, now. And I do nothing that I don't choose to
do, but don't let any thoughts of the future disturb you.
You're not beholden to me. I make my own choices."

He shook his head, surprised that he was oddly
shaken by guilt, and irritated by it. "Miss Fox, none of
us really makes our own choices in life. A great deal

is handed down to us, and there are always matters at hand that are far greater than you and me."

"And I do believe we're both trying to deal with those *matters at hand,*" she told him. She started to rise. He caught her arm, pulling her back to him.

"I didn't mean to anger you," he said.

"You didn't anger me. I am my own person, and that is all."

"Tara, we do live in this world, and even if we're at war, and even if we face an insidious enemy, the world will go on, and eventually, God help us, the war will end, and—"

"Don't you listen!" she said angrily.

"I'm trying to say—"

"Well, there's the difficulty right there. I believe you should cease talking!"

"Tara—"

She started to pull away again.

"Where do you think you're going?" he demanded.

"I'm getting up—it's day."

"You haven't slept."

"I don't need much sleep."

"You need some...."

"The cabin is feeling quite crowded at this moment!"

He held her tight; she struggled against him for a moment. "Please, take this time, get some rest," he told her.

She stared at him with anger still flashing in her eyes. Again, he felt the rise of desire that she could so easily inflame. Her eyes touched his, and he knew that she felt it, too.

"Stay, please," he said softly.

"On one condition," she said primly.

"And that is?"

"You stop talking!" she told him.

He smiled slowly. "What if I were just to say something like…I believe I would die if you were to leave me in this moment. The tiniest streaks of golden sun are slipping through, and slight as they are, they make spun flames of your hair, and create emeralds and rubies in your eyes, and you feel like the most precious satin against me, and—"

"I'd say, sir, that you were nearly as full of hot air as a politician."

But she was smiling, and she laughed. He pulled her back into his arms, and the instinct and desire that had begun so unwittingly with anger flared hotly. They became lost again in the wonder of each other's arms. He forgot her anger, forgot the world he had reminded her existed, and in moments they were entangled and sensations overcame and overwhelmed them, until they lay panting again.

But she didn't stay. When he held her, she resisted, and he had no real choice but to let her go.

"Tara," he said. "You still haven't slept."

"Please, don't be concerned. I'm not a sailor, not the captain, nor the ship's physician. I'm a prisoner, remember? I can rest at will."

She dressed quickly, and stepped out into the daylight.

He closed his eyes. Rest wouldn't come. He rose himself, and went out to face the new day, wondering again when the next attack would come.

TARA KEPT CLEAR OF RICHARD, speaking with Captain Tremblay, and then finding Billy Seabold, who was preparing a meal of dried beef and the ubiquitous beans and mushy hardtack of sailing vessels.

Billy was cheerful, whistling while he worked. He spoke to Tara about the island of Key West.

"I never minded," he told her. "The men complain so much about the mosquitoes and the heat, but I find that I love the heat compared to the snow, and I think I might try to find my way down there and buy property—when the war is over, of course. They say that we'll not pull out of the fort until that time, and I don't mind at all. Of course, I love the sea. I love sailing and being aboard the ship, and I hope that I can buy myself a fishing vessel, and make a new life there."

"Where are you from originally, Billy?" Tara asked him.

"Originally? Oh, that's hard to say, miss. My parents were wanderers. I've lived many places." He turned to ring the bell, signaling that the meal was ready for the sailors with leave to dine first. "When the war broke out, I was working in a printing company in Maryland. I joined up quickly, when I found I could enlist as a seaman."

"Have you spent much time in D.C.?" she asked him.

"A bit. We were close, you know, to the capital."

"Ah, beans!" Dr. MacKay said, joining them toward the aft, where Billy had set up his mess operations.

"Beans, yes, but with some excellently salted and dried beef!" Billy said.

"A fine meal, lad, a fine meal," Dr. MacKay said. Apparently, the good doctor was hungry. He was ready with his plate and fork, and helped himself from the large pot. "Miss Fox, shall I make a plate for you?"

Before she could answer, they heard a loud bellowing from the crow's nest. "Ship on the horizon!"

Tara and MacKay quickly looked to the man. She hurried toward the helm where Captain Tremblay had his glass on the horizon.

Finn stood by him. He was tall and straight, striking in his posture, and his eyes were fixed on the sea, narrowed slightly.

Tara swallowed down the emotion that seized her as she watched him; she didn't know exactly what she was feeling, why she felt that she was in such turmoil. *I do what I choose!* she reminded herself. And she had done what she wanted, but the problem was that she wanted to feel him constantly by her side, to know more and more about him....

And to believe that he would be in her life, that there would be more than this time when life and death and tension seized them constantly. Blinking, she reminded herself that they were both concentrated on preserving the life of Abraham Lincoln—a man she had yet to meet. And still...

"She's Union," Finn said.

"You can see that already?" Tremblay asked him.

Finn nodded. "I see her flag."

"Fire a shot! Recognize her position!" the captain bellowed. "Bring her around to rendezvous."

Tara stood behind him as the men hurried to follow orders. As the Union ship came closer, she could see the seamen on the other ship arranging to draw near. The men busied themselves on both ships, and more orders were called, ropes where thrown and the ships were brought flush together.

Captain Tremblay greeted his counterpart across the few feet that divided the two ships. "Tremblay, sir!"

"Gazersin, Captain Tremblay. With news from the front."

"Aye, sir!"

"I believe, sir, that you'd been apprised that President Lincoln and the rebel Jefferson Davis had planned a peace conference. Southern delegates had been chosen to meet with President Lincoln and Secretary of State Seward, but you must be aware that the conference will not now take place. Mr. Davis demanded that the United States recognize the sovereignty of the Southern nation, and the president will not meet under such circumstances. Be aware, sir, that all possible negotiations for peace have fallen through. Any Confederate ship you encounter remains an enemy ship, and you are to capture or disable any such vessel, and take prisoner any survivors."

"Aye, then, sir! Thank you for your information," Captain Tremblay said. "Is there anything else, sir?"

Captain Gazersin hesitated a moment, frowning as he noted the group surrounding Captain Tremblay. "General Sherman has routed the forces in South and North Carolina. The land has been laid waste. War efforts continue in the West, but General Grant is harrying the troops in Virginia, and major action is expected there."

"Where do you travel now, sir?" Tremblay asked him.

"Back to Florida. I bear army personnel to help rout the Cow Cavalry there, sir!"

"God be with you," Tremblay said.

"A strange meeting," Finn murmured to Tremblay. "He has stopped you to tell you that we are not at peace. None of us expected that we were."

"What else, sir? Is there something that you need from us?"

Tara felt a palpable tension. She looked at Finn, who was staring intently at the other captain. Always the detective, she thought. He sees a man, and knows that there is more.

She found herself wondering how he saw her, and she bit her lower lip.

Obviously, the man didn't see everything.

Which was good. She didn't want him knowing how she felt. The strange bond they had formed was one thing; the exquisite sensual relationship they shared was another. But she didn't want him ever believing that she was growing dependent. She didn't need *him*. She was strong, and she had lived her life with Richard as a brother and Pete as a mentor for years.

But she had never imagined this *feeling*. A very different kind of *need*.

Ah, yes! And it did seem that he could so easily turn from the handsome, smiling lover to the ruggedly stone-faced agent, ever a man of duty! He continued to stare hard at the other captain, waiting.

Captain Gazersin was silent a moment. Then he said. "Coffee, sir. Our store of coffee was in a barrel that leaked, and it is filled with maggots. My men would be heartily grateful for a store of coffee."

"Coffee?" Tremblay said quietly to Finn.

Finn shook his head. "Captain, note that there are only a few men topside. Where is the rest of his crew? There is something not quite right."

"Sir, where have you sailed from?" Captain Tremblay asked.

Captain Gazersin stared at him blankly for a moment.

"Call the men to arms!" Finn warned quickly. "Now!"

As he spoke, men suddenly burst out from below-deck. There was a cry from a man in the crow's nest, and he came leaping down to the deck.

"Swords, men, to your swords!" Tremblay cried.

In droves, men appeared on the attached ship; the

first three tried to leap the distance from ship to ship, but Tremblay's crew was ready.

Tara scrambled for a weapon, as did the others. As the crew of Captain Tremblay's *Freedom* gave fight, she saw that Finn intended to leap across the way to the other ship.

"Finn!" she cried, but he didn't hear her. He intended to ferret out every last man from their attacking visitor.

She couldn't let him go alone. Seizing her sword, she ran to the edge of their vessel, and as she leaped past a man, she realized she recognized him. She couldn't remember from where—and then she knew. He had come from the Union fort on Key West, and he had disappeared in the midst of the fighting on their first night in Key West.

Shouts and screams abounded from both decks. The men on the *Freedom* seemed to be holding their own, and the enemy was cut down while trying to board. Every man on the *Freedom* knew what to do, and when one man downed an enemy, another stepped forward to make sure that the head was severed. On board the grappled vessel, Tara quickly realized that the enemy was newly turned. They were not adept at daylight, nor were they possessed of exceptional strength. She and Finn soon faced each other over a pile of six or seven corpses, and the ship was still, while on board the *Freedom,* the last of the cries were dying down.

"Dunne! Agent Dunne!" Captain Tremblay shouted.

"Aye, Captain!" Finn called back.

"Come back aboard. I'm blowing her out of the water! We'll see that no infection travels again so cruelly in the guise of a Union ship!"

"Aye, sir, give me ten minutes!" Finn shouted back.

"What are we doing?" Tara asked him.

"You're going back to the *Freedom*. I'm going below." She stared at him and he said, "Tara, if there's an experienced vampire aboard this ship, he'll survive an explosion, and even days at sea. You know that."

"You're not going alone."

"Good God, Tara, I've been at war. I know what I'm doing."

"And I've been learning."

"Tara—"

"We've got ten minutes," she said, setting her jaw.

"Stay behind me!" he warned fiercely, his voice almost a growl.

She wasn't going to argue the point; he started for the stairs below and she followed. They moved carefully, and found that none remained in the quarters here.

She started suddenly, hearing a muffled cry.

"Finn, there's someone below...ballast deck!"

He listened, and they both stood there quietly.

They heard it again, a cry that began to rise on the wind, along with a thudding sound and finally the scream of a single word.

"Help!"

"It is coming from the ballast.... Someone needs help!" she pleaded.

"Vampires *kill*. They don't take hostages," he told her harshly.

"Finn, listen, please, we have to see!"

They heard the desperate rapping against the hull again, and then another cry.

CHAPTER FIFTEEN

IT WAS A TIME OF WAR. The ballast hold was stacked with kegs of powder for cannon balls. There were boxes upon boxes filled with rifles and swords, most probably on their way to troops fighting on the western front before the ship had been deterred. Finn, ever aware of Tara moving carefully behind him, came down the steps to the bowels of the ship and began making his way through the labyrinth of boxes and supplies. The banging on the door and the cries had become louder. They heard something that was almost like weeping, and in the sound of it there was both hope and fear. As they neared the aft end of the ballast hold, Finn could hear the sound of whimpering, and whispers within a closed section in the far rear.

"Stop calling! They'll…they'll kill us!"

"If not, we'll drown here, caged together," someone else said.

A heavy door sealed off a small compartment; Finn hesitated in front of the door, looking at Tara. She backed away and he lifted his leg and kicked the padlock that chained the door shut. The padlock shattered and he wrenched the door open.

The small hold space held five men. One, whiskered and grizzled, was clad only in a cotton shirt and breeches while the others wore shirts with the insignia of the United States Navy. One was barely a boy, perhaps thirteen or fourteen, and the other three men looked to be in their early twenties.

The older man stepped forward. "Captain Gazersin, United States Navy," he said. There was a tremor to his voice, as if he waited.

The young boy stepped forward next, "God A'mighty, have you come to eat us? If so, by God, do it! *Do it!*"

"We're not here to eat you," Tara said, stepping forward, and staring at the group incredulously. "How are you here?"

Another of the men spoke up. "Lord save us! It was horrible, miss. We came upon a man floating in a ship's dinghy, and we figured he was a survivor from some naval battle. We dragged up the poor soul, only to find there were two of the blokes. We pulled them on board and tended to their wounds, and the next thing you know, we're being picked off and ripped to shreds—I mean it! Throats ripped and blood flowing and the bastards drinking up the blood. Then our ship's mates were herding us down here, because someone was saying there was too many created, and those what tore up the first would starve if they didn't come on another ship, and..." He paused a minute, choking on his words.

The captain picked up the speech for him. "We

started off as ten down here. They've been pulling us out, one after another, over the past few days."

"God help us!" the boy said. "You're really not going to eat us?"

"We're really not going to eat you," Finn assured the boy. He looked over at Tara. She was staring at the group with such empathy in her wide eyes.

"Saved by an angel!" the boy whispered, staring back at her.

"We've got to get topside," Tara said, looking at Finn. "Captain Tremblay wants to blow the ship out of the water."

"No," the real Captain Gazersin pleaded. "She's a good ship, a fine ship. We were carrying arms down to the fort at Key West when we thought we were saving men from the sea. God help me, but I brought this plague upon us all, trying to be merciful!"

"Let's get topside. The choice will go to the captain of the ship we're aboard, the *USS Freedom,*" Finn said. The ship they had boarded did seem to be a sound, and her cargo *was* valuable. "Come on, men, hurry topside."

They urged the small group before them. When they reached topside, the young man paused, looking at one of the headless corpses on the deck.

"Dr. Leery!" he cried. "A good man, and taken from us just a night ago."

Tara caught the young man by the arm, leading him away. "Son, he is gone now, but truly in God's hands."

Aboard the *Freedom,* tension filled the craggy features of Captain Tremblay, who greeted them with Dr. MacKay at his side.

"They were keeping hostages—prisoners to be feasted upon one by one!" Finn shouted over to him.

"Sir! She's a sound ship. Bound for Key West!" Captain Gazersin shouted.

Tremblay looked at Finn with surprise. "Hostages?"

"There was an intelligence at work," Finn said. He turned to look at Gazersin. "Sir, I'm going to need you to go through the corpses, and tell me which of the men were the ones saved, to assist in this mystery we've been chasing. Captain Tremblay! I'll need a few men over here to help with the disposal of the corpses. The ship does carry valuable cargo. Send me London, sir, and Griffin, if you will. And Billy Seabold. We'll scour her from top to bottom, and see to it that no monsters remain aboard."

The boy sniffed. "Dr. Leery was no monster!" he said.

"No, son, in his soul, never. But the disease makes hideous monsters of good men, and there is nothing to be done. He is gone now, and as Miss Fox said, he is in God's hands now," Finn told the boy.

Captain Gazersin said, "We can attend to the men. They were my men, so I would see to that they were buried at sea with honor."

"We need our men, sir. I have to know if those you rescued came from the fort," Finn told him. He turned to Tara. "You don't need to be here for this."

She shook her head. "But I do. What if the men who were rescued and turned the ship to monsters were citizens from Key West?" She offered him a weak, grim smile. "Finn, I don't need to be protected—not at this point."

He turned away from her. The requested men were coming aboard the ship, and they quickly began the grisly task of identifying all the bodies. He walked the ship with Charles Lafferty and Captain Gazersin while Tara went with the boy and Grissom and London. Toward the mainmast, Captain Gazersin stopped, pointing down at one of the corpses. "There! There is one fellow who we rescued from the dinghy!"

Finn stooped down by the man. He recognized the man himself.

It was Lieutenant Bowers, who had greeted him and brought him to Captain Calloway when he had first arrived in Key West.

"Sever the head and body, then into the sea," Finn said.

"Wait!" Captain Gazersin protested. "They were surely God-fearing men! Please, sir, you are our savior this day, but I'd have good Union men met by their God!"

"Aye, Captain. We need to find the second man who began the infection on the ship. Gather the…body parts here. You may say the prayers for those who died at sea, and we will finish with this sad business."

Tara discovered the second man from the dinghy who

had come aboard to infect the ship; Finn heard her cry of dismay when she came upon him.

He bent down by her. "It's the young man who was in charge of my meals," she said. "He was terrified when the attack began. He thanked me for saving his life, and protected me from the other men by telling them I'd done so."

"I'm sorry," he said.

He rose, both sorry and touched to see the pain that was in her eyes. So much! And she still hurt for those around her. He wondered about himself, and feared that he had grown so hardened to war and death that he had little left of a soul himself.

"The infected men did come from Key West the night of the attacks there," he announced, shouting over to Tremblay.

"What of the others?" Tremblay demanded. There was suspicion in his voice; Tremblay would never be quite the same man again, Finn knew. He had learned that those who appeared to be friends or comrades could be monsters, and those who appeared to be the enemy could be friends. War, of any kind, was complicated, with God-fearing men killing God-fearing men. But another dimension had been added here.

"We will ascertain with the five of the living," Finn assured him, his voice rising ominously in the air.

Tara stood by the captain while the men gathered all those who had been killed—and decapitated—and then Captain Gazersin said the appropriate prayers. As the men's bodies were at last shrouded and their heads covered in old canvas sailcloth and cast over the side, Tara took Finn's arm and asked quietly, "What now?"

He looked back at the *Freedom*. Most of the men were topside, hovering near Captain Tremblay, watching the events.

He turned to Captain Gazersin. "Sir, were the five of you together at all times, after the real fighting on your ship began?"

"Aye, we were. We waited with the other living, as I told you, and they came for us, one by one."

"Can you take her into Key West with your crew of five?"

"I can, sir," Gazersin told him. "She's mightily ill-staffed with a crew of five, but we can limp her in. But, surely, your ship can spare a man."

He lowered his voice. "Sir, I'm afraid that the infection may be simmering aboard our ship. I even fear that the men who boarded your ship did so with the ultimate goal of delaying us from our goal of D.C., knowing we would stop for you."

"Infection!" Captain Gazersin said.

"It's an infection, sir, yes," Finn said. "It turns men to madness, as you've witnessed. And as you and your men discovered, it's insidious. Men can appear to be as they were, sad wretches adrift at sea and in need of rescue—and then monsters who slowly slip within a group. You need to take this ship to port in Key West, and find Captain Calloway. He has seen the illness, as have the people there. You'll be watched with suspicion by those with whom you should be allies, but you mustn't be dismayed. In Key West, they have now learned to deal with the disease, and every man there watches every other man."

"We can bring her to port, eh, men?" Captain Gazersin shouted, looking at his five remaining crew members.

"God help us, aye, Captain!" called one of the men. "Lord willing, and the Rebs don't strike!"

Finn looked over at Charles Lafferty, who had proven to be such stalwart help after first mocking him on the island.

"Lafferty, gather Grissom and London. We return to our own ship," Finn said.

In another twenty minutes, Tara, Finn and the crew from the *Freedom* had returned to their own vessel. Captain Gazersin stared across the hull and the few feet of water separating the two ships, facing Captain Tremblay.

"May God speed us both now, Captain!" Gazersin shouted to Tremblay.

"Aye, sir! Do you know if the information your imposter gave us was true? Negotiations have failed—and we remain at war?"

"Aye, sir! That's true," Gazersin replied. "Sherman has now marched through the Carolinas, and General Grant plans his offensive in Virginia. The war in the West continues, but there is progress against the Rebels.

May God grant us all a speedy end to this great conflict!"

"Amen," Captain Tremblay said.

"Men! Clear the grappling hooks!"

The ships were separated. Captain Gazersin shouted orders to his men, and added his own effort to hoisting the great sails of his ship.

Finn stood at the hull by Tremblay and the others as the ships parted, and the *Freedom* continued north, while Captain Gazersin disappeared on their voyage south.

"Captain," Dr. MacKay said. "Perhaps we've made a grave mistake, sending her off after such an event with a skeleton crew."

Billy Seabold was standing next to him. "I know what Agent Dunne was thinking. He couldn't put a man from this ship aboard her. Agent Dunne doesn't really trust a one of us."

"Ah, Billy!" MacKay said. "He trusts *one* of us. He trusts Miss Fox. And I believe we all trust Captain Tremblay, don't you think?"

"Or," Finn began, "I didn't trust *them* enough to leave one of ours aboard their ship."

As if to end all speculation on allegiances, Captain Tremblay suddenly roared orders, showing his authority. "To your stations, men! Stay in threes! And full speed ahead!"

TARA SPENT MUCH of the day in her cabin, lying down. She couldn't shake the image of the dead man—the young fellow who had brought the tray to her at Key West. He'd been grateful to her—in shock but still so grateful—and then…

She wondered how many men they had presumed missing or dead had fallen victim to this plague. And she couldn't help but wonder again if many who had been such good men couldn't have been helped.

There was a tap at her door as evening came. It was Richard, and he brought her a tray of food. "There's a vial there, as well," Richard said gruffly. "Compliments of Agent Dunne."

She nodded, murmuring, "Of course."

Richard sat at the cabin's desk, looking at her where she sat at the foot of the bed. "Tara, what would happen if you didn't…if you didn't have a vial now and then?"

She stared at him. She'd known him most of her life, and she couldn't help but take affront at the question.

"I'd find a bilge rat," she told him.

"And if the rats were all gone…?"

She stood. "Richard, get out. Please."

He walked over to her. "Forgive me, dear friend—sister!" Richard said. "It's just that…I have known you forever. And I had never imagined that what you are could turn into…what those men became."

"Richard, I would die myself before besieging an innocent man or woman, no matter the circumstances. And when I'm forced to kill—as we all seem to be in this—I am at heart remorseful, and careful to see that the dead rest with God. And so help me, if there is a way to save a man, I will save him."

He went down on his knees at her side and took her hands. "I'm so sorry. Please forgive me. I was so wrong to speak. But we've seen so much that… God help us all! And it's true—Dunne thinks that someone aboard this ship is a monster."

She nodded. She touched his hair, looking into his eyes. "Richard, you needn't fear. He knows that it's not you."

He shook his head. "They say that the two men 'rescued' from the sea came from Fort Zachary Taylor."

She nodded. "I knew the one man, Richard. He'd been kind to me."

He sat next to her on the bed and she leaned against him as he slipped an arm around her. For a long moment they just sat together. "I never thought that I'd be praying to live long enough to reach a federal prison," Richard said lightly.

"You'll live, Richard. You'll live!" she said passionately.

"Ah, Tara, you always think that you can change the world. You want to stop all the pain everywhere. No one can do that, you know."

The door started to open; they both went still, looking toward it. Tara felt the tension that filled Richard's muscles.

Finn had come.

"Captain Tremblay would like your advice on the coastline, Richard," Finn said.

"Aye, then."

He turned to Tara, kissed her on the forehead and rose. The two men left and the door closed. Tara rose and exited the cabin, as well. She stood by the door to the cabin and felt the night breeze rush around her.

Darkness again. But they were still far from the port, far from Washington, and although she believed that perhaps they had been fated to have an encounter with the Union ship devastated by the monsters, she thought that now they would be waiting again.

Feeling the tension aboard the *Freedom* rising, she walked over to the captain's station near the helm. Richard was pointing out an area where the shallows could tempt a man by night, and advising Captain Tremblay on an alternate route. The sky was growing dark; some men sat with their mess kits, quietly conversing while they ate. There was a man up in the crow's next, on lookout.

The air was crisp; the breeze remained with them and, against the velvet sky, the sails billowed, oddly beautiful.

Finn stood at the stern, looking northward.

He turned as if he knew that she watched him. Then he looked to the sea again.

Tara returned to the cabin. She browsed through the books she found there, but a tract on the speed of mid-Atlantic storms did nothing to hold her attention. She ate and paced, and considered heading out on deck again, but the tension on the ship held her back. While they had sailed with good camaraderie previously, even with the weight of fear upon them, tonight seemed to bring with it something different.

At length, she lay down. She didn't believe that she fell asleep, but she felt as if she left the place where she was, as if the air around her became an opaque rush.

She was back in Washington, D.C., again, sitting at the desk before Lincoln.

He looked up at her and smiled a welcome. "I'm about to give another inaugural speech, my dear. It's so important, always, to say the right thing." He paused, flushing. "At Gettysburg, I didn't want to speak too long as people had already sat through a great oration. No words, of course, can ease the pain for those whom death touches personally. I hope that they know—the Rebel soldiers, just as the Union soldiers—that they all died to create a nation that must stand firm under God, and will one day rise to prove itself a bastion of freedom for all men."

He sighed deeply. "Of course, I wish to speed recovery. I wish that the last of the battles may come, and that we may begin to heal the great rift between us. But I cannot approve any constitution for any state that is ready to return to the Union if they don't grant equality for all men—white and black." He paused, looking at her. "You're coming closer, aren't you?"

"Yes, sir. And it's more important than ever that you take care of yourself."

"Ah, don't worry! My good friends—military, civilian, Pinkerton—watch out for me. It hurts me, child, to see one so young worry so much."

"You must understand, sir, that you have become the embodiment of the Union."

He smiled. "Ah, yes. Well, the years have been hard and bitter. I think so often of my poor wife. It was a great day when I could come and tell my dear Mary that my enemies had not triumphed, that God himself was on my side, and I won the election the second time."

He cleared his throat. "Tell me, what do you think? I will end my simple words—for a second speech should not be a long one!—with this sentiment, one that we must embrace. 'With malice toward none, with charity for all, with firmness in the right as God gives us to see the right, let us strive on to finish the work we are in, to bind up the nation's wounds, to care for him who shall have borne the battle and for his widow and his orphan, to do all which may achieve and cherish a just and lasting peace among ourselves and with all nations.'"

"I think, Mr. Lincoln, that you are one of the finest politicians and men to ever hold public office," she told him.

He smiled, looking at her. "Do I imagine you?" he asked softly. "Do I need to believe that the enemy will again be my friend, and so I speak to an unknown angel?"

"I, too, often wonder if I am dreaming when we speak," Tara replied.

"So you are real. Are you living? Or perhaps I brought you to me when I attended one of my dear wife's séances in the Red Room?"

"I'm most certainly real, sir. And I'm *coming to help you....*"

He didn't hear her, Tara realized. She was feeling the rush of misty, opaque air again, and she was coming back to lie in her bunk in the captain's cabin aboard the *Freedom.*

She started, almost screaming. She wasn't alone. Finn was seated in the desk chair, opposite her, watching her. He wore a grave expression as he did so.

"You were…gone," he told her.

She eased up against the paneled wall in the niche where the cot was positioned, looked at him, and let out a long sigh. "I told you. I dream that I am with President Lincoln. Or, perhaps, it's some kind of vision. I don't understand myself. I have never met him. When the war began, I understood so little of what was happening. And then, in the summer of 1862, I began to have these dreams."

"We were losing badly in the summer of 1862," Finn reflected.

"Men were dying and Mr. Brady and other photographers were on the battlefields, and we, at home, were able to see how horrible the cost of war!" Tara said. She shook her head. "Finn, I don't know what it is—it's something that I see and feel, but perhaps it's all in my mind, and I am going mad. But then again, as we both know, there are so many things that the world can't see or accept—such as what we are. So perhaps my dreams or visions are real."

"Perhaps," he agreed. "And perhaps you have a talent that I do not."

He didn't touch her; he didn't come closer. It was almost as if he needed to keep a distance. She was surprised by his words when he spoke again. "Have you ever had any such similar experience?"

She frowned, looking back at him. "I knew the night my mother would die," she said. "But she was ill. I believe that other people have had such sensations at the crux of the life of a loved one. Maybe we just see when the illness has run its course. We love someone so much that there's something inside of us that warns us when the end is near."

He was thoughtful for a moment. "I try to come close to each man in the crew. I *should* be able to see through the monster among us, but I can't. I'm somehow blinded, and I can only think that it's someone old, and very adept and experienced. And I feel that we've been playing a game, and that we've been behind each step of the way. And because we're sailing north, and we're coming closer and closer to Washington, I fear that the monster is Gator himself, and that I am bringing him straight to his target."

"We can sail elsewhere," she said.

"That won't solve the situation. I have to ferret out the enemy," he said.

"I don't know who it is," she told him. "I know that it is not me, and that it is not Richard...."

"I've said it many times—I'm not here to accuse you."

"Then?"

"I'm here because I need you."

She sat up in the bed, looking at him. "What do you mean?"

"I'm not at all certain that I believe that those truly dead can rise, that ghosts come back to speak to us, or that poor Mary Lincoln or even President Lincoln have any hope of reaching their lost children. But I do believe that maybe, just maybe, there are more avenues to the human mind than any of us knows. And your mind may be the one that sees," he added quietly. "And, of course, you were in Key West, you were near the fort.... There might have been something, some clue, that just hasn't reached the forefront of your mind as yet."

"What do you want me to do?" she asked.

"Tomorrow, we'll be off the coast of the Carolinas, and soon after that, we'll reach the Washington Naval Yard. Every step of the way, we might well have fallen into the perfect trap. Led to believe that Gator was a Rebel, we hunted down a blockade runner. And once that was achieved and our ship was lost, we were beset. But each battle that we've fought so far, I believe we were intended to win. Except, perhaps, the last. If we'd grappled onto the Union ship yesterday, those men would have taken over, and the *Freedom* would have reached Washington with a company of men ready to create real havoc—while Gator himself got to the president. We have to discover the truth tomorrow, Tara. We have to."

"What is your plan?" she asked.

"Bait," he said softly.

"Bait?"

"You."

She was surprised to feel a chill ripple along her spine. She'd begun this in innocence of what horror could truly await them, but she had followed him every step of the way, and though she remained horrified by the carnage, she knew that she had done well enough.

"What do you want me to do?" she asked him. "I would do anything, you know," she added hastily. "The president must live!"

He lowered his head, smiling. "I'll be at your back, though you may not see me, through every step you take."

"How am I bait?" she asked.

"I have to get you alone with each man," he told her.

"But you've ordered that everyone must stay in threes."

He nodded. "Except, of course, when someone comes to see you aboard the ship. You're right on the main deck here, with activity just beyond the door. There will be a way and a reason to send each man to you."

She shook her head. "Still, I don't see what you will accomplish."

"Gator, I believe wholeheartedly, intends to take over the ship before we reach port. That means he will strike tomorrow or tomorrow night. The men on this ship have learned well, but none has the strength that you and I possess. Given the chance, Gator will want to destroy you as a threat."

"And not you?"

"Oh, yes. But I believe that he sees you as an easier target."

"I'm not an easy target!"

"I didn't say that," he assured her, smiling gravely. "But I have far more experience. If he is able to take you down, he will believe that he can rip through the men. When he's created enough havoc...well, then, he can come for me, without my having hope of any assistance. He's been laying traps for us since I arrived in Key West. It's time for us to lay a trap for him."

Tara nodded. "I will do whatever you think we must. I know that I must reach the president. So...do we start now?"

He looked at her. He lowered his head again for a moment, and then met her eyes. "Tonight, we rest and gather strength," he told her.

She looked at him, and she was ready. But also afraid.

"All right," she murmured.

He started to rise. "I should leave you to that rest."

"No."

"No?"

"Don't leave."

He smiled. "I rather thought that you were angry with me."

"I am."

"Then…?"

"Well, you see, I'm really not that tired. And I do believe a bit of physical exertion would help greatly in that matter," she told him.

There were a dozen arguments they might have had. There were many things they might have said. But they didn't speak at all.

He took her into his arms, and his mouth found hers.

Whatever the morning would bring, Tara thought, she would have the night.

CHAPTER SIXTEEN

FINN STOOD BY CAPTAIN TREMBLAY near the helm; Billy Seabold held the wheel. The wind was staying with them, and the sails billowed beautifully against the bright blue sky.

"Coming closer, and the sailing goes smoothly," Captain Tremblay said.

"Coming closer," Finn agreed. He looked at the captain. "I'm hoping all will be well. I've asked Tara to use a few of her special abilities to ensure it."

Tremblay frowned. "Her abilities? The young woman *is* quite amazing, more adept with a sword than a good portion of the army, I dare say. But, with good luck and God's help, we'll not come across another ship laden with diseased!"

"Well, sir, I know this sounds quite absurd, but then, the situation we've been in has been quite absurd. Tara has other abilities." He spoke loudly. Dr. MacKay was seated on a barrel not far from them, writing in a journal. Grissom was repairing a sail near the helm and several of the other men were involved in mundane tasks of one kind or another in the near vicinity. Whatever he said would be repeated over and over again, until his words were heard by every man on the ship. "She has a strange sense of inner sight, I suppose you might say. There are times when she can *see* what others are thinking. And when something is dire, or eventful, she can sometimes use that to predict what's going to happen."

Tremblay frowned. "Ah, but did the young lady *see* any of the events that have so recently plagued us?"

"A few of them, sir," Finn said. "The human mind is an amazing puzzle, so, no, Tara doesn't *see* all events, just some. It's extremely strange, more than just all the talk you hear about mediums and séances from other venues. Tara can sometimes tap into someone else's mind. I know it to be true, because she's told me about events and people that only I know about."

"I'd have said that all 'spiritualism' was botch!" Captain Tremblay said. "Not long ago, aye, that's what I would have said. The armed forces and half the country have whispered about President Lincoln and his wife, Mary. They say she went off the wall when they lost little Willie in the White House. Séance practices going on—and even the president taking part! I thought it all true rubbish! Now...well, now I say that anything is possible."

He looked at Finn and said seriously, "If only she soon sees into the heart of the traitor who has caused the death and destruction of so many good men!"

"Yes, we can certainly pray that happens. The time grows short before we reach the naval yards at D.C.," Finn said.

"Aye, we'll be on fierce guard!" Tremblay said.

Finn nodded, and walked down the deck toward Dr. MacKay. "A journal, Doctor? It will be interesting to see how you have recorded these days."

MacKay looked up at him sheepishly. "It's interesting recording the truth, and should anyone read what I've written, the truth will surely be regarded as fiction. Actually, I'm thinking of writing it all up as fiction, and perhaps repairing my prewar business by selling this wild story to some publisher."

"Where do you hail from, Doctor?" Finn asked.

"Massachusetts. A little town just outside Boston. My grandfather fought in the American Revolution," MacKay said proudly.

"Was he a doctor, too?" Finn asked.

"No. He was an evil-doer!" MacKay said, laughing. "A politician, but he went to war, fought with General Washington and survived Valley Forge. He lived to tell the tale, and see that I made it through medical school at Harvard."

"Well, then, all the best with your...fiction," Finn said, nodding and walking away. Heading toward the portside rail, he found Charles Lafferty fishing. They were moving at a good clip, but Lafferty was still sending out a line.

"Any luck?" Finn asked him.

"Aye, believe it or not. Three big cod so far! Hoping to have fresh fish for all by suppertime tonight," Lafferty said cheerfully.

"Continued good fortune. I confess, I couldn't begin to fish under these circumstances," Finn told him. "We're moving at a good speed."

"Keeps the bait moving, which the fish like," Lafferty said. He shrugged. "And I come from a long line of fishermen, so it's something I've done since I was a child."

"Are you from Massachusetts, too?"

"Too?"

"The doctor is from the Boston area," Finn said.

"Ah, yes, of course. I did know that. Our pasts have all been lost in the years of the war, I'm afraid.... I'm not from Boston. Gloucester, man, Gloucester! A beautiful place, but brutal sometimes, when winter comes. And still, in winter, we went out to make some of our finest catches, that we did!"

"I daresay, it's almost time that we may look to our old lives again," Finn said, and nodding, he headed down the steps, anxious to see what was going on below. Three of the men were sleeping. Richard and two others were watching over the sleeping men, playing a game of cards.

"All is well here?" Finn asked Richard.

Richard nodded. "One of us dozes off now and then. No one has slept well. But we're doing all right."

"Have you slept?" he asked Richard.

"Enough," Richard assured him.

Finn bid good day to the others and returned topside. He walked back to Tara's cabin, knocked and entered.

She was awake and pretending to give her attention to a book. It was upside down. He righted it for her.

"It has begun," he told her.

"What do we do now?" she asked him, her beautiful hazel eyes as bright as a brushfire.

What was going to happen when they reached Washington?

If they reached Washington.

They had to. The threat aboard the ship was great, and as the days passed, he found himself growing ever more concerned. He had never felt torn like this in his life, lost in a pair of eyes, the scent and every movement and breath of a woman....

And such a fear for the future.

"Finn?" she said, puzzled as she stared back at him.

He couldn't allow his feelings for her to jeopardize the discovery they must make, and the ultimate shipboard battle they must win.

"We wait," he told her. He smiled. "You now have truly remarkable powers! They'll all be watching you."

"And you?"

"I'll be watching them," he told her quietly.

FINN WAS STRANGE. But, of course he was; she was surely strange herself. They were tense, waiting for the horrible event that was sure to occur.

As the day wore on and the afternoon arrived, Finn was convinced that his words about her "abilities" had traveled through the men on the ship. She wandered out on deck with her book—carefully held in the upright position—and found a seat near the helm where the breeze was cool but the day bright, and the sun like a sweet beacon in the sky.

She wasn't there long before she heard her name called softly.

"Miss Fox!"

She turned. Billy Seabold was standing by the rail behind her, staring at her with a curious expression.

"Yes, Billy?" she said, turning to look at him.

"Would you…would you talk with me in private a bit?"

Tension gripped her muscles as if a great hand had clamped down upon her.

"Of course, Billy," she managed to say.

Captain Tremblay was standing by the helm; Charles Lafferty had the great wheel.

Finn was down in the center of the ship talking with Dr. MacKay, and Richard was topside with Grissom and London, cleaning and filleting a cache of fish.

She stood, and eased toward the stern with Billy. She tried to make sure that she kept a distance of a few feet between them.

He struggled to speak for a minute. "I hear that you have very special powers, Miss Fox."

"Perhaps that information is something that shouldn't have been shared by Agent Dunne," she murmured.

He touched her arm, as if reaching for her. She gripped the rail hard, not wanting to appear to be frightened of him. He started to speak again, and then hesitated. He moved a bit closer to her, and she looked around, hoping that the others were watching.

"Miss Fox, I have to know," he said.

"You have to know what, Billy?"

He let out a long breath. He was even closer. She was nearly pinned to the rail.

"I need to know about..."

His face was so close to hers. She felt that she could almost see him change, almost see something come over his face and his eyes. She was afraid that when he opened his mouth again, she would see that his fangs had extended, and that he wasn't the young man she had thought that she had known.

"Eric Wordsmith," he said.

"Pardon?"

Billy began to speak quickly. "He was my mate. My best friend. We opted into the navy together, and he was killed in a sea battle early on in the war. He was terrified of hell, but he was a good fellow, he really was. He thought that God would damn us all for taking arms against our brothers. I think about him night and day, and I'm praying that you can *see*...that Eric rests in heaven."

"What's going on here?" Finn demanded suddenly, breaking between them.

Billy flushed to the roots of his hair.

"It's all right, it's all right!" Tara said quickly. "Billy just had a question for me, Finn. That's all. Just a question."

Billy backed away. "I mean, begging your pardon, please?" he said to Tara. "You see, it was my fault that Eric was in this thing. I wanted to be in the navy, and Eric joined up because of me."

She smiled at him. "Billy, I believe that God knows that men were forced to make a choice. I think He knows that Eric was a good man, caught up in a horrible war. God weeps at the loss of life, and we all have to hope that it's been for a greater cause, and we'll all go on to a better life. I doubt you need to worry, Billy. I believe that your friend rests with God, in heaven, and that all will be well for him."

Billy reached for her hands in a sudden motion that brought Finn instantly stepping between them.

"It's all right!" she said softly. She squeezed Billy's hands.

He smiled at her gratefully. "Your pardon, Agent Dunne," he said to Finn, and then he walked away, heading toward the fish-cleaning project, whistling a sad tune as he walked.

Tara looked at Finn and grimaced. "Most likely, the men will just be asking me about their loved ones who have died," she said.

"I'm sorry, but I needed to start something about your mental powers of observation. I hadn't anticipated that *those* would be the primary questions they'd have...."

"It's fine. It's just that I can't see behind the veil of death. How will I know if someone is asking me about a human monster?"

He studied her intently for a moment. "Your dreams of Abraham Lincoln seem to be so intense and real. Maybe you do see more than you imagine."

"I can't see who the monster might be," she said quietly. She shook her head. "Finn, perhaps he or she isn't aboard the ship. You have been a detective for a long time. And," she added softly, looking around, "you are half vampire—you should be able to *see* who this is!"

He was frustrated; she saw that instantly. His fists clenched at his sides and his features tightened, but she knew that he wasn't angry with her.

"I can't see, and that makes me really afraid. Believe me, this vampire is here. And he's old, and far more experienced than me."

She tried to appear strong and confident.

"Perhaps then, you shouldn't spend so much time with me. Let the others come," she said.

He nodded. "I will be near. I will be watching. At all times."

"So I pray. And now, sir, if you will please…go."

Finn walked away, heading to the helm where he spoke with Captain Tremblay. Soon after, Richard left his work and came to stand by her.

"All is well?" he asked softly.

She wrinkled her nose. "You smell like fish."

"You won't be looking down at me like that tonight when you dine on cod fillets, Miss Fox!"

She smiled, but her smile faded quickly. "I am fine. How are you doing? Richard, I fear for you. You are so

often among the men, and with this building air of dis-
trust...."

"They're tired," he said. "Even spelling one another
in groups of three to see that we are on guard for one
another. Today, I was on guard shift with two of the
men—Samuels and Humphrey—and Humphrey dozed
off. Samuels went to wake him, and I nearly panicked
and attacked Samuels. The anxiety among us *is* growing, but not for nationalistic reasons."

"With every mile," she said. "Every man walks
about, doing his duty. But I see that they are strained. I
see it in their faces."

"Nothing will happen by day," Richard said.

"You're so certain?"

"Aye, this man will wait for the darkness," he told
her. He smiled then. "I smell that badly of fish? I will
go wash up, and leave you to your observations."

Richard left her. She gave her attention to her book.
It was an excellent book—*Tales of the Sea*—but she
couldn't make her eyes focus on the words and they
began to blur before her. As she read, a man would approach her now and then, asking what she saw for them,
if anything.

Many asked about their loved ones.

The wind shifted direction. Captain Tremblay shouted
orders, and the men scurried about to trim the sails.

And finally, the sun began to lower in the western sky.

Billy Seabold and several of the men prepared a
smoke over with a large pot and coal from the steam

room, and soon the smell of the fresh-cooked fish began to waft across the deck. Rum portions were ladled out, and limes and coconuts and other still-fresh produce completed the meal.

Everyone was topside; none of the men were sleeping.

As she ate, Tara tried to speak with all the men, pretending that she wasn't aware of the way they all looked at her, wondering just what might lurk in her mind.

When she had finished with her fish and thanked Billy Seabold and the others, she found that Captain Tremblay was behind her. He wanted to lure her back to the helm with him.

She looked at him. *No! It can't be this man, it can't be!*

But she let herself be led.

The captain excused Grissom, who had been at the wheel, and took over the helm himself. And as he looked ahead he asked her, "Can you see the future? Can you really see the dead?"

"I see some things," she said.

He nodded, still looking ahead. Richard and Finn were together, she noticed. And she was certain they were both aware of her situation.

She forced herself to stand still; Tremblay seemed to be shaking. His hands on the wheel were knotted hard.

"God help me...is the war ending?" he asked.

She tried not to let him see the instant frown that creased her forehead. "I believe so, sir."

"But you don't...*see* it?"

"No," she told him quietly. "I know what you know, sir. That the South is drastically short on supplies, that the young men die and cannot be replaced. That the North, with its great manufacturing abilities, is making more and more guns, and that more and more immigrants are stepping off ships to join the Union ranks. I believe that generals such as Lee are desperately hoping for a great victory to turn the tide—and God knows, Lee is a great general—but his men and his resources are being depleted."

Tremblay winced. "Do you see *me* surviving the war?"

Tara was surprised by his question, but even more surprised when it seemed that her vision clouded. She was looking at Tremblay, but she was not seeing him as he stood at the helm. She saw him, stricken, holding his chest, with a pool of blood surrounding him. The image was so strong that for a moment she felt as if she would cry out loud. She gave herself a mental shake, and she spoke quickly, "Captain Tremblay, I can't see all futures—really, I can't."

But what had she seen?

Shaken, she excused herself quickly.

She headed back to the center of the ship where others were still milling, finishing their meals. Grissom sat up on the rail, playing his harmonica. But no one was laughing or joking, and the songs that Grissom played only added to the melancholy.

She walked over to stand by Richard and Finn and she said quietly, "I think I should go back to the cabin."

"I'll escort you," Finn said.

When he entered the cabin, he made a thorough search of the small space before sighing and taking a seat at the desk, the look upon his face one of deep frustration.

"Anything?" he asked her. "Anything at all?"

She wanted to go to him, to touch his face, to curl up on his lap and somehow be able to reassure him that they would be all right. But they weren't all right, and she was afraid. She shook her head. "I'm sorry. Tremblay...I was afraid that I saw him dying when he spoke to me. And Billy wanted to know about a friend. And I tried to look at each man and see how he looked at me in return, but...nothing."

Finn nodded, looking toward the curtained windows. "Darkness is coming quickly," he said. "And now, I'm afraid for you to go out among them, afraid of what I've done. Still, I see no other alternative."

She didn't get a chance to answer him; she wasn't able to say that it was all right. There was a demanding knock at the door and a cry for help. "Finn! Agent Dunne!"

Finn rose quickly and threw the door open. Dr. MacKay was standing there. There was a slash on his face and blood oozed from it; he seemed unaware.

"What is it, man? For God's sake, what is it?" Finn demanded.

"Down below…we don't even know how it started, but the men are all at one another—they're afraid of each other…. It's horrible!" MacKay shouted.

"I'm coming," Finn said. He turned to Tara. "Lock yourself in here. Don't let anyone in, anyone but me!"

He hurried out the door. MacKay stared at Tara so long she thought that he was going to smile suddenly.

"MacKay!" Finn said.

Dr. MacKay turned and followed Finn out of the room.

Tara began to pace. She looked at the door and longed to follow the men below and find out what was happening.

The ship gave a sudden pitch, nearly sending her to the floor.

There was no one at the helm, she thought.

She chafed, catching her balance, standing for a moment to feel the yaw and move beneath her.

She couldn't just stay there!

"Tara!"

There was a banging at her door, and the muffled sound of someone calling her in great distress.

Don't open the door; Finn had told her not to open the door.

She stood still, waiting. She heard the voice again.

"Tara, please! Tara, it's Richard!"

Richard! Of course he had not meant Richard. She walked quickly to the door, drew the bolt and opened it.

Richard staggered in. There was blood dripping

down his forehead, covering part of his shirt and crusted around his neck.

"Sit down, sit down, quickly, before you fall!" she told him, grabbing his arm and dragging him to the chair. "What happened? What's going on? Where's Finn?"

"Finn…he's trying to…restore some kind of order."

"What happened?" she demanded.

"I don't even know…don't know where it started. We were suddenly all defending ourselves from…from one another. One of the men…London! He looked at me and cut me with his knife. And then the others thought it was me, and I cried out that London had started it, and he cried out saying that it was another…and suddenly we were all belowdeck, and no one knows who started attacking who and—"

"Let me see to your wounds," Tara said.

"No, no!" he said, trying to push her away.

"Richard, damn you, sit still!" she said.

She jerked his hand away from his throat, and it was then that she saw the marks there that told her the truth. He had been bitten. He jumped to his feet with a sudden strength and energy that astounded her, and she fell back, staring at him.

"Richard, you need a doctor, and you need one fast," she told him.

He looked at her, shaking his head. "I have to stop you," he said, his voice thick. "I…" He paused, as if in great confusion. "I…have to stop you."

He lumbered toward her. She gripped him by the shoulders, and was surprised by the electric feel of him, and the strength in him.

"Richard! Stop!" she commanded.

To her relief, he fell back. Again, confusion reigned in his face, and a sudden sob escaped him. "I don't know...I don't understand. My God, what has taken hold of me?"

He fell back against the wall. "I am to kill you," he said, horrified.

Then he brought hands to his temples, as if he could squeeze his mind between them. "He's telling me that I have to kill you, but I cannot—a thousand bees are stinging my head!"

He pushed away from the wall. He shook his head and stared at her, and it seemed as if his eyes burned, and then went blank. Her sword rested on the desk. Richard reached for it. She knew that he was an excellent swordsman; he had taught her how to fight.

He came at her, and she waited. When he was almost upon her, she sprang into a leap and jumped over his head, pushing off the ceiling as a springboard and coming down hard upon his back. She latched onto him with a vice grip, but he shook her off and turned.

"Richard, it is me, Tara. I am your best friend. I am your sister, and you don't want to hurt me. God knows, I don't want to hurt you!" she cried.

He paused. His arm went slack.

There were tears in his eyes. "I love you!" he said.

She went forward swiftly, hoping to wrest the sword from him while he stood in weakness.

But the fire shot back into his eyes. He clenched the sword with an iron grasp and she nearly impaled herself upon it.

"Richard, no!"

He came forward in a single bound, pinning her to the desk. He started to raise the sword.

"Richard, it's Tara, your friend, your lifelong friend! Stop!"

He stood, frozen, staring at her, and again the tears appeared in the depths of his eyes.

"No, no, no!" he cried out.

He was frozen above her; she didn't know if he would gain control, or if the sword would fall.

But the door burst open.

Finn rushed in, and the sword was ripped from Richard's arms. Finn spun him around, ready to use the sword to decapitate Richard.

"No!" Tara cried, rushing forward, and forcing Finn to stay his blade.

"Tara, he's been bitten, infected," Finn said harshly.

"But he can be cured! I know he can be cured. Finn, no!" she cried.

They heard a scream from the deck.

Finn drew his pistol. Tara screamed herself, certain that he meant to ignore her for the good of the nation and shoot Richard point-blank.

But he didn't.

He brought the gun smashing hard against Richard's skull, and her old friend went down without a sound and lay in a heap on the floor.

"Bind him well," Finn ordered. "Make sure he cannot escape, do you understand me? Next time, I will have to kill him."

More cries had arisen from the deck. Tara did as bidden, using sheets and ripping down the curtains to assure herself that she could bind Richard's wrists and ankles, and then tie him to the bed.

When she finished, she heard more cries from the deck. She couldn't stay there when beyond the door men were dying, and a demon had created mayhem.

She threw open the door. Captain Tremblay stood before her.

Stood, as he had in her vision, earlier that day.

His crisp white naval shirt was covered in blood.

She cried out and hurried to him.

And he fell into her arms.

Looking around, she saw that the men all engaged in battle against one another. It was horrible to behold. She looked at Captain Tremblay's throat, and she found no marks. She dragged him back into the cabin and laid him upon the stripped bed.

Quickly, she ripped open his shirt and discovered that he had taken a stab wound to his chest. She staunched it the best she could, and tried to feel the depth of it. He was losing a great deal of blood. She had to stop the flow.

As she did so, the door burst open.

MacKay. He was gasping for breath, and like the others, he seemed to have been sprayed with blood. His eyes were wide and panicked, and he stumbled into the room. He grasped her arm, hard, and for a moment, panic seized her. She leaped to her feet, throwing him off. He went flying against the cabin wall, and sank down, dazed. He didn't even seem to realize that she had thrown him off.

"It's bedlam! Blood, there's so much blood—everyone attacking everyone!"

Tara walked over to him, reached down for his hands and jerked him to his feet. When he was standing, she slapped him hard against the cheek.

He let out a cry of indignation, and his eyes flew wide open. And then he stared at her and let out a long breath, moaning softly.

"My God, I am a coward," he said remorsefully.

"You have to help the captain. He is bleeding to death. I've tried to stop the flow, but you must do something," she said.

"The captain!" he said, and he seemed to recover his senses. Richard groaned, and MacKay seemed to notice him for the first time.

"What…you have him trussed like a Christmas pig," he said, staring at Tara. "Not Richard, oh, Lord, not Richard…"

"No, not Richard, but he's been bitten. Don't let

him up. Go over there, and help the captain!" she commanded.

"Yes, yes, of course, the captain."

MacKay rushed to Captain Tremblay's side and quickly removed the wad of cloth Tara had used to stop the flow of blood. She saw him probe the captain and study the wound. "No vital organs have been hit. It is not too deep, though it bleeds severely. I can staunch the flow and clean the wound—alcohol, whatever you have in here—but he'll need proper stitches," he said.

Tara hurried to obey his request, digging in the desk for a bottle of rum.

"I need my bag," he told her. "I need my sutures and needles."

"Where are they?"

"Below, beneath the lowest bunk closest to the aft," he told her.

"I will get them. Whatever you do, don't let Richard loose!"

She rose and headed to the cabin door.

The cries and the awful sound of swordplay, steel against steel, could still be heard from the deck.

She started out. As she did so, Billy Seabold fell back against the wall of the cabin. He looked exhausted; his sword had fallen to his side.

"Billy, are you injured?" she asked quickly.

"I don't know...I don't know.... Help me, oh, God, please help me, Tara!"

He was about to topple over fully but she caught

him, dragging him back into the cabin. It was growing crowded but she found a place on the floor, near the bunk.

"Another!" MacKay said, groaning. "My supplies will not go so far!"

Tara bent over Billy herself. His eyes had closed, and she touched his cheek.

When he opened his eyes, he looked up at her and smiled. "You are really so sweet, Tara. What a pity. I began to tell you that tale about Eric, and all you wanted to do was reassure me. But, of course, there was no Eric...."

It wasn't until his last words registered in her mind that Tara realized the awful truth of it all.

He gripped her shoulders, and his hold was so powerful that she thought her bones would shatter. He threw her from him and came to his feet. MacKay cried out with a sound of horror, and remained frozen next to the unconscious captain.

Tara kept herself from falling back. She looked quickly for the sword, but it was down by Richard. She didn't know if she could reach it in time.

"Why?" she whispered to Billy. "Why all this death and mayhem?"

He barely moved; it was as if he leaped in a puff of smoke, and was directly in front of her again, staring into her eyes.

"Why? Because the predators among us will be strong. And because the idiots on the battlefield aren't doing enough." He smiled, and worked his jaw, and it opened wide. All she saw were eerily long fangs gleaming with an opalescence she had never witnessed before.

"Why?" he asked again. "Because I am Gator, and Lincoln must die. But I'm ever so afraid, my lovely little creature, you must die first."

CHAPTER SEVENTEEN

"STOP! STOP NOW!" Finn roared, leaping atop a barrel and shouting down at the men who were desperately fighting one another for their lives. He cried out, using the power within him to create a megaphone of his voice, a sound so loud that it shuddered with the breeze and seemed to bring with it a sudden warm wind.

"Now!" he thundered.

As fierce as the noise on deck had been, the sudden silence that followed his shout was just as menacing. While swords ceased to clash, the men looked up at him, suspicion and fear still clouding their eyes, their grips still taut on their weapons.

"You've become madmen!" he said. "You're lashing out with no knowledge of what you're doing. Where did this start? Damn you, men, speak up! When did it start?"

Grissom cleared his throat and nervously moved forward. "Down below, Agent Dunne. All I know is that Richard Anderson was suddenly upon me and I shoved him off, and London moved in on me—"

"Because you were attacking Richard Anderson!" London said, stepping out of the group.

"I wasn't attacking him—I was warding him off!" Grissom returned angrily.

"Who was below?" Finn demanded.

"Everyone rushed down when the fighting started—"

"No! Who was there when it started?" Finn demanded.

Grissom spoke up. "It was me and London, Richard Anderson, Billy, the Doc and Lafferty."

"Where are the others?" Finn demanded. "Step forward, men!"

"I'm here, sir," Charles Lafferty said, moving around his latest combatant.

"Where are the captain, the doctor and Billy Seabold?" Finn demanded.

No one spoke; everyone looked around.

"I think I saw the captain. He was wounded," Lafferty said.

Wounded, and now not to be seen. Richard was in the cabin with Tara....

"Stop your fighting. It's not a man among you," Finn shouted, thrusting his way through them to reach her quarters.

He didn't knock, or call out; he threw the door open.

And there he saw the missing men—and Tara.

The captain was lying on the bed, bleeding. MacKay was at his side, holding a cloth to the captain's chest, staring across the cabin with stricken eyes.

Richard still lay trussed on the floor.

And Billy Seabold. No longer looking like a fresh, young seaman.

He had Tara. He had his hands on her, and there was now no missing the fact of his nature. His form had changed entirely, as if he had cast off a costume. He was larger, his muscles far more heavily honed. And his features had shifted, too. His face was narrower.

Cruel.

And he had long, long fangs, and they dripped the saliva of expectation over Tara's neck.

He had to know what she was! He had to know that he would sicken if he drank the blood of another vampire, even a half-breed.

But he had to be old, old and powerful, to wear such a complete disguise, day after day. Maybe he had lived so long that such rules no longer applied to him.

Maybe he didn't care.

Maybe he just meant to rip her throat to shreds.

"Billy Seabold," Finn began, thinking and playing for time.

Billy smiled, except that it wasn't a smile, not when his fangs were so grossly visible. It was a terrible grimace of amusement, power and cruelty.

Tara's eyes met Finn's. She didn't appear to be afraid, and yet, he could see she trembled slightly in the monster's grasp.

"Agent Dunne! Ah, yes, Agent Dunne, the great detective. What a race you have run, eh? Convinced that you must be looking for a Southern spy, a mad patriot to the Southern cause! It's been so much fun watching you. Fun, actually, since I joined the Union Navy, and hunted here and there, planting my newly made comrades where they could best serve. Some of them were quite happy, you know—they enjoyed their newfound power. And, of course, I did find a few old friends to join me along the way."

"A few old friends," Finn said. "Very old friends, I'm assuming. I believe we met a few of them on the island when the ships were destroyed? Before going to Key West?"

Billy laughed, never moving an inch from Tara. His fingers moved over her neck as he held her hard against him. His mouth remained close to the alabaster flesh, and Finn could see where her pulse pounded against a pale blue vein.

"I believe old Cutthroat Bennigan was among them, yes. Old pirate friend of mine from days long gone by. Met him years ago, off the coast of Bermuda."

Finn shook his head, as if bewildered. "So, where did you really come from, Seabold?"

"I was born in the midst of Revolution, my friend. Born as I am now. Born at a time where the founding fathers were putting together a country, and now, the Northern autocrats would dictate the freedoms we died for then. So, while I do enjoy ripping a human to shreds once in a while and feasting on blood, it's the cause that sends me on this mission. And, Agent Dunne, you will not stop me!"

Billy lifted his head; he looked like a cobra about to strike.

Finn used all of his strength in his movement. Tara was ready to fight. And yet, even with her formidable strength and him flying to the rescue like a speeding bullet, they might not have moved quickly enough to save her.

It was Richard who suddenly kicked out with his still-bound legs. Richard who, with his infected power, had more impetus and speed than ever. He managed to lash his legs against Billy Seabold's, and as he did, Tara swung around with an elbow, catching Billy Seabold in the soft flesh beneath his ribs. Finn was immediately before him, gripping him by the neck, avoiding the lash of his fangs and lifting him with all his power. Throwing him headfirst into a wall.

Now a distance from Tara, Billy rose, a horrible hissing sound of rage issuing from his lips. He kicked Richard where he lay on the floor, and Finn was sure that he heard a rib crack.

Richard cried out.

Tara dived for a sword.

Finn drew his weapon and advanced on Billy.

But the vampire saw that his cause here was lost.

He reached for a decanter on the desk, threw it and cried out, "Death to you all, death to tyrants! You will not stop me!"

And then he was gone.

Finn knew that he hadn't *vanished*. But his speed had

been such that he had seemed to disappear into thin air, and now he couldn't be seen. Billy Seabold had lost the ship, and he knew it. He had tried to get the majority of the men to kill one another, likely hoping to change just enough to sail the ship straight into a destination where he could tear apart the country. But he hadn't succeeded. Alone, and with his battle among the others lost, he had to abandon the ship.

Finn raced out on deck, but the vampire was nowhere to be seen. Men were now helping those they had battled just moments before; Charles Lafferty had taken the helm, and the *Freedom* was on her way again, heading for the naval yards of D.C.

"Agent Dunne!" Lafferty roared to him, a question in his voice.

"It's over, Charles. Keep your heading steady!" Finn called back.

He turned, quickly heading back into the cabin. Tara was on her knees by Richard. MacKay, a little unsteady, had risen. "I need my doctor's field kit. The captain is breathing and his pulse is steady, and already, the wound seems to be healing. But I'll stitch him up."

"No need," Finn told him. "Not if you believe he's healing already." He hesitated because MacKay was looking at him in surprise. "The captain has Tara's blood now. He will heal."

Finn came over and hunkered down by Tara. "I have to go," he told her. "Billy Seabold is off the ship and headed to Washington."

She shook her head, tears in her eyes. "Richard! Richard needs blood," she said.

He set a hand on her shoulder. "Dr. MacKay can do a transfusion. We know that Richard will do well—even infected, he wouldn't kill you. You stay with him. I'll see you in Washington."

"No. You need me. You can't go without me," Tara said. Her eyes were brilliant, burning red-gold, and her chin was set stubbornly.

"Tara, you'll have to stay here if you want to save Richard. And I should face Gator on my own. I'll need to move quickly."

Tears sprang into her eyes. "He's older and more powerful than you, Finn. You can't go alone. You can't!"

"He doesn't need to go alone."

The voice startled him and Tara, as well. Finn swung around.

Captain Tremblay was already sitting up. He patted his chest, and then moved the bandages that had been pressed against it. Barely a scratch seemed to remain. He looked down on his wounds incredulously and then looked at them again, smiling. "I have your blood in my veins, Tara Fox. And I imagine the wonderful healing power in yours has now taken root in mine. I can help to save your Richard, with the assistance of the good doctor here."

Tara stood, facing Richard. "I must go with you, Finn. Surely, you can see that. He is powerful. You need me."

He walked over to where she stood by Richard, who lay with his eyes closed, scarcely breathing.

"He needs *you*," he told her softly, pulling her to her feet. "And I need you to stay with the ship, because if I fail, you will be all that's left to stop him when he reaches the capital. Tara, I'm going to take one route, and you're going to stay with the ship. When I reach land, I'll put the call out for help. But we know exactly where he's going. I believe that he'll reach land, find himself some other conveyance and head straight back to the shipyards. You must stay with the *Freedom,* and be ready in case…in case he gets to me first. Tara, before God, I wish that we could do this together, but we can't."

She stared back at him, and he knew that she was searching his eyes to discover the truth of his words.

"Please," he added softly. "Time is everything now. I could meet up with him, slow him down and still survive to fight with you in the capital. Or we could come upon him together, and both be killed, and there would be no hope."

She nodded slowly, but the look in her eyes showed him that she felt she was losing her soul. He didn't know if he could tear himself away, watching her.

He had to.

He pulled her to him, heedless of anyone around him, and he dared take a moment to hold her close, and kiss her lips, and savor the touch and scent of her, beautiful memories to warm his flesh in the frigid waters that awaited him, thoughts to remember that he had everything to live for.

They kissed, and kissed, and he felt her arms and her lips and the heat of her body.

And then he pulled away, his hands still holding hers. "Captain Tremblay, make all haste to the Washington Naval Yard."

He dropped her hands and hurried out on deck. He judged the distance from sea to land and plunged into the water. The Atlantic seemed unaware that spring was approaching; the sea was bitterly cold.

TARA WAS IN AGONY.

While Tremblay insisted that he could afford the blood to save Richard, she could not allow it. The captain had healed remarkably, but he still didn't have the strength that was hers, nor had he been born with the blood that could save. She fought him tooth and nail and with complete logic, assuring him that he was the only one who could bring them to their destination with all speed.

And so, she lay quietly while Dr. MacKay gingerly performed the operation with needles and tubes that would send her blood through Richard's veins, and save his life. When it was over, she was weak, and she rested on the cot, just thinking about Finn, and still reeling at the fact that Billy Seabold, who had seemed so young, earnest and *normal,* could have proven to be such a monster.

She could hear the commotion on deck, and she knew

that Tremblay was busy sailing with Charles Lafferty as his right hand, and that Dr. MacKay was busy patching up the men who had been injured.

She heard the sad sound of Lafferty's harmonica after the captain's words over those who hadn't been saved, but had to be sent to watery graves, heads separated from their bodies, just in case.

Then the precious darkness of sleep overcame her.

She dreamed again that night of the president. He had been sleeping, just as she had been. He was in a long nightdress, and he lay next to his Mary, who was resting at his side. Seeing her, the president rose, and walked to meet her at the foot of the bed. "Let's go to the hallway, shall we? Sleep is essential to Mary. It is the only time that she doesn't grieve."

They stepped into the hallway.

"We're almost here, sir," she told him. "Finn has left us, because he is in pursuit of Gator, and you can't imagine what that one man can do. He is extremely powerful. He can turn the city into a sea of traitorous monsters, heedless for their own lives. Finn believes he will reach land and find another ship, and he will make it into the naval yard and, from there, descend upon the men by stealth, picking them off and making them his followers, one by one. I am still with Captain Tremblay, and we are racing here, as well."

The president set his hand on her hair gently. "As the war dies down, the capital is now, at last, very well defended."

"No, sir, you must understand. This one man can infect hundreds, and quickly."

"I've been aware, my dear, and I know those who have fought such wretched disease and insanity before. They will be there to help you." He smiled. "I know your sister and your brother, and they have both done their share, along with others, in this war." Like a father, he pulled her to him and kissed the top of her head. "We'll be ready."

She stared at him, still so afraid. But he smiled. "It's the country that must be saved, Tara. No man is greater than the country."

He began to fade, and she awoke with a start.

She discovered that Richard was sitting by her side. She almost jumped away, but he winced quickly, seeing her expression. "It's over, Tara. I am me. You saved me."

She eased back, allowing herself a little smile. "You were well worth saving, Mr. Richard Anderson. Under the worst of circumstances, you fought the killer instinct. And you actually managed to save the day, you know."

He was pleased with the compliment. "We all need one another in this world, I think." He rose to answer a knock at the door. It was Dr. MacKay, and he carried a tray. There was a delightful scent of something cooked over their brazier, dried beef freshened with salt and pepper in boiling water, hardtack coconut meat and a small tankard that she was pretty sure was filled with blood.

"How's our patient?" he asked.

"Strong and rested," she assured him.

"Good. The captain says we'll make the naval yard by tomorrow dusk. You'll need to be rested," he said, and leaving the tray, he went out to attend to his other patients.

Richard followed him, but paused at the door. He looked back at her and smiled. "You know, Miss Fox, we all do need one another in this world. And it's rare when a man or woman finds that perfect person. There's no one in government of society who can stop them from being together. So, my darling friend, sister, I'm telling you this as one who loves you deeply—stop being a stubborn fool and stop being afraid that you may love someone more than a person loves you. For God's sake, Tara, marry that man!" he said.

"He hasn't asked me," she told him.

Richard grinned. "Then ask *him!*"

She felt a strange trembling seize her and she was surprised when she spoke with quivering lips. "Richard, we may not survive that long."

"All the more reason, Tara," he said seriously, "that if you do, you be honest with yourself, and with him, and seize the happiness you are both surely due."

With that, he left the cabin.

FINN MADE LAND IN Northern Virginia. Exhausted, he lay on the ground, breathing, gathering his strength again. He closed his eyes, and the thunder of his breath was so loud, and he was so exhausted, that he didn't hear the approaching men.

When he opened his eyes, he was surrounded by soldiers.

Union men, he saw with gratitude.

Someone poked him with the business end of a rifle. "Get up, man! Identify yourself!"

"Phineas Dunne," he said, "Pinkerton agent. It's imperative that I reach the capital as quickly as possible." He tried to get to his feet, but he staggered. A man reached out to help him.

"We'll get you to the general," he was told. "Have you credentials?"

"Who is the general in charge here?" he asked.

"Ulysses S. Grant, and he'll know the truth of you, that's for sure. And if you're lying, and you're a Reb spy, you'll hang, sir! General Grant shows pity on fighting men, but spies…spies hang from the neck until dead!"

"Just get me to him. Speed is of the essence now. By God, speed is everything!"

Finn chafed at any time spent away from his pursuit, but the swim across miles of ocean had cost him dearly. Nor did he wish to cause harm to these officers. He allowed himself to be escorted and seated atop one on the soldier's mounts, again chafing at the time it took to reach the federal encampment. There was more time when lesser officers argued his position, and then finally agreed that Grant must have the final say. By the time he was ushered into the field tent where the general sat with maps, a bottle of whiskey and a cigar before him, he'd been given dry clothing, and he was feeling the return of warmth and power to his muscles.

"Dunne!"

Finn was surprised when Grant recognized him immediately. They had only met briefly, and that before the general had been sent to the Western campaign, years before. Grant actually rose, and reached for his hand. "A glass, man, bring a glass," he ordered his aide. "This man is in sound need of a drink!"

Yes, a small portion of blood would be nice right now, Finn thought.

But he accepted a whiskey instead.

"I must make Washington, D.C., with all haste, general," Finn said. "There is a spy about to land in the area, and I believe he will have killed somewhere along the coast to acquire a ship for access into the capital. I need to send a special warning to the president, and to certain men in the capital who have dealt with such a man and his life before. Can you get a telegraph out for me?"

"Indeed, I can, and if this matter be so grave, I can send men with you," the general replied.

"I must find this man myself, sir, and the problem is that he spreads a disease. It is better to trust no man than take a chance trusting one who has been infected. I need a conveyance into the capital—the quickest route possible."

Grant nodded, still watching him.

"General, the president's life lies in the balance."

Grant stood. "I will see that you are accompanied to Lieutenant Dickson, who will get your telegraph out. And I will help you with whatever provisions and God's speed that I am able to supply."

"Thank you," Finn told him.

Grant nodded. "If you get to the president, let him know this personally from me. I have General Lee all but pinned down here." He pointed to the map. "He is low on men, and the land is all but stripped. He is feeling the noose of the blockades and knows that there is nothing more than what he has. If Lee will surrender, the South will be broken. God help me, I fear that I will sacrifice thousands more men, but we will corner Lee, here in Virginia. A good man, a brilliant commander, one who might well have stopped the war years ago, had he only agreed when Lincoln asked him to head the Union army." He lifted his glass. "To my enemy. May he survive, and may we end this quickly, while American men—of all states—still live."

Finn lifted his glass in turn, feeling Grant's determination, and his sorrow.

DUSK FELL AND THE *USS Freedom* made its way through the waterways, halted time and again by the guards of the defense system that surrounded the capital.

Tara was on deck when they at last made port, and she eagerly examined the yard and those who were working there. It had taken them nearly two full days to arrive, and she was heartily afraid that danger and death might well have arrived before them. But, there was a bustle about everywhere, and it seemed that the men were fine. Even at dusk, men were working in the shipyard, and the guard that greeted them as they debarked was fierce.

Captain Tremblay immediately wanted to know if there had been any disturbance in the area; they were assured that there had not been.

Lieutenant John Dahlgren, in charge of the yard, was absent, overseeing the launch of a new ship, but a Captain Myers was at the officers' building, a beautiful residence with terraces and built-in brick, cleanly painted and welcoming, and had insisted they report there.

Beneath the glow of a bright new moon and the many lamps that burned around the busy area, the yard presented a strange spectacle of peace; across the river Tara could see sloping fields and farms, all restful as night fell. Following Captain Tremblay, with Richard and Dr. MacKay at her side, she hurried toward the officers' building.

Many soldiers and sailors were housed there as the war progressed. Tara kept a sharp eye on the men they passed as they were escorted in and led to an office on the second floor. They entered alone, and soon after, Captain Myers came into the room, ready to greet them.

Myers was a young man, perhaps in his late twenties at best. He greeted them with a salute, and while he asked them to sit, Captain Tremblay remained standing. "Sir! It's imperative that we know of any ships that might have made port in the past forty-eight hours, and of any disturbance, no matter how small, that might have occurred in that time," Tremblay told him. "We have immediate knowledge of an especially heinous and…diseased spy who was attempting to arrive and, from here, attack the president of the United States!"

"Captain Tremblay, please, sir, take a seat. We've had no such arrivals, nor have we endured the least disturbance. I can see to it that you and your crew are housed for the night, and that your ship is refurbished, and then send you on your way again." He stared point-edly at Tara. "Miss…what would your function be on this journey?"

"I know the spy," she said. "I can point him out to you."

He lowered his head, his lips curving into a half smile. "Miss, trust me, at this point of the war, we have dealt with many spies. Indeed, one of the finest ladies in Washington society, Mrs. Rose Greenhow, was caught for her espionage for the Southern front. She abided for a while in prison, and was sent south. I hear that the woman died, drowned, after attempting to procure for-eign assistance for the Rebels. You see, we have learned, and we will prevail."

Tara stood, placing her hands on the desk. "Lieuten-ant, this is a spy like no other. The men from this ship and I need to mingle with the officers, enlisted men and shipbuilders here. This man, called Gator by many—a known figure wanted by the Pinkerton agency—is talented beyond all expectations. We are also expecting a Pinkerton agent to have arrived here in pursuit of this spy."

"Dunne isn't with you?" Lieutenant Myers asked.

He knew about Finn. There was only one way.

Tara gave a hard look at the man's eyes. And she saw the little rim of red around the irises.

Myers realized that she recognized him for what he was—diseased.

He let out a hissing sound, curling his lips back as he pounced from behind his desk. He leaped toward her, but he was no Billy Seabold. Captain Tremblay pushed back, drawing his naval sword, but Tara didn't need his assistance to ward off the man. She caught him by the neck as he struggled to reach her. Captain Tremblay skewered him through the back, and straight through to the front, but not before the man managed to choke out a loud cry.

As Tremblay retrieved his sword from the body and Tara threw the man down, they heard the pounding of footsteps in the hall, men answering the cry of alarm from their commander. "His head, his head, be thorough!" Tara cried, wrenching Myers's sword from its hilt. Tremblay decapitated the man with a now-practiced swing.

"Lord, they'll think us murderers!" Dr. MacKay said.

"He's here—Billy Seabold is here," Tara answered him. "We've got to defend ourselves. And try not to kill the innocent."

"He might already be headed to the White House," Richard warned.

There was a thunderous pounding at the door. Tara hurried to it and threw it open. "He's diseased! The lieutenant was diseased. There are others out there now who will try to kill you, as well," she quickly told the five men—weapons posed—staring at her. "Help us. Before God, you've got to help us."

"Murder!" one of the men cried. "Take them!"

Richard grabbed Tara. "Get out of here while you can. They'll imprison the rest of us—you go!"

"They'll *kill* you!" she argued.

One had raised a rifle. She flew at him, grabbing the rifle and twisting the rod. He stared at her, backing away in dismay and fear. She spun around, taking hard swings at two others. Captain Tremblay stole a paperweight from the captain's desk and smashed it against the head of the fourth man while Richard gave the last a right to the jaw. They could hear footsteps on the stairs and all around them.

"Let's go!" Tara cried.

She ran toward the stairs and met the men racing up them. "Out the window! The attacker leaped out the window!" she cried, and the troop of men went racing down the stairs.

They followed.

But when they reached the serenity of the terrace, they were suddenly met by another, larger group of men. Tara paused, and those who had come down the stairs shouted that they were looking for an attacker that had gone out the window.

The group didn't move.

"What's the matter with you men?" a lieutenant demanded of the stilled men. "We've an assassin among us!"

The men opposite stood dead still, staring. And then, a hissing sound. Those in the front began to bare their fangs and move forward with deadly intent.

"Their heads! Go for their heads, men!" Captain Tremblay shouted.

Tara found herself in the midst of a melee, men coming after her, one after another, as if they knew she was the enemy to beat. She fought them off, aware of the tremendous numbers against her. Even as others tried to step in to come to her aid, they were batted off, stabbed, attacked and left behind.

And as she fought, trying and then failing to keep Captain Tremblay, Richard and Dr. MacKay in view, she realized that she was being herded back toward a smaller house that stood behind the officers' building.

She had no choice; she kept backing away, defending herself, slipping away with all speed only to discover that at least ten of the men knew her moves, and that they would be in front of her again. She killed one, two, three…and still, they kept coming. She was forced up the steps to the house, and the door opened, and she was forced in….

And suddenly, the men were gone.

She turned, and saw Billy Seabold, now wearing a Union brigadier general's uniform. He smiled at her from the bottom of the house's staircase.

"Welcome, Tara Fox!" he said. He approached her, and she realized again what a magnificent disguise he had managed as a lowly seaman, disguising his much taller, older and stronger self.

He smiled. "I have command of the naval yard. Come on in. I have a lovely cognac here, and it's been blended with the most delicious mixture of blood!"

"Human blood?" she asked. "I think not."

"Oh, come, come. You're going to die, which is such a shame—you're truly such a beautiful creature! But... alas, I don't think I can bend you to my way of thinking, and thus, my dear, no matter what you were to say, you'd always be a danger to me."

Tara followed him to the table. He didn't seem to be afraid of her behind him; he was barely aware of the bloodied sword she still carried. He knew that she couldn't leave by way of the front door; she would be forced back by the number of his creatures.

"What I want to know," she told him. "What I'd truly like to understand, is *why?*"

"Because I like the South!" he told her gleefully. "Lincoln must die, and our way of life in the South must be preserved. The hospitality, the grace, the horsemanship—"

"The harnessing of other human beings?" she demanded.

"Tara! You are a Southerner," he said with mock dismay.

"Yes, and I believe in preserving the hospitality, the beauty of the country, the horsemanship and the friendship. But we've been wrong, and I believe that this war is proving it. No man can own another man!"

He laughed. "Own another man? I say, own a huge food buffet!" he told her, laughing. "Oh, I enjoy blood of all varieties, but in the South… How many question the death of a slave?"

"The death of a human being!"

He slammed the decanter of fiery red liquid he had lifted back on the table.

"I have the power to make it happen. And I will. You're not going to drink with me? Really, you should have. It would have given you a bit of strength. A fighting chance…"

He smiled, and he started toward her.

FINN ARRIVED IN THE MIDST of chaos.

Men were battling men everywhere; it was much as it had been on the ship. He procured a horse near the rail line and rode into the melee of men bitterly battling other men with swords. He shouted out to the group of them. "The eyes, men, it's in the eyes! Look to the eyes for a hint of red, and don't kill those not infected!"

He was surprised when the clash of swords ceased, and then began again.

"Finn!" His name roared over the cacophony of battle.

Urging the horse forward, he found that Richard, bloodied from those he had fought but unhurt himself, was eager to meet him.

"Tara!" Richard cried. "We haven't been able to get to her! She's back that way. Go! He had her forced into his place, and, oh, God… Please go!"

Finn didn't wait for a second urging. He kneed the gelding he'd taken and rode the great horse through the crowds of fighting men. As he neared the smaller dwelling near the officers' building, they began to form against him in huge ranks. He brought his sword down again and again. The gelding reared high, but he held his seat, and he made use of the horse's fear, causing the animal's front hoofs to beat down some of the enemy before him. The men began to throw themselves at the horse, willing to die to stop him. He felt a sword rip through the back of his arm, and he winced, twisting quickly in the saddle to bring down the offender, and ruing the weakness the injury would cause. He kneed the gelding again, and kicked its ribs, silently apologizing to the animal as his kick sent the horse leaping forward.

He'd reached the porch, and he jumped from the horse and burst into the house, closing the door behind him and dropping the heavy wooden bar bolt, stopping the minions from entering. He heard a crash, and he rushed from the entry into the parlor.

He arrived just in time to see Tara flying through the air. She crashed against the wall near the fireplace, and sank to the floor. Billy Seabold strode toward her, aware that Finn had entered, though apparently not at all alarmed.

"Love! True love!" Billy Seabold said. "Or is it honor? Whichever, foolish emotions." He paused in his pursuit, turning to look at Finn. "What idiots," he said flatly. "You might have joined my ranks, and we might have lived as we were intended to live, the top of the food chain, rulers of the world. Well, pity, but you both shall die." He laughed. "And how strict and stern and uppity you were, Agent Dunne! A Pinkerton. How amusing!"

Finn moved slowly toward him, trying to keep his attention from Tara as she pushed herself up the wall and attempted to regain her feet.

"You can't live among men if you can't learn to live in peace, Seabold," he said.

"Peace? The humans are ripping one another up!"

"Because they believe differently on issues," Finn said. "But they don't seek to murder one another."

"But they *do*."

"When they want nothing but blood lust, the law catches up with them. North and South."

"I'm just helping them all along," Seabold said. "They want to kill one another? I'm taking the task on for them."

"There will be peace. Abraham Lincoln will live, and there will be peace."

"No, I think not," Billy Seabold said. He turned his attention back to Tara, walking toward her. She had lost her sword. As Seabold approached her, Tara suddenly hissed and showed her own fangs.

Seabold laughed. "Bite me, and I think you will die!"

"And you just might, too," she told him.

He reached out for her. Tara was like a cornered badger, fighting, ripping. Finn made his move, flying for Seabold. Seabold caught him—his hand shooting out, his fingers winding around Finn's throat. He was weakened from the slash on his arm, but he knew that he couldn't show the least frailty. Seabold thought that he had them both.

And he did. He had their throats.

But as he laughed, avoiding Tara's gnashing fangs, she twisted suddenly, and caught him in the arm.

And as she did so, Finn managed to lift his sword, and thrust it into their enemy's side.

Taken off guard, Billy Seabold dropped them both. Tara fell to the floor, but Finn was immediately ready when Seabold drew his sword. Finn placed his injured left arm behind his back, and began to fight for his life with his right.

They thrust and parried; Seabold bounced away, skimming off the wall to come at Finn from the back, but he turned in time and avoided the deadly thrust. He sought the weakness in the other man—sought the vampire's throat. He ducked one blow, and jumped over another when Seabold would have sliced his legs.

At last, with desperation and deadly aim, Finn got in a fortunate thrust. He pinned his enemy by the shoulder to the wall. Seabold looked at him with fury and amusement, laughing as he went to reach for the sword to remove it.

But even as Finn tried to figure his strategy—a way to maintain the lock on the monster before him and finish him with his wounded arm—Tara staggered up from the floor. She made her way toward them, her own bloodied sword in her hand, and she managed to thrust it into Seabold's gut before falling down again herself.

Finn withdrew his own sword, backed away, and swung.

Seabold's head fell to the floor while his body convulsed, pinned to the wooden paneling by Tara's weapon.

Finn stood still for a moment, shaking. He became aware of the pounding at the door, and then a crash of glass as Seabold's creatures broke through the windows. He forced himself to come to life, hunkering down by Tara and lifting her into his arms. As he wondered how he'd get her through the mindless horde outside, the world suddenly fell to silence.

Holding on to his neck, Tara whispered, "Where have they gone?"

He heard an explosion and realized that someone had shot their way through the front entry. With Tara dearly in his arms, he hurried to the hallway, ready to take any means of escape until he could lay her safely down to shake off the effects of Seabold's blood.

But there were no monsters in the hallway.

There were two men, and two women.

"Cody Fox," one said, stepping forward. "We were called here on a discreet matter through the executive office. "I believe that's my sister you have in your arms."

One of the women at his side stepped forward. "Megan Fox," she said. "This is my husband, Cole. And I'd like to introduce you to Cody's wife—Alexandra. I believe we have things under control now outside. We have some very good friends working with the post-battle cleanup. *We've* been asked to bring you to meet someone."

Finn heard a soft sob and looked down. Tara was just staring at the foursome who had joined them. Then she looked up at him with wonder. "I have family, Finn!"

He smiled. "So you do," he told her warmly.

"We're delighted to go with you," he said, smiling at the newcomers. "But I guess since you're Tara's brother, Cody Fox, I should get this out right now. I'm really quite in love with your sister. And, I must say, I've compromised her, or we've compromised one another. That being, I really do believe that you should give us your blessing to marry."

EPILOGUE

TARA SAT IN A STRAIGHT-BACK upholstered chair, across the desk from Abraham Lincoln. She was tempted to draw out a hat pin and prick herself; it was still difficult to believe that she was here, and he was here, and that they were facing each other, in the flesh.

But they were. The night when they had finally bested Gator, they had come to the White House. She discovered that her family had, indeed, been involved in the "war beneath the war," and that they were all acquainted. Finn had made the introductions, and Abraham Lincoln had taken her hands, met her eyes and said, "We've met, I believe, many a time, in a dream."

She hadn't been well. She'd needed rest. And they had all seen to it that she had gotten it, and it had been wonderful. Her sister—*her sister*—had assured her that Richard and Captain Tremblay and Dr. MacKay had all been found and were safely recovering from the minor wounds they had received, and she would have her audience with the president the next day.

She had been so well guarded, and so well loved!

And Finn had asked to marry her.

He wasn't around in the morning, though. It was Alexandra, Cody's wife, who brought her to her appointment, and then left her. And so, at last, she faced the real Abraham Lincoln, and they sat, a pot of tea between them. It was so good to see him, and see him alive and well, that she fought back tears.

"First, of course, I must thank you," he said. "I've heard you were highly instrumental in saving many lives. I'll not say Union lives—I pray daily that, soon, our great nation will begin the healing process, and those lives you saved, on the ship and in Key West, will be nothing lesser or greater than *American* lives."

"I see the world as you do, sir," she told him. "And yes, Mr. President, that's why your life is so important, and why, I believe, I have haunted your dreams. Even with the war dying down, sir, and with the latest deadly effort stopped, you must know that you still have enemies. God knows, men are good, North and South, and men are fanatics, North and South."

"Of course," he said. He rose, walked to the window and looked out on the city of Washington, beautiful as spring now intruded fully upon the winter. "We are born, we love, we see the world around us, and we find our place within it. We all know laughter and happiness, and tragedy. We are the same, really."

He turned and smiled at her. "I have given my second inaugural address, you know. And I believe those who watched and listened are as eager as I to see the healing begin."

"There will be those who cannot accept defeat," she told him.

He looked back at her. His face was grave. "I had the dream…" he said.

She nodded. "I know," she said softly. "You saw yourself walking through the rooms, and you heard the people sobbing. You saw the catafalque, and you wanted to know who had died, and they told you the president."

He walked back to the desk, but he didn't take his chair. He sat on the edge of the desk, close to her, and said quietly, "No one man can create a lasting peace. What must be understood is this—slavery cannot be. In my heart, I know that it's an abomination against God. But there will be a long road ahead to educate those who were slaves, and it will be a far longer road ahead for men ever to look upon one another as equals. States must still retain certain rights, because we are a nation of different areas, with different liabilities and different wonders. And despite the pain and the bloodshed and bitterness that have been, we must learn to forget. That can't be just one man, my dear. That is a mindset that we must create, and it must build and grow. Wounds take time to heal, and this country has been wounded to the core. It will take years for the lesions to heal. And yet, it's the people who must band together, like the blood in a man's body, the flesh upon him. Every man and woman is part of the great body. I know that you will go on, as others will go on. And your words and your actions will help that healing. That's what you must understand. I have known you in my mind, and I have seen you in my dreams. You've been like a guardian angel. But no matter what the future might bring, you must remember that you, and those like you, will be the heart and soul of the new nation."

"But, sir, you don't understand, truly you don't, just how important you are," Tara said.

He smiled. "I am important only if the words I have said can live on in the hearts of others. No man is greater than the nation. Please, remember that. Pray for the nation, Tara, and create a world wherein we can find peace."

They talked awhile longer, and when they had finished, she exited the White House to find that the sun was setting, and darkness was falling.

And her family and Richard, Captain Tremblay, Dr. MacKay and Finn were all waiting for her.

Finn stepped forward, and enfolded her into his arms.

"Come along, come along," Cody said. "It's getting late."

"Where are we going?" she asked.

She looked into Finn's eyes. She tried to remember when they had met; she'd never imagined then that he could look at anyone with such tenderness.

"You're about to become my bride of the night, Miss Fox. That is, if you're willing," Finn said. His voice was rich and husky and his eyes were a fire that promised a lifetime of both tempest and delight.

"Aye, I'm willing, my love," she told him.

And the darkness was descending, but she heard church bells ringing.

And the church was beautiful, hastily adorned with flowers by her newfound family.

Cody gave her away while the others stood witness, Richard acting as best man and Megan acting as her matron of honor. The words were all said, and she was married, and when they stepped into the street, Finn looked at her.

"For us, the healing has begun!" he said softly.

She kissed him, and the others applauded. They had found their own peace, and in it, the strength to fight for a new nation, and a new beginning.

* * * * *